SKINNER ALIVE!

APPALACHIAN TALES FROM KENTUCKY

CRAIG CAUDILL

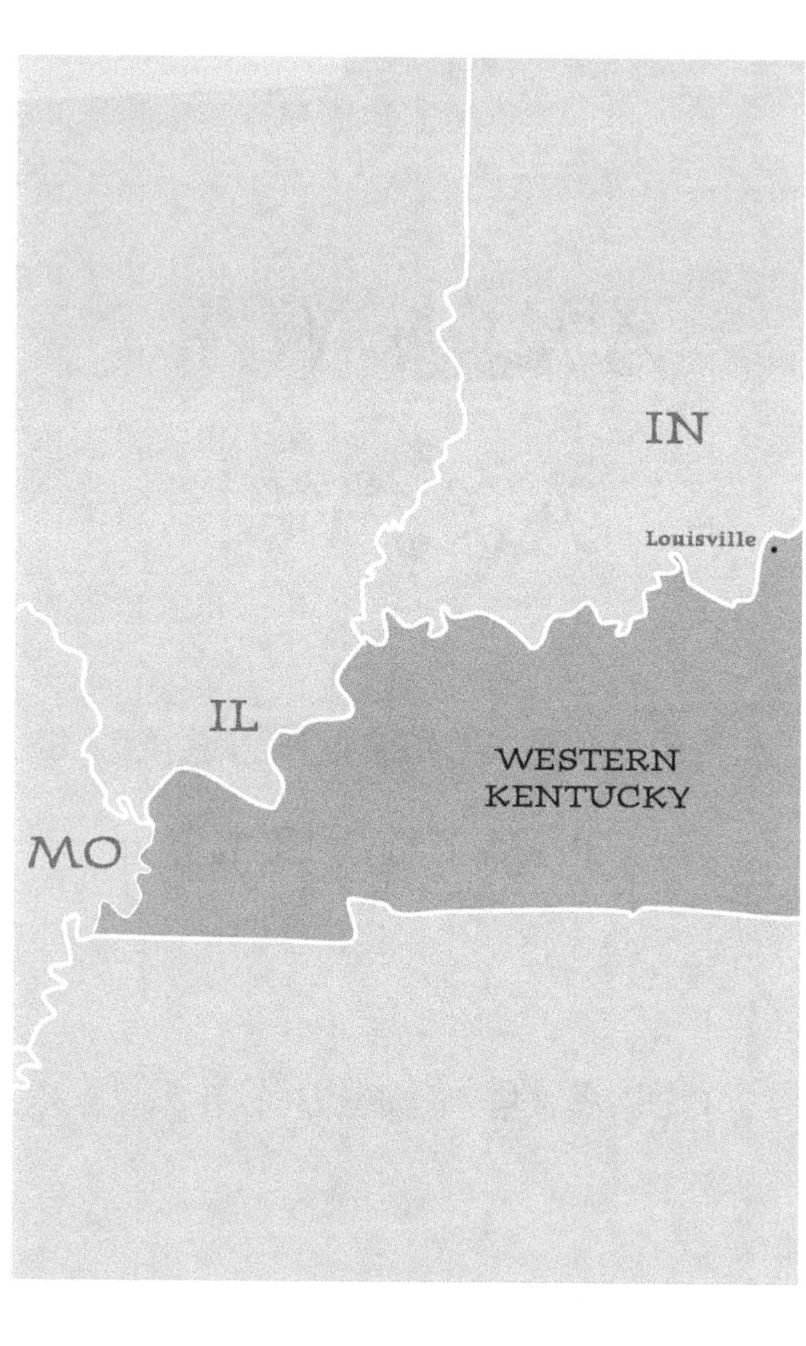

IN
Louisville
WESTERN
KENTUCKY
IL
MO

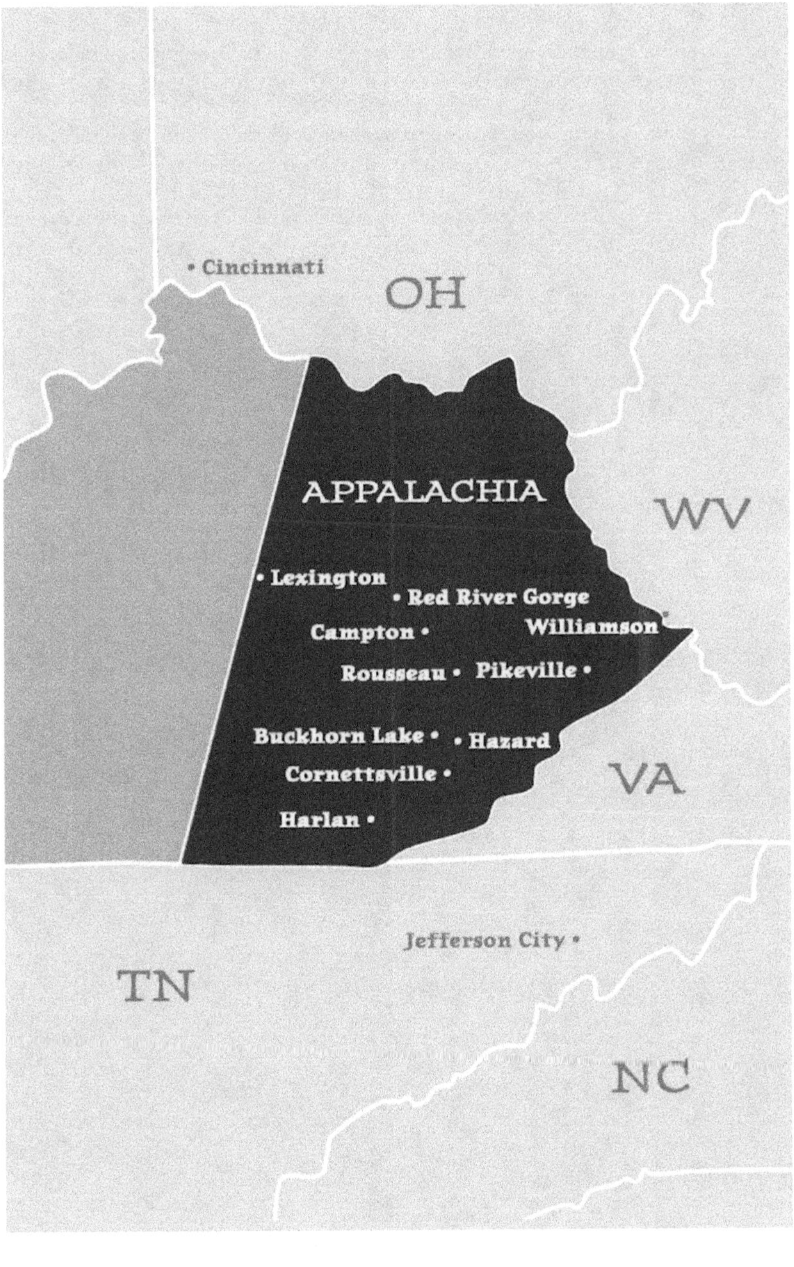

Cincinnati
OH
APPALACHIA
WV
Lexington
Red River Gorge
Williamson
Campton
Rousseau
Pikeville
Buckhorn Lake
Hazard
Cornettsville
VA
Harlan
Jefferson City
TN
NC

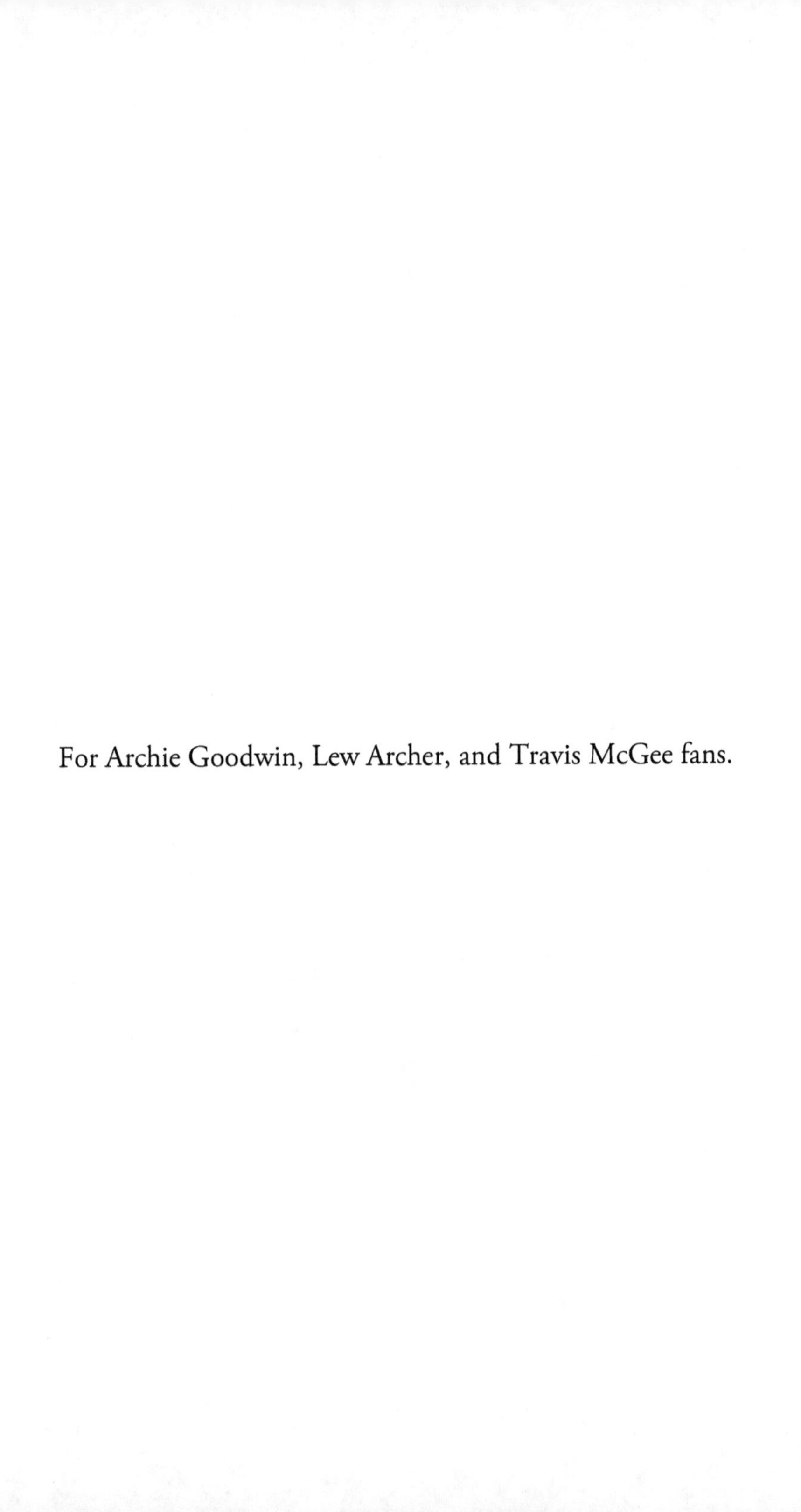

For Archie Goodwin, Lew Archer, and Travis McGee fans.

Contents

It's Not About Money

If ever a name fit a person, it was that of six-foot-seven John Money. He could beat defenders off the dribble, post up, shoot lights out, and run the floor like a cheetah, not to mention rebound over rim protectors and play defense better than most guards. Money was considered the best white player to lace up a pair of high-tops since Larry Bird. Duke, North Carolina, Kansas, Kentucky, and seventy-five other colleges craved his services, even if he'd only be around for one year. He had yet to announce his college choice, which puzzled the sports world, especially since the final game of the Boys A state tournament was tomorrow. Hazard High won titles in 1932 and 1955, and because of Money's thirty-eight points a game, was about to do it again.

On the Saturday night before the final game, Maude Skinner sat in a shadowy corner of Malone's Steakhouse in Lexington between the two men in her life, her husband and brother. She owned and ran Vigneron Winery, financed by her brother, Marcel Sutherland, who was wealthy, and had married Marcel's best friend and silent partner, Brock Skinner, who was also loaded. The newlyweds bought a log cabin on a small farm behind her wine operation in Hazard, and spent the second half of last year turning it into a Taj Mahal. Most people with their money would have left the mountains, but the two of them loved Appalachia. They also owned a place in Lexington for a taste of city life when the urge hit them, where they could occasionally party with Marcel, who lived in Harrodsburg, forty minutes away.

Brock said, "John called after the semifinal game this afternoon and wanted to see me at nine thirty in the hotel lobby where the team is staying. He sounded troubled."

Brock Skinner had gotten to know John last fall when Hazard's coach, Ed Brewer, asked him to participate in practice a few times to rough John up under the basket. That kind of treatment wasn't strictly legal, but Money had asked for it. He was a nice kid, and knew he needed to get tougher to be a better player. "I'll be back at the condo in an hour or so," Brock declared as he threw his napkin on the table and headed out to climb in his Lamborghini.

John Money peered vacantly through the bank of tall lobby windows in the direction of the backlit fountain on the other side of Broadway Street. His trance broke when the loud sports car streaked in front of him and turned into the parking garage of the hotel.

"John, you okay?" Brock asked when he walked up a few minutes later. Money was an imposing figure with a friendly face that perpetuated his choir-boy image. Brock, on the other hand, at almost thirty-five, was a battlefield mercenary, experienced at handling tough situations.

"Yeah," John replied brusquely. He looked at the floor and tapped his toes.

"Out with it. What's wrong?" Brock prodded. John reached in his pocket and pulled out a typewritten note. It said:

John Money

You must attend the University of Tennessee to play basketball, or I'll make sure you can't play anywhere else.

The Volunteer

Brock glanced up and said, "I guess recruits receive these kinds of letters once in a while. When and how did you get it?"

"Somebody dropped it off at the school office last Wednesday."

"Have you told your parents about it, or the police?"

"No, and I'm not going to," John stated defiantly.

Brock walked over to the windows to stare at the alluring fountain across the street. He pivoted to face John. "That puts us both in a bad position. If anything happens to you, and anybody finds out you showed me this, my goose is cooked, along with yours."

"I figured you'd say that. I came to you, Mr. Skinner, because I thought you'd be able to find who's threatening me. I don't want to worry my parents or get into a big hullabaloo."

"John, just be sure to keep your eye on the ball. After a year of college, if you don't get hurt, you'll get an NBA contract that will set you up for life. That's the best thing you can do for yourself and your parents."

"Yeah, but I don't want to be looking over my shoulder everywhere I go. Is there any way to find who this person is on the QT?" Money wondered aloud.

"I suppose. You can't tell anyone I'm snooping around, though." Skinner crossed his arms and put his head back. "After you win tomorrow, announce you'll name your college choice on Tax Day, April fifteenth. That will give us a month. Also, I'll buy two hundred programs at the game. You can set up an autograph session for your fans at school next week. I'm guessing this person will come around for a visit. We just have to pick 'em out."

"Okay. I really appreciate your help." Money appeared relieved. He shook Skinner's hand vigorously before taking the elevator up to his room.

Marcel Sutherland, holding a port wine and watching *SportsCenter*, saw Brock come through the condo door at ten o'clock. He asked, "So, what did Money want?"

"He got a love letter from somebody who told him if he didn't play basketball at the University of Tennessee, his ball-playing days would be over."

"Uh-oh, please don't tell me you're going to help him find this person."

"I am," Brock answered as his wife, Maude, emerged from the bedroom wearing a pearlescent green robe. He recounted his meeting with John verbatim to her.

Money poured in forty-seven of Hazard's sixty-eight points on the way to a fourteen-point victory over Trigg County. The press seemed pleased that John had nailed down when he would reveal his college choice. After the game, Brock carried the four boxes of tournament programs he bought to his car. When he and Maude were driving back to Hazard late on Sunday, she said, "You know, there are about two million Tennessee fans who could have written that note. I'm going to start calling you Brock Quixote."

"And you are my Dulcinea del Toboso."

"Who's that?"

"The Man from La Mancha's girlfriend. In his head, that is. She was the picture of perfection, sort of like you."

"I'm glad you see things so clearly." Maude grabbed her husband's ear and gently twisted it.

On Monday morning, Brock drove the winery pickup truck through a nippy breeze into Hazard High's parking lot. He cleared security and found his way into the walled-off administrative office. A woman in her late forties was visible through the glass. Her name, Joan Miro, was etched on a metal plate mounted on a block of wood. Brock had heard of Joan Miro, a twentieth-century male Spanish artist. A reproduction of one of his paintings, *The Farm,* hung on the lemon-yellow wall behind the woman's desk. Brock said, "Hi there. Last week I asked my brother to drop something off for John Money. It was a letter of encouragement for the team to win the state tournament. Looks like it worked."

"How can I help you, sir?" She acted as though she hadn't heard what he said.

"Are you the person my brother gave the note to? I just wanted to make sure he got it."

"He got it. It wasn't your brother who dropped it off. It was some girl."

"What? Maybe it was his wife. What'd she look like?"

"Late twenties. Pale. Had canker sores all over her face, like a meth addict."

"That's her. Thanks for your help." He nodded respectfully as he stepped away. Joan Miro went back to the work on her desk, hoping he'd move along.

Brock only knew of one drug house in Hazard, and was sure there were others. Many times, he had driven by the place on High Street, fittingly named, to watch patrons march in and out every half hour. He parked the pickup truck across the street from the grungy white door at eleven in the morning. At one thirty, the girl with cankers on her face strolled toward the entrance, her head down. She had the hollow eyes of a dead woman walking. He jumped out and hollered at her. "Miss, do you have a second?"

She recoiled like a scared cat. "Leave me alone." Her clothes were frayed around the edges.

"I've got a hundred-dollar bill that has your name on it. I just need a little information."

She hesitated, shoved her dirty hands in her jacket pockets, and shrugged. "What do you want to know?"

"Somebody gave you a letter to deliver to John Money at Hazard High last Wednesday morning. What can you tell me about it?"

"Show me that hundred first." He handed it to her discreetly. She looked at his face, then away. "Somebody left an envelope in my mailbox with instructions where to deliver the letter inside. There was a lot of money in there for me, so I did it."

"Was there anything else in the envelope?"

"Yeah, your picture. If the police ever wanted to know who asked me to deliver the letter, I was to say a man who drives a Lamborghini. The photo was so I could pick you out of a lineup if I had to."

Brock got angry but felt bad for her. He watched her fidget. "Would you consider going to rehab if I paid for it?"

She gazed at him wistfully. "Oh, God yes. I can't take this anymore."

Brock said, "Come on over and sit in my truck for a minute." He called the only limo driver he knew in Hazard, asking him to come get the woman and drive her to a Christian-based rehab clinic he had heard about in Lexington. Before he closed the limo door, he asked her, "By the way, what's your name? I'll call the clinic and let them know you're on your way."

"I go by Amanda Lockhart." She gave him a half-hearted smile. As the vehicle pulled away from the curb, he made the call, telling the rehab facility to expect her. He asked them to keep her for thirty days if possible.

Maude had made turkey chili before she went over to the winery on Monday morning. When she got home at ten after six that evening, she heated it up and set two bowls on the table. Brock tried a big spoonful. "Mmm, good. You know, this thing with Money is a setup of some kind. Whoever is behind the letter expected Money to go to the police. The police were supposed to investigate and be able to pin the note on me. The troubling part is the mastermind wanted me caught up in the affair. Locating the girl who dropped off the letter for John was pretty easy."

"Try not to get yourself killed. We just got married," Maude interjected dryly. Brock told her all about Amanda Lockhart and how he had convinced her to check in to rehab in Lexington, at his expense, of course. Maude commented sadly, "Drugs are a big problem around here."

"Not much different than big-city ghettos, I suppose. A way to make money when there aren't many others."

Hazard's sheriff, Nathan Connors, sat behind his desk signing papers on Tuesday morning when Brock came into his office. By nature, Connors was decidedly calm and understated. He asked sarcastically, "Staying out of trouble, Skinner?"

"For the moment. Nathan, can I see the mugshots of the drug arrests that've been made around here over the last couple of years?"

"Looking to make some new friends?"

"No. Actually, I want to be sure that none of Maude's employees at the winery have a drug problem."

Connors hollered through the door, "Mark, set Skinner up on a computer with the drug-arrest mugshots."

Brock was stunned by the number of pictures in the file. The one he'd been searching for hit the screen as an arrest a year ago. Her real name was listed as Amanda Critchfield—no known address.

He thanked Connors and walked six blocks to the post office. He happened to see his mailman in the fenced-in back lot, opening the door of his postal truck. Brock asked him through the fence, "Do you have an Amanda Critchfield on your route?"

"Sure do. Forty-eight eleven Fourseam Branch. Place is away from the road, down by Buffalo Creek. Hardly ever gets any mail."

"Thanks."

Brock bounced through the ruts along the car path until the driveway at the address became a turnaround in front of a beige-colored trailer. Rough gravel had been spread under and around the base of the dwelling, and rotting tree twigs left over from winter were on the roof. Weeds had begun to pop up in the yard. He got out, tucked the pistol in his belt, and tried the door. It was locked, so he picked it.

The place smelled like stale peppermint oil. The refrigerator contained eggs, milk, bread, lunch meat, mayonnaise, and oranges. Boxes of instant pasta mixes, cereal, and cans of soup were on the countertop. No dirty dishes were in the sink. There was a wadded-up counterpane at the foot of the bed, with two snapshots of Amanda, when she was younger and bright-eyed, on the side table by the bed. One was her grinning, wearing a cap and gown at a graduation ceremony. Brock wondered if the other two people in the photo were her parents. They looked a little old. He found a bag to put the perishables from the refrigerator in, and took them with him when he left. When Brock looked in the rearview mirror as he sped away, he saw a sedan with two older people turn into Amanda's driveway.

The low, gray clouds swallowing the mountaintops heightened the claustrophobic feel of living in Hazard. It was one thing for troughs of sunlight to disappear long before sunset, yet another to be immured incessantly by the craggy hillsides of trees that lined every road fanning out from town. Brock coasted to the rear of Vigneron Winery to park the pickup close to the building. He came through the back door carrying the bag of food, aiming to join his wife in the tasting room.

Maude said, "There's my meal ticket. What can I get you for lunch?"

"Corned beef sandwich and a pickle. Had any customers today?" Brock set the bag of food on the counter.

"It's still early in the season, but a wacky couple did come by and talk my leg off. Sometimes I think people are on a quest to find anybody who will listen to them. They asked a lot of inappropriate questions, like, was my husband here," she said.

"Huh. Listening seems to be your calling," he replied. "This is the food I found in Amanda's refrigerator. I didn't want the place to start stinking."

"Been breaking and entering this morning, have we?"

"Yes. Her real name is Amanda Critchfield. Here's a picture of her when she wasn't on drugs." He reached in the bag of food to retrieve one of the photos of her.

"Not a bad-looking girl. Wonder what happened to her?"

Brock Skinner left in his Lamborghini after lunch, headed for the courthouse. When he got there, he asked the clerk in the property tax division who owned the homestead where Amanda Critchfield was living. The deed showed that Edward Brewer bought the property nearly three years ago when he came to Hazard. Brock thanked the clerk and decided to call on the coach at the high school.

Ed Brewer was sitting at the cheap metal desk in his office when Brock popped in. Pictures of action shots were on the wall behind him. "How 'bout those Bulldogs," Ed spouted. "Money's one hell of a player."

"Boy, you ain't a kiddin'," Brock seconded. "Good resume builder for you too, Ed."

"This is my third championship at three different schools."

"Good for you. Where was your last stop?"

"Jefferson City, Missouri, and before that Jefferson City, Tennessee, which is just south of here. I had heard about Money. That's why I jumped on this coaching job when it came open."

"Are you married?"

"I was, but we separated many years ago." A sudden diminuendo in Ed's voice signaled he didn't want to talk about it.

"Sorry to hear that. Did you buy a house when you came to town?"

"No, a trailer out on Fourseam Branch. I looked around that summer until I found the house I wanted to buy east of town. I kept the trailer. It's rented out."

"What are John's parents like?"

"He's an insurance agent. She's an elementary school teacher. Really nice people."

"Any idea which college Money's going to pick?" Brock knew if he kept asking questions, Ed might start to get suspicious and begin asking him questions he didn't want to answer.

"He keeps telling me that if he doesn't go to Kentucky, the people around here will disown him, or worse."

"He's got a point. Congratulations on winning another championship," Brock said as he prepared to leave.

"Thank you." Ed leaned back in his chair, put his hands behind his head, and grinned smugly.

Wednesday afternoon, when school let out, John Money started signing programs in the gymnasium at a table set up in front of the bleachers. A line of about sixty people had formed within ten minutes. Maude sat behind John, high up and off to one side. She took pictures of every person who worked their way up to him. Outside, Brock photographed the license plate of each car that came and went. In all, there were seventy-nine cars and one hundred thirty-six photos of people.

After everybody had left, Brock said to John, "Anybody look suspicious to you?"

"Not really. I knew most of the people from around town. Have you found out anything?"

"Just the person who brought the note to school. She goes by Amanda Lockhart. Ever hear of her?"

"The name doesn't sound familiar."

"What about Amanda Critchfield? That's her real name."

"I've seen or heard that name somewhere, but I don't remember where," he replied.

"Okay. My wife and I will go through the photographs we took and see what turns up."

Thursday, late morning, the Skinners pulled under the portico of the Light of Life rehab center in Lexington. A white, blue, and orange EMT vehicle with a caduceus spanning the folding rear doors was at the curb next to the giant cross between the sidewalk and building. Maude got out. Brock parked at the side of the facility, away from other cars. They asked to see Amanda Lockhart, but were denied. Policy didn't allow it. A middle-aged nun came out from behind the reception desk to introduce herself. The three of them moved across the room to take seats in the waiting area. "Are you the folks who sent us Amanda?"

"We are. Is she doing okay?" Brock asked.

"She's in the toughest part right now."

"Can you tell us anything about her? We really don't know her very well," he commented politely.

"I can only share basic information we found in the public domain that she has confirmed."

"Such as?" Maude urged.

"Well, she's twenty-six years old. Her given name is Amanda Critchfield. She was born and raised in Jefferson City, Tennessee. She went to Carson-Newman University, graduating five years ago with a degree in theatre. She worked in Jefferson City for a couple of years, and then moved to Hazard, Kentucky, changing her name from Amanda Critchfield to Amanda Lockhart. She has one drug arrest from about a year ago. Her parents are still in Jefferson City, but she asked us not to contact them." The nun sat up straight and placed her hands on her lap.

Brock asked, "When do you think we can visit her?"

"Our policy is after five days, provided she is stable and wants to see you."

"Thanks for the information," Maude said with a warm smile as she stood.

"Who may I say will be calling on her?"

"Maude and Brock Skinner."

When the Skinners keyed open their condo in downtown Lexington, a cold drizzle had started to fall. They took off their shoes and turned the heat up to sixty-eight. "Call over to Columbia Steak House and put in a to-go order for a couple of salads and hamburgers. I'll walk over and pick them up." When Brock returned with the food, Maude had plugged the cameras into the TV screen and was clicking through pictures and license plates.

"Brock, I didn't notice this when I was taking the pictures, but this is the guy who talked my leg off Tuesday morning at the winery. Here's his wife. I ran through the license plate pictures. I remember their car. This is it." She pointed at the screen. The car had Tennessee plates.

They ate lunch, and then Brock placed a call to Sheriff Connors. "Nathan, could you run a Tennessee license plate for me?"

"I can. But I won't unless you tell me what kind of trouble you're stirring up."

"The couple in the car came up to the winery Tuesday morning. They were asking a lot of questions for no good reason. I guess I'm too suspicious."

"Yes, you are. Will there be anything good in this for me if I get you the name?"

"On a stack of bibles."

"Give me ten minutes. I'll call you back."

The car was registered to Cooper and Alice Critchfield from Jefferson City.

Brock retrieved the pictures of Amanda from his jacket pocket and showed Maude the graduation shot with the other two people in it. "This is them, isn't it?"

"Yep."

"Must be her parents."

Maude said, "Old, aren't they? Let's go back to Hazard tonight. You can drive down to see them tomorrow."

Early on Friday, Brock Skinner stood on the stoop of the clapboard Critchfield house in Jefferson City, waiting for the knock on the black tongue-and-groove door to be answered. Hazard was a rough place compared to Pikeville and Whitesburg, but all three were rustic up against Jeff City. When the door finally swung open, there stood Mr. and Mrs. Critchfield. "Come in. My name's Cooper, and this is my wife, Alice. We've been expecting someone to call." Skinner gave his name, and they directed him to take a seat on the divan before sitting in the side chairs themselves.

"I take it you're Amanda's parents."

"Yes, you could say that," Cooper said. He tapped his fingertips together.

"What do you mean?"

"Well, we raised her. She thought we were her parents until we had to tell her the truth three years ago."

"You adopted her at a young age?"

"Something like that. A man brought her to us when she was just a couple of weeks old," Alice stated.

"Let me guess: the man was Ed Brewer? Why'd he bring Amanda to you?"

"We knew him from church. He claimed his wife was leaving him, and he didn't want to raise her by himself."

"So, it wasn't a legal adoption, then?"

"No," Cooper said dejectedly.

"How come you had to tell her you weren't her parents?"

Alice explained, "Because when she went to get her driver's license renewed, the clerk told her that her birth certificate was a fake. We had the forgery made when she was very young. She had to have some kind of identification. The clerk traced the number on it, and nothing came up. That started Amanda on a quest to find out who she was. She began to get crazy. We had to tell her."

"So, I take it she found out who her father was and decided to make contact with him?"

"She went to Hazard, and by some stroke of luck, Ed Brewer, her father, had a trailer for rent. She took it, but didn't tell him who she was right away. She only did that a little over a year ago."

"What did he say?"

"We don't know. All we know is she started taking drugs. The police called us when she got arrested last year. There was nothing we could do for her."

"Tell me about the letter to John Money."

Cooper said, "I don't know what you're talking about. Someone taped a letter to our side door last Monday afternoon that told us you would have some important information about Amanda. We went looking for you Tuesday morning at your wife's winery. When we left there, we tried to visit Amanda at her trailer. She wasn't home. We tried again Wednesday, and then went to a program-signing by John Money, hoping to find Ed Brewer. We hadn't seen or heard from him in over twenty-five years. Couldn't locate him either. We're worried about Amanda."

"Let me see the letter," Brock said. Alice pulled it from a drawer next to her chair.

Alice and Cooper Critchfield,

Go to Vigneron Winery in Hazard, Kentucky, on Tuesday morning. Brock Skinner, the owner's husband, will have some very important information for you about Amanda.

Amanda's Friend

"Well, maybe this is a bit of good news. I took Amanda to a rehab center in Lexington on Monday afternoon. She wanted to go. I'm paying for it."

"That *is* a relief. At least she's safe," Alice said.

"I'll let you know how she's doing after I see her. You can reach me at this number. Please call if anything comes up. Thanks for your help," Brock added as he took down Cooper's number, feeling something good had come from his visit.

Maude wouldn't be home from the winery until six fifteen. Brock made it back to the log cabin right after lunch. He spent the afternoon trying to learn why Ed Brewer left Tennessee for Missouri several years ago. He had given away his child, and his wife had purportedly left him. He coached at the high school in Jefferson City, Tennessee, for many years, winning a state championship. Then he decamped and went to coach in Missouri, where he won a second championship. Brock called and talked to the school principal there. The principal reported that Brewer left on good terms.

Brock grilled a couple of filets after Maude got home. She asked, "What did you find out in Tennessee?"

"This thing doesn't seem to be about basketball. Those people got a letter like John Money did that told them to find me because I had some information about their daughter. It looks like both letters were to push me to her, but I found her on my own, which messed up the plan. The mystery person writing the letters was counting on the police finding her. Nonetheless, Amanda must know something that's supposed to make me spring into action."

"Oh boy, I see another trip to Lexington in our future," Maude remarked.

"Yeah, like tomorrow."

The Saturday morning sun had begun evaporating the dark puddles of water on the roads. The Lamborghini was covered in dirt before the pavement dried out, so Brock stopped at a car wash in Lexington that he trusted before rolling into the parking lot at the rehab center. The nun greeted them at the front desk. "She's in the courtyard getting some fresh air." Brock ushered his wife through the heavy double doors leading to the chairs outside.

"Hi, Amanda. This is my wife, Maude."

The sores on Amanda's face had liniment on them, and a flicker of hope could be seen deep in her green eyes. Her hands and hair were much cleaner than when Brock had last seen her. She wore a loose yellow cotton top and cinched baggy gray pants. "Pleased to meet you."

"Feeling better?" Maude asked.

"Different. Tired," Amanda replied meekly.

"Would it be okay if we asked you a few questions?" Brock asked.

"Why not? I've been talking about the garbage inside my head for three days now. What do you want to know?" She twisted in her seat and pushed the wavy brown hair out of her face.

"What happened when you asked Ed Brewer if he was your father?"

"Boy, you go right to the final act. He denied it."

"Denied that he was your father?"

"Yes. I had traced everything carefully before I confronted him. I was absolutely sure he was my dad."

"So, what happened then?"

"I insisted that we both get a DNA test."

"And?" Brock put his foot on a chair, rested an arm on his thigh, and leaned toward her.

"It came back negative. He isn't my father."

Brock looked at Maude. "That doesn't make any sense." He absentmindedly scratched his head with both hands. "Either he's not Ed Brewer, or the real Ed Brewer isn't your father."

Amanda said, "The way I got it figured, my real mother, Sonja Brewer, must've had an affair with someone, and Ed found out

I wasn't his child. They gave me to the Critchfields and decided to split up because of it."

"Brewer should have confirmed that for you. Have you ever talked to your birth mother about it?" Maude asked.

"She took off twenty-five years ago. Nobody seems to know where she went."

"Let's forget about that for now. Amanda, when you're completely healed, we want you to assemble a theatre troupe to put on plays at Maude's winery and other spots in the area."

"I'd love that." Amanda blinked away tears. After a few seconds, she looked at Brock wanly. "Thank you for saving my life."

The Skinners went to their condo to watch March Madness games on Saturday afternoon. They met Maude's brother at Tony's that evening for steaks and seafood. Marcel asked, "What's new with John Money?"

"Oh man, it's been a wild week. I'm starting to believe that John sent the anonymous letters himself. He must want something about Coach Brewer to come out without him being implicated. Brewer told a girl mixed up in this thing that he wasn't her father, but didn't say that her mother had an affair with another man. There's something fishy about that."

"I take it this adventure is still pro bono," Marcel remarked.

"It's worse than that. Moneybags over here is paying for the girl to get clean." Maude jerked a thumb in Brock's direction.

Marcel quipped, "You jealous?" Maude gave him the look he had seen many times in his life.

~ ~ ~

A little after three on Monday afternoon, a vehicle drove into the winery parking lot, coming to rest under the big maple tree farthest from the tasting-room entrance. Brock recognized Ed

Brewer as he deliberately got out of the car. He wore a light polo jacket. The glare from the sun and moving shadows cast by the fluttering tree branches almost made Brock miss what Brewer did, which was to tuck a pistol in his belt, down his lower back. "Maude, call Connors and tell him to get over here as fast as he can." Brewer casually walked up the gentle hill toward the veranda steps. He looked side to side, making sure no one was around. Brock came out to greet him. "What's going on, Ed?"

Brewer stopped and lifted his hand. His face had a hollow expression. Brock reached behind his back, preparing for gunplay. "Why are you doing this? You trying to ruin me?" Ed squawked.

"Doing what?"

"This." He put his hand in his pocket and pulled out a folded piece of paper.

Brock said calmly, "You'll have to turn around, Ed, and let me remove your gun. Otherwise, one of us is going to get hurt." Maude, after calling the sheriff, positioned herself at the front window, peeking out from the edge.

"I never did anything to you. Hell, I let you participate in our practices last fall."

"Whatever this is about, you'll have to put down the gun." Ed backed up and went for his pistol. Brock bull-rushed him, hitting his sternum. Ed gasped, flew backward, and his gun went off, sending a bullet into the wood siding of the winery, above the window to the right of the door. Brock fell on him, bounced up, and grabbed the gun lying eight feet away. Ed rubbed his chest and coughed after he sat up. Brock retrieved the folded note that had fallen to the ground.

Mystery Man,

Why are you impersonating Ed Brewer? What have you done with him? You better have a good explanation.

Brock Skinner

"When did you get this?"

"It was on my desk this morning when I came to school. How did you put it there?" Brewer got to his feet and rotated his neck as though he had whiplash.

"Never mind that. Who are you?"

"Ed Brewer."

"I doubt it," Brock said. "If you are, you're going to have to prove it." Brewer made a run for his vehicle. Just as he opened the door, Skinner kicked it shut again. "Where you going?"

Ed pleaded in a raspy voice, "Please, man, just let me take off. You'll never see or hear from me again."

Sheriff Connors gunned his car as he raced up the hill recklessly. When he approached Vigneron Winery, he saw the two men standing in the parking lot. He skidded to a stop behind them. "What's the trouble?"

"I think you know Ed Brewer." Brock grabbed the back of Ed's collar and pulled him close to Connors, who had gotten out of his car. "Only problem is, he's somebody else. He tried to shoot me. The bullet's in the wall over there." Brock handed over the gun that had been fired.

"What's your side of it?" the sheriff asked. Brewer looked down and said nothing. Connors used handcuffs and put him in the back of the police car. "I'll run his prints to see if I can find out who he is, or maybe he'll just tell me." Brock saw Brewer exhale and lay his head back.

Brock said, "There's something else going on here, Nathan. Call me when you find out anything."

Maude came out to the parking lot when the sheriff's car went over the hill and dropped out of sight. "Are you okay?"

"Sure. Finally, this saga is about to break." Brock handed her the letter. "We'll get some answers when Nathan finds out who that guy really is."

Connors called Brock's cell at five fifteen. "You better get down here and fill in a few of the blanks."

"On my way." He grabbed the camera with all the pictures they took and threw it on the passenger seat of his car.

Connors shut the door to his office after Skinner entered it. "There's a hit on Brewer's prints from the FBI. The guy's name is Jared Wardlow. He's suspected of stealing a Salvador Dali from the museum he worked at in Columbia, Missouri. He went missing when the picture did."

"When was that?"

"It'll be three years ago this July."

Brock said, "Okay, let's see if the man has anything to say." Sheriff Connors led the way to the interrogation room and brought the coach in with handcuffs on. Brewer had an angry expression on his face. Brock decided to needle him. "Go figure. On top of the mountain one day, in the depths of despair the next."

There was no reply.

Connors said, "Tell us what you know, Skinner."

"Well, Wardlow here must have found out somehow that he was a dead ringer for Ed Brewer, the basketball coach in nearby Jefferson City. It looks like he cooked up a plan to step into Brewer's shoes, and must have stolen the painting in Missouri and disappeared."

"What do you mean, step into his shoes?"

"I can only guess. He probably followed Brewer here, and found out he lived in a trailer out on Fourseam Branch. Most likely, he killed him and disposed of the body. Then, he took on the identity of Ed Brewer. Somebody's figured out he's not the real deal."

"Who's that, you reckon?"

"John Money."

The sheriff turned to Wardlow. "I don't suppose you'd like to tell us what happened to Brewer? I didn't think so." Connors motioned for Wardlow to get up. He escorted him back to his jail cell. When Connors returned, he said to Skinner, "Since you served this guy up to me on a platter, I'm going to let you run with the Money business for a little while. Don't stub your toe. I want to hear from you the minute you have something."

"The thanks I get." Brock stood, patted the sheriff on the back, and sauntered out.

Skinner's car was at the open gate to the high school parking lot on Tuesday morning, before classes began. The sun had started to warm the cool, fresh air that blew in gentle gusts. The kids who drove by were playing their music so loud, Brock couldn't hear himself think. When he saw John Money pull up, he honked at him. Money veered past the Lamborghini and came to a stop. Both of them got out of their cars. "Hello, Mr. Skinner. What are you doing here?"

"I need to talk to you."

"About what?"

"Your sophomore year, when Coach Brewer first came to Hazard, did you notice anything unusual about him?"

Money frowned. "Sure. He didn't know basketball lingo or any of the common drills that coaches use. Over time though, he developed into a good coach. Have you found out who wrote that letter to me?"

"You wrote it to yourself, John. I'm just trying to figure out why."

"I did not. What are you talking about?"

"There are four letters out there. One to you, another to a girl named Amanda Critchfield, one to her parents, and the latest to Coach Brewer. I think you're behind them. You need to tell me what's going on."

"You've got it wrong. I don't know what you're talking about." Money, at that moment, looked as sinister as Brock had ever seen him. "I can tell you one thing. I remember where I saw the name Amanda Critchfield."

"Where?"

"A woman at the program signing asked me to address my signature to her."

Skinner went to the passenger side of his car to retrieve the camera from the front seat. "Here. Click through these shots. See if you recognize her."

John punched the camera button fifty times or so before he stopped. "Here she is."

"You know her, don't you?"

"I do." John handed the camera back to Brock.

~ ~ ~

Nathan Connors and Brock Skinner were seated across from the woman in the bright-white conference room, peering into her brown eyes. She seemed too relaxed for comfort. Brock broke the ice. "You're Sonja Brewer, aren't you? Amanda Critchfield's birth mother. You want to tell us about it?"

"What do you want to know?" She leaned back in her chair.

"Let's start at the beginning. You and Ed Brewer were married. You lived in Jefferson City, Tennessee. The two of you had a daughter. What happened after she was born?"

"Ed insisted that we give her to another family."

"The Critchfields."

"Yes."

"Why?" Skinner put his hands in the air like a charismatic preacher.

"Because Ed said he wasn't going to raise a girl."

Connors said, "Why didn't you just take her and leave him?"

She became animated, slapping her hands on the table. "He told me he would kill me, or her, or both of us."

"You could have gone to the police."

"Yeah, right," she muttered.

Brock asked, "Then what happened?"

"I had not seen Ed in over twenty years. I was introduced to him three years ago when he came to Hazard, and he didn't recognize me."

"So, you thought it wasn't him," Connors surmised.

"I knew it wasn't. Ed had a little star-shaped scar on his left hand, between his thumb and first finger. I really didn't care that some guy was impersonating him."

"Until a year ago, when you heard about a girl claiming he was her father," Brock said.

"Yes." She became somber and lowered her head. "I figured it was my daughter."

Brock asked, "What made you spring into action recently?"

"A couple of weeks ago, I was in a burger joint when the help behind the counter yelled for an Amanda to come up and get her food. I looked at the girl and knew she was my daughter. I could also tell she was on drugs. She looked pitiful. I had to do something."

"So, you wrote all the letters to expose Brewer and get Amanda some help."

"I did, and I had heard from some of the basketball players that you were a pretty salty character who could handle himself. That's why I pulled you into this."

"Why didn't you just go to Amanda and tell her you were her mother?"

The look on Sonja Brewer's face was the epitome of guilt and shame. "I was too afraid."

"We're going to fix that," Brock assured her. "Tell me, why did you start going by the name Joan Miro?"

"I left Jeff City twenty-five years ago and came to Hazard looking for a job. I decided to use it because that's what I named my baby girl who was taken from me. Joan Miro Brewer."

"You have some affinity for the artist?"

"Yes. Have you ever studied his painting *The Farm*? It captures the feeling of living in Appalachia. Lonely. Depressing."

"No. Why do you keep such a grim reminder behind your desk?"

"When I look at the picture, I think of the daughter I lost." Her expression oozed with pain.

"You'll want to let Amanda know her real name when she comes back to town. She's up in Lexington at a rehab center getting off drugs."

Sonja Brewer, known at the high school as Joan Miro, put her head on the table. After a few seconds, she groaned, "Thank God!"

~ ~ ~

On a radiant Saturday afternoon in May, Maude stood to announce the theatrical production that was about to begin. The crowd of wine-bibbers on the veranda stopped conversing long enough to listen. "Ladies and gentlemen, today we will see a Shakespearean vignette put on by Joan Brewer and her cast of three." John Money, Sonja Brewer, the Skinners, and the Critchfields were seated together right up front. Joan's eyes sparkled like emeralds as she belted out the opening lines.

John Money announced he would be playing ball for the University of Kentucky, where Brock and Maude's brother, Marcel, had successfully matriculated. What a coincidence.

GETTING TATTOOED

Savory air, redolent of late spring flowers, and the royal-blue translucent sky were glorious that Friday afternoon in May. Maude Skinner left the winery at three thirty to give herself plenty of time to get ready for the big celebration that was on for tonight. David Sturges, a decorated World War II veteran, had turned a hundred years old two days ago, and all the nabobs in town had been invited to his home for a gala. Maude's husband, Brock, was on his way to fill the Lamborghini with gas. She waved to him as he sped by, going the other direction.

As Brock neared the gas station, he could see it was overrun with vehicles. SUVs with trailered boats, heading to the lake that evening, hogged several of the pump lanes. He got in behind a black Mercedes, waiting to move ahead when the cars cleared. The two in front that had finished filling up pulled off together. The Mercedes took the forward pump. Brock parked at the one in the back. Later, he would scold himself for what happened after that.

The young man up ahead, in camel-colored slacks and a black golf shirt, gassed up in a hurry. He smiled innocently and started walking in the direction of the Lamborghini. Brock anticipated he would make some comment about the car, but instead the man hit him in the chin with a right hook that just about knocked him out. As he was falling, drops of blood spewed from his mouth onto the passenger door of the Lamborghini. The man began kicking him viciously. All Brock could do was ball up and try to protect his face and stomach. "This is a warning. Keep your nose out of Sturges Lumber's business. You got it?" The man crouched and gave Brock one more punch to the face before he got in his car and pulled away.

The people who saw the beat-down ran over to offer assistance. A young girl in jeans and a Marilyn Monroe t-shirt helped Brock to his feet. When she noticed the blood now gushing from his mouth, she fainted. He was still foggy, yet had the presence of mind to say, "Thanks, folks. I'll be all right. Get her some water." Brock, a skilled boxer, had never let a person approach him without being ready for a sucker punch. He let his guard down this time, and paid a heavy price.

"What in the world happened to you?" Maude howled with panic in her eyes.

Brock went to the pantry and got out the container of salt. He poured a half inch in the bottom of a glass and turned on the hot water. "Some guy beat me up at the gas station." He filled the glass, took a big mouthful, sloshed it around, and spit it in the kitchen sink. He did that a dozen more times, now able to feel the cut in his tongue and gash in his cheek on the inside of his mouth.

"Who?"

"He was in a black Mercedes with tinted windows. Told me to stay away from Sturges Lumber."

"What does that mean?"

"The accountant for David Sturges called me this morning and asked if I had any interest in buying fifty percent of the company. I told him to send me the financials and I would take a look at it." Brock poured more salt in the glass and repeated the saline rinse several more times. He took a clean washcloth and stuffed it in his cheek and around his tongue.

Maude turned angry. "Damn it, Brock. I can't even send you to the gas station. I was looking forward to the party tonight. Look at that bruise on your cheek."

He took the washcloth out of his mouth so he could speak. "I'll eat soup and wear makeup. Think nothing of it. Now, let's get ready and have a glass of wine on the patio before we go."

The Sturges homestead, on the narrow spine of a mountain southwest of Hazard, Kentucky, was an English Tudor affair with more than two hundred globular bushes around the driveway and pool. Red herringbone brick filled in the spaces between the timbers that were the structural elements of the walls. Two dozen cars were parked along the grass on both sides of the road leading up to the house.

The main structure was rectangular, and on the back, a big open room had been scabbed on for entertaining. The southern exposure allowed shafts of sunlight to shine through the clerestory and side walls in the afternoon and early evening. The vaulted ceiling, over twenty feet high, had dark brown timbers spaced every five feet. A wood-burning fireplace at the far end, with a black stovepipe that extended up fifteen feet before going through the wall, was purely decorative.

David Sturges made his grand entrance to the raucous applause of the thirty or so people who were in attendance. He waved to them with the arm motion of a puppet on a string. He was slightly bent over, using a walker, and the watery skin around his eyes drooped. David tottered over to where Brock was standing against the wall. "Are you Mr. Skinner?" he asked.

"I am. This is my wife, Maude."

She stepped forward and said, "Nice to meet you, sir."

He nodded at her and grinned feebly. "I want you all to sit by me this evening."

"We'd be honored."

To demonstrate his lucidity, David threw out some clever opening remarks for the crowd. He asked everyone to take a seat so dinner could be served, and afterward he would tell a few war stories. Maude sat across from Brock, next to David, who was seated at the head of the table. Brock chose the soup over salad when asked what he wanted as his first course.

David put his forearms on the end of the table and fluttered his hands, preparing to speak. "So, Mr. Skinner, what's your position on tattoos?"

"Pardon me, sir?"

"Tattoos, are you for them or against them?"

"That's a loaded question," Brock said.

"Come now. Surely you can do better than that." Sturges leaned back and to the side, pulling one arm away from the table.

"How about this?" Brock wove his hands and stuck out his chin. "Leviticus chapter nineteen says do not put tattoo marks on yourself. That's good enough for me."

"Hot damn. I knew you were my kind of man. You don't have any tattoos, do you?"

"Well, no."

"All right, then. Did my accountant call you?"

"He did," Brock confirmed.

David turned to Maude to engage her in a little witticism. She escalated the conversation to cultural badinage about art and life in general. Brock did the best he could to down the pan-seared fish that had been served with a beurre blanc sauce. When he finished eating, he excused himself and went to the bathroom while David and Maude continued their banter.

Brock rinsed his mouth out after washing his hands. At least no more blood was coming from his wounds. He touched his tender jaw and wiped his lips with a spare hand towel from under the sink. When he saw a closet in the mirror behind where he stood,

Brock tried the door, but it was locked. He defeated the lock quickly and looked to see what was inside. Letters were piled on the lower shelf, in a stack nearly a foot tall. The blueprint on the top left of the stationery read: *Colonel Corey G. Powell, USAF (Ret.).* On the right was a swooping eagle and line underneath it across the entire page. The letter on top was dated two months ago. Brock pulled a few out of the stack to read them.

Dear David,

I am eating licorice made in Finland. Can you believe this? Truly, there is nothing that surprises me anymore. The rest of the world has figured out the things America likes best, and they cater to our whims. Why not? That is where the money is, right?

"Ride to the sound of the guns, you fools!" That is what Custer said and got his rear-end blown off. Custer was last in his class at West Point, academically. I believe he was fortunate to get his diploma. He was always in some kind of mischief. Still, that is the stuff good generals are made of.

Arrivederci! Best wishes to your children.

Corey

Dear David,

If I didn't know better, I would swear one of two things was happening as you were writing your last letter to me. 1) You were pissed to the eyeballs with bourbon, or 2) You were leaning up against a B-25 with the throttle to the firewall. Bob Simmons was the lead navigator in that B-25. The only time we saw him and his crew was taking off from NATAL.

My biggest mistake after leaving Ascension Island was not making landfall at TAKORADI which was a short distance from ACCRA. Because we were late taking off, I elected to head directly to ACCRA. The course heading, as I recall, paralleled the coast between TAKORADI and ACCRA. Result, a landing in Lagos and a lot of scotch whiskey with the RAF. War was hell!

Stay well, my friend.

>*Corey*

Dear David,

Do you remember the guy with the ill-fitting uniform whose hat was perched on a knob on the back of his skull? He had flunked out of pilot training, even bombardier school. I asked him how he did that. His answer was simple: "I couldn't hit the target." That explained it. The tactical officer spotted this stubble under his nose and made him shave it off. Har, Har, Har.

Then, of course, there was "Big Al" Karloff, a.k.a. "Stud Horse." I can still hear his voice resonating off the walls at Mather Field in the early morning hours as he described his sexual conquests of the previous night. "There I was, operating." He was always at the bar of the Senator Hotel in Sacramento picking up women.

Regards to your kids.

>*Corey*

Dear David,

I will always remember when an Army general ordered his staff car to stop in North Africa when our classmate A. L. Morgan failed to salute the flag on the car. The general ordered the driver to stop, back up in front of Morgan, where the general jumped out and asked him, "Young man, don't you recognize a senior/superior officer's flag?" Morgan's response: "I guess I had my head up my ass, sir!" A very good answer, but not the correct one. The general then proceeded to chew Morgan's ass out unmercifully. Do you recall the incident? I think the chewing out was related to Morgan's lack of command of the English language.

My best to you.

   Corey

Dear David,

I did enjoy our trips to Cairo and our visits to the pyramids. Those forlorn flights between Dakar and Marrakech. I did take advantage of a ride on the back of a camel. Those camel drivers needed a bath. I seem to remember that the camels could and would bite if you didn't keep your eyes open. How fortunate we were. Remember the per diems, etc.?

As a finance officer, I used to strap the cash belt around my waist. At night, the time of the loss, I took the belt off and put it under my pillow. The thief managed to take the money anyway, and I had to make full restitution. A thousand bucks was a lot of money in 1943.

Stay well and write.

   Corey

Dear David,

My television set is turned on to an Alabama vs. Kentucky football game. I believe the Crimson Tide will dominate. I hope I am wrong. Have you seen the Red Lobster ad? Endless shrimp, my favorite! Alabama has scored again on a pass in-terception.

I don't know why Kentucky does not fare better in the foot-ball department. I recall when Paul "Bear" Bryant coached at Kentucky and then left for Alabama. Bryant always had to ask one of his assistants if his players were attending classes.

The assistant would say, "I thought he was kicked out of school last year."

The dinner bell has sounded. Arrivederci.

Corey

Dear David,

I remember when our crew was taking a C-54 to Frankfurt, Germany, from Hickam Air Force Base in Hawaii. The pilot was a great guy named Joey Chula. Joey was married to a fine young woman named Babs. We had taken off from the Azores headed for Germany and even made a few passes at the Greenway at Rhein-Main before the tower and Air Traffic Control waved us off and told us to proceed to our alternate, ORLY AIRBASE.

We were stuck in Paris for five days! Ooh La La! As a bachelor, I made sure I enhanced my education. The Louvre. The Bastille, etc., etc. I was even able to employ my rudimentary French language skills. By then, I knew I had not wasted my time in French class. I'm glad I did all those things before I met my beloved, Sharon. She was the love of my life. My soulmate. God rest her soul.

Au revoir.

Corey

Dear David,

I always told you that you had your snout into the sauce too much! That picture you sent me was taken at Forbidden City, a night club on Powell Street in San Francisco, after we transferred to Hamilton AFB from Memphis. Remember? As I recall, Forbidden City was located in the Sir Francis Drake Hotel. Why is that bottle of scotch in front of me? Where is my date? So many unanswered questions!!!

Oh, just to let you know, I'm giving my half ownership in your lumber company to my great-grandson, Adam Powell. He's nearly thirty years old now, and his wife's name is Eve. How's that for biblical significance?

Stay well, and most importantly, stay in touch.

Corey

Brock saw an envelope on the upper shelf that had a return address on it for Oaks Life Community, 72 Franklin Road, Roanoke, Virginia. He put the letters back in the stack except the top one that declared Corey's great-grandson, Adam, would be receiving the 50 percent ownership in Sturges Lumber.

Maude looked over and said to Brock when he returned to the table, "You okay?"

"Fine."

Thankfully, the dessert was chocolate mousse.

David Sturges stood after dinner and told three war stories, one that included his best friend, Corey Powell. He was presented with a couple of gag gifts and a gilded plaque of his military service and association with Sturges Lumber for the last seventy-five years. The crowd stayed and mingled for another hour or so, and on the way out, each person personally paid their respects to David Sturges for his long, fruitful life.

~ ~ ~

Monday morning, an express package came to the Skinner house with ten years of financial statements for Sturges Lumber enclosed. The volume of the business had consistently been around $10 million. Profits fluctuated from one hundred to three hundred thousand a year. The book value of the company was a little over four million, with no debt on the balance sheet.

Brock picked up the phone and placed a call to the accountant who sent the information. "Is this Ron Harris? Brock Skinner here."

"Yes, Mr. Skinner."

"I've got a few questions for you. First, how come David hasn't given his interest in the business to his children, grandchildren, and great-grandchildren?"

"Because they all have tattoos."

"You're kidding."

"No."

Brock regrouped and asked, "Well, who's running the company?"

"His great-grandkids. David let his son run it years ago until he retired, and then his grandson took over. He just retired, and now one of the great grandsons is running it."

"Who owns the other fifty percent?"

"I'm not quite sure. For the last seventy-five years, David's war buddy, Corey Powell, was his silent partner. The last twenty-five years, since I've been David's accountant, I've sent dividends and tax information to Mr. Powell annually, but he died a couple of months ago. I think he had dementia for several years before his death. I don't know what has been happening to the money."

"Hasn't David told you who was going to get that stock?" Brock asked.

"No."

"I have reason to believe it will go to his great-grandson, Adam Powell. Why is David selling now?"

"All he told me was Corey's death complicated everything, and that he needed to sell."

"Well, tell David I'll give him book value for his fifty percent, which would be a little over two million dollars cash," Brock said. "The only condition I have is that we find out who owns the other fifty percent, and make sure everything is legal on their end."

"Okay. I'll tell him."

"One more question. Who gets the Sturges Lumber stock if David dies right now?"

"You're not going to believe this. Upon his death, his fifty percent position is to be auctioned off and the proceeds given to the National Museum of the United States Air Force in Dayton, Ohio."

"What about his other assets?"

"Split equally among his blood relatives," Harris replied.

Brock reflected on that. "Sounds to me like he set it up that way to keep his family members from trying to kill him for his money. His heirs will end up getting a lot of cash if he sells to me. If David says yes to the deal, I'll want to meet with him right away."

~ ~ ~

Maude decided to ride along on the trip to Roanoke, Virginia. They located Oaks Life Community, went in, and asked to see the manager. She was young and slightly overweight, her thick blonde hair smartly styled. She ushered the Skinners into her office. "What can I do for you folks?"

"Can you tell us about Corey Powell?"

"Oh, poor Mr. Powell. He was here eleven years, and nearly made a hundred before he died a couple of months ago."

"Did you notice him writing letters every day?"

"He only started doing that a couple of years ago, when his dementia got worse. The nurse would bring one up to be mailed just about every day."

Brock pulled a letter out of his jacket pocket and gave it to her. "Is that his handwriting?"

"Yes." She handed it back.

"Did he ever have any visitors?" Maude asked.

"Just two. His great-grandson and great-granddaughter-in-law. It was all the family he had left. His wife died over twenty years ago. Mr. Powell had a son, who had a son, who had a son. The great-grandson's parents and grandparents were killed in a car accident right before he moved in here. Mr. Powell was living with his grandson then. He had no place to go, so they moved him in here. He seemed to have plenty of money. The great-grandson was eighteen at the time, I believe."

"Adam and Eve Powell," Brock said. "How well did you know them?"

"Not well. They scared me a little. Something wasn't right with them."

"Who paid Mr. Powell's bill?"

The manager wrote down a name and address on a sticky note. "His accountant."

The accountant was a one-man operation, desperately hanging on until retirement. It looked like he'd been in the same office for forty years. The walls were brown from the tar of cigarettes. Brock lied to him, and said, "I own fifty percent of Sturges Lumber in Hazard, Kentucky. I just bought it from David Sturges. I'm trying to locate the owners of the other half of the business so I can try to buy them out."

"Corey signed the stock over to his great-grandson two months ago, and a couple days later, he was found dead at the nursing home."

"You suspect foul play?"

"Wait until you meet Adam and Eve. Judge for yourself."

"Do you know where they live?"

"I suppose in Blacksburg, Virginia, where Corey lived until he moved into the nursing home in Roanoke."

"What about the rest of Mr. Powell's assets?"

"You mean the million dollars he had in the bank? He left that to David Sturges."

"Does Sturges know?"

"I called him a few days ago and told him to expect a check. You see, the account was transfer on death, which means it bypasses probate and goes right to him."

"Thanks for your time."

~ ~ ~

Brock was led into the study at the Sturges home by the Man Friday. David was teetering back and forth in the cherry rocking chair next to the desk. Wilma, David's wife, died of cancer nearly fifty years ago, and the last Christmas present she gave him was that chair. "Ah, Mr. Skinner. Nice of you to stop by."

"You in the mood to fill me in on your family affairs before I buy half of the lumberyard?"

"Why, of course. You're going to be up against it a bit," Sturges admitted.

"Start by telling me the real reason you're selling. I know that Corey Powell's great-grandson now has the other fifty percent of the company, and you're going to inherit a million dollars from your deceased friend in the next few days. And I'm not buying the story about not giving stock to your kids because they have tattoos. You're far too broad-minded for that."

"I haven't given the company to my family members because they don't have enough sense to get along with each other. I just use the tattoo business as an excuse. I figured if I just let 'em all work there, there'd be less infighting. They've all had jobs, and have had to work together for their own good."

"Okay, then. Why didn't you try to buy Powell out to get complete control?"

"I'm not prepared to answer that. I did tell Adam Powell a white lie when he called me wanting to buy my half. I told him I had a deal to sell my ownership to you." David stopped rocking.

So, that's why the guy beat me up at the gas station, Brock thought. "You understand that if you sell out to me for two million and change, and get a million-dollar check from Powell, your heirs will have several million reasons to want to kill you."

"I'm going to change my will and put the money in trust so they won't get it for ten years. Surely, I'll be dead by then. That should remove any incentive they might have to bump me off."

"Better do that in a hurry, and let them know about it," Brock warned. "My goal is to buy Adam Powell's shares, and sell forty-nine percent of it on installment to your family members working there. I want them to have some skin in the game. How many of your kin are there now?"

"It's down to seven of my eight great-grandchildren. The other great-granddaughter left town after she graduated from high school many years ago, and we haven't seen or heard from her since."

"That makes the math easy. Seven percent for seven people is forty-nine percent."

"I wish you luck in that endeavor," Sturges said.

Brock did the deal and bought David's shares by the end of May. He had yet to meet Adam Powell, unless he was the man who beat him up at the gas station. If it was him, he'd likely be coming around again soon. Brock would be ready for him next time.

~ ~ ~

"Maude, I'm going over to Blacksburg to see if I can find out anything about Adam and Eve before they take another bite from the apple. I'll drive a pickup truck from the winery."

"Try not to get beat up again, or something more," she cautioned.

"I'll stay the night and be back after lunch tomorrow."

Brock parked in what looked to be a popular spot in Blacksburg, the River Birch Grill, at five thirty. He sat at the bar, nursing a glass of wine, searching for the right person to engage in conversation. A dapper man in his seventies, wearing a porkpie hat and houndstooth sport coat with brown-felt elbow patches, came through the door holding a taupe rain coat draped over his left arm. His face was slightly gaunt and he had a full day's growth of gray stubble. Brock conspicuously waved him over. The man's eyes brightened as he approached. "Do I know you, sir? One of my former students perhaps?" he asked.

"I don't think so. I'm just visiting Blacksburg, and you look like a man who knows something about this town."

"Well, you're right on that score. I've been here over fifty years. Retired history professor from Virginia Tech. Taught there forty years. My name's Raymond Crickmore. And you would be?"

"Brock Skinner. Can I buy you a drink?"

"You certainly may. I'll have a Dewar's and water."

"Are you meeting anyone?"

"Heavens no. Since my wife left me, I try to get out a couple times a week to be with the proletariat. You know, keep the mind active," Crickmore offered.

"Better them than the apparatchik or bourgeoisie."

Crickmore heaved his shoulders, and said, "I see you're an educated man. I wouldn't have thought so. You look rather disquieting."

"I'm trying to find out about a car accident that happened around here nearly a dozen years ago."

"What were the names of the people involved?"

The bartender brought Crickmore's scotch.

"Powell. Father and son, and their wives," Brock said.

Brock's new acquaintance stiffened. "Oh, yes. Artemis Powell and I were friends. He was my age, you know. His wife, son Lionel, and daughter-in-law all vanished at one time. A tunnel caved in on top of them. What a tragedy." He took a long pull on his drink and looked past Brock, deep in thought.

"Did you ever meet your friend's father, Corey Powell?"

"I'm afraid not. I am acquainted with Art's grandson, Adam Powell. He and his girlfriend, Eve something, were in my history class together at VPI."

"What do you remember about them?"

"Just one thing. I was afraid to give either of them anything less than an A, if you know what I mean."

Brock kept the conversation going. "I guess the two of them got married. You don't happen to know if they're still around here, do you?"

"Unfortunately, they are. They live on Pine Valley Drive out by Blacksburg Country Club. As far as I can tell, the only thing he does is play golf for money. I played with him once. That was enough for me. She's a bit of a mystery."

"Do you happen to know their address?"

"The corner of Pine Valley and Augusta National Road. It's a gaudy-looking stone thing."

Brock Skinner and Ray Crickmore had a delightful dinner together. There was no more discussion about the Powell family. When the two men parted company, Ray expressed his sincere appreciation for being able to spend time with someone in lively conversation, like he had been able to do when he was still a teacher. Brock got a real sense of loneliness from the man, something he hadn't fully appreciated until that moment.

The thick blanket of inky clouds, gearing up for drizzle, hastened the evening darkness. Light shone from many of the windows in the stone house on Pine Valley. Brock coasted past it slowly, parking in the driveway of a new home for sale up the way. The sidewalks had become damp from the heavy air. He walked right up the driveway of Powell's house, followed the path around to the back patio, and then hugged the wall by the sliding glass door. Faint conversation could be heard coming from inside, and as it got louder, Adam and Eve came into view. Recognizing Adam, Skinner focused intently on Eve's face. The couple turned the lights off in the room where they were standing before moving into another part of the house. Skinner snuck away and left the neighborhood quietly.

Brock marched into Blacksburg Country Club at 7:30 the next morning—high, wide, and handsome. The cloudy weather had moved out, and a fresh breeze of dry air had moved in. The morning tee times were packed with golfers. He went into the pro shop to look for a directory, but all he saw was the computer used for posting golf scores. He searched around on it until he found the online listing of members. Adam Powell's cell phone number was shown. So was Eve's. Brock scrawled them both on the pad next to the computer.

Maude called her husband late that morning to see if he was in one piece and on the way home. "Did you enjoy your visit?"

"You won't believe my luck. I ran into an old man who knows the blaggard who owns the other fifty percent of the lumber company. He even knew where he lived."

"Is he the guy that beat you up?"

"The very same."

"Do you have more lumps on your head?" she asked half facetiously.

"I do not. I was more interested in figuring out what the deal is with his wife, Eve. If my hunch is right, things are going to get interesting."

"When will you get here?"

"Later today. I'm going to David's house for a few minutes before I come home."

When David's Man Friday opened the door, he said he would see if Mr. Sturges was accepting visitors. After a short wait, Brock was taken into the study again, where David was sitting at the desk this time. "What can I do for you, Skinner?"

"What is the name of your great-granddaughter who ran off years ago?"

"Monica Sturges."

"Does she have a middle name?" Brock asked.

"Evelyn."

"Do you have a picture of her?" David reached to the corner of the desk and turned around a photo that had been taken fifteen years ago of his eight great-grandchildren. David pointed Monica out.

Brock studied the girl's face. "Okay. I have her phone number here."

"You found Monica? Where?" His eyes widened as he sat up in his chair.

"We'll talk about that later. I want you to call this number and ask if it's Monica Sturges."

David dialed the number on the antique black phone perched on his desk. After some delay, he said into the mouthpiece, "Is this Monica Sturges?" He listened for about five seconds. "This is your great-grandfather calling." He looked at the phone, put it down, and said, "She hung up."

"What'd she say?"

"She asked who was calling."

"That seals it, then," Brock said with a modicum of satisfaction.

David slumped back down in his chair. "Where is she?"

"I can't tell you right now. You'll have to trust me. Everything's going to work out. Look, I need to go home and plan out some things. I'll be back in a couple of hours. I want you to call Adam Powell when I get back." Brock showed himself out.

David Sturges rubbed his eyes and exhaled.

Skinner returned to the Sturges house after dinner. David asked, "Can I get you a cup of decaf coffee?"

"Yes, thank you." The Man Friday took leave. "David, call Adam Powell and tell him the deal to sell your stock in Sturges Lumber to me has fallen through. Tell him you want to sell to him. Ask him to come and visit you at one thirty tomorrow to discuss price and terms. Tell him to bring his wife in case any papers have to be signed, but let him know that you want to meet with him alone to talk money. If he balks, and wants to discuss it over the phone, tell him you have some information about his great-grandfather, Corey, that will be of interest to him."

"Why are we doing this?"

"Lots of reasons. Mainly for your well-being, and that of your family." David's helper returned with two cups of coffee, and David made the call. "What'd he say?" Brock asked.

"Very little. He said to expect him at one thirty. What do I say when he gets here?"

"We'll talk about that in the morning," Brock assured him.

David lapsed into a saturnine temperament. "I guess I owe you the truth about tattoos." He gingerly took a sip of the hot coffee, his hands shaking from old age.

"Yes. And a few other things. Let me give you my opinion."

"Go ahead," David said.

"Over the years, you've seen a few Holocaust survivors with concentration camp tattoos on their arms. Every time you see one, it brings to mind the horrors of war."

"You're a perceptive man, Skinner. The things Corey Powell and I saw were unspeakable. What is this information I'm supposed to have about Corey that will interest Adam?"

"I think you know." Brock set his coffee cup on the desk. He thanked David for going along with his plan.

David got to his feet slowly and spoke ardently. "You know, my missing great-granddaughter is what has troubled me the most. She's a lost sheep that must be found."

"She will be." Brock nodded as he turned to leave.

On the ride home, he thought about the many things that could go wrong tomorrow; he had to be sure to account for all contingencies.

~ ~ ~

Brock walked into Sheriff Nathan Connors' office at eight o'clock sharp the next morning. "Uh oh. Captain Trouble is here again," Connors said.

"Nathan, I need you to help me collar a murderer."

Connors looked at him. "Get out of here. I don't have time to do your bidding."

"You know David Sturges, don't you?"

"Of course."

"And you know he still owns part of the Sturges Lumber Company." That was a lie. Brock owned it now.

"I do."

"The man who owns half of the company is coming to visit Sturges at one thirty today. He wants to buy the rest of it. I'm afraid the guy might threaten him, or worse."

"What exactly do you want, Skinner?"

"Three men."

"For how long?" The sheriff rolled back against the wall in his chair and put his legs out.

"Two hours. From one until three."

"Promise me that I'll get a feather in my cap for this charade."

"From an Amherst pheasant. On an El Dorado black leather hat," Brock replied.

Skinner spent the rest of the morning prepping Sturges on how to handle the negotiations with Powell. At noon, he parked off to the side of the road Adam Powell would use to enter town. It was one fifteen before the black Mercedes with tinted windows sped by. There was no way to tell if Eve was in the car.

Adam followed his GPS up the mountain in the direction of the Sturges house. There was a strong wind up there that pushed the car off course several times. Drawing near, he slowed down and looked side to side and in the rearview mirror, making sure he wasn't going to get ambushed. He drove up to the front door, turned the car around, and parked a hundred yards down the driveway, facing away from the house. Adam said to Eve, "Stay here. If anything happens, drive to safety and call me. If I need you, I'll bring papers out for you to sign." She nodded and went back to looking at her phone. Adam put his pistol in the holster under his arm, grabbed the papers he brought, and got out of the car.

The Man Friday ushered Adam into the study. David Sturges said, "It's been a long time since I've seen you. I think the last time was when your family came to Monica's graduation. Are you doing okay?"

"Fine," he said, without expression.

"I was sad when I heard of Corey's passing. His mind had gone soft the last couple of years. I guess it's a blessing. You and your wife were the only family he had left."

Adam sat down in front of the desk. "Yes. So, what happened to your deal with Skinner?"

"He couldn't come up with the money."

"That's strange, I heard he was rich. What was the price to him?"

"The same as it is to you. Book value for the shares. A little more than two million."

Powell got up and moseyed over to look out the windows on the front of the house. He could see the Mercedes. After a few seconds, he said, "I could probably afford to pay that if my great-grandfather hadn't given you the million dollars in his bank account."

"Adam, you surely understand I gave Corey half interest in the lumber yard, and paid him dividends for seventy-five years. Don't you think that's generous enough?"

"That doesn't help me. I'm offering you book value, less the amount of money you got from our family."

"Well, that's not enough, Adam. I'm sure Brock Skinner could come up with more than that." David suddenly beamed with confidence, like he had the ability to seriously challenge Powell.

"Why were you ever interested in selling to Skinner?"

"I figured he'd do right by my seven great-grandchildren who work there now." David leaned forward and put his arms on the desk.

Adam turned to face him. "Which means you don't trust me to take care of them?"

"I don't know you, Adam. From what I can tell by looking, you're a little on the shifty side."

"I'm not going to stand here and listen to your insults." Adam pointed to the papers he had brought, on the front of the desk. "You're going to sign those for the deal I just explained."

"No, I'm not. If you want the deal I offered, you can have it. Otherwise, clear out." David wasn't short on courage.

Adam pulled the pistol out of its holster. "Maybe this will persuade you."

David stood up more spryly than a man of his age usually does, and said, "Now I know for sure what kind of character you are. A bad one. How about this? What if I give you book value for your shares, in cash, right now?"

"Show me the cash," Powell said. David lifted a briefcase next to his chair up onto the desk. Powell opened it and sifted through the bills for a few seconds. He put the papers he brought with him on top of the money and closed the case. "I'm taking the money, and I'm not selling you my stock. You owe me this money."

Sturges looked down and said sotto voce, "Yeah, I probably do. But you're not taking it unless you sell me your stock."

"Just watch me," Adam retorted.

From the study door leading to the front of the house, Sheriff Connors called out, "Drop the gun." Adam pivoted and sprinted toward the door to the dining room. As he went through it, a deputy hacked his arm, sending the gun flying. The deputy tripped him, dug a knee in his back, and put handcuffs on him. Connors called Skinner and instructed the deputy to get Powell's cell phone.

Eve heard and saw a pickup truck barreling toward her. She shimmied over to the driver's side of the Mercedes as fast as she could, but it was too late. By the time she had the car started and in drive, the pickup was within a foot. The driver's door flew open and a policeman who had been hiding behind a nearby shed reached in and pushed the off button before dragging her out. He found the keys to the vehicle and put them in his pocket. Brock told the policeman, "Hold her here for a few minutes. I'll wave when I want you to bring her in."

Skinner entered the house to find everyone sitting silently. He said, "Sheriff, this is the charming Adam Powell, great-grandson of Corey Powell, David's best friend. Adam here knew that his great-grandfather owned half of Sturges Lumber. He got the bright idea to kill his parents and grandparents by rigging the collapse of a tunnel, thinking he would be next in line to inherit whatever Corey had when he died. To his dismay, Adam found out that Corey was going to leave everything to his friend, David Sturges. Adam and his wife, Eve, worked on poor Corey for eleven years, trying to get him to part with either some cash or the company stock."

Sturges interrupted. "And it finally worked. Corey relented and signed the stock over to Adam. He didn't, however, give him the money he had saved up over the years."

Brock continued, "And that made Adam mad. So, he killed Corey. Most likely by poisoning."

Connors sat up with interest. "Think we can prove that?"

"Have his body exhumed and check for toxins. I'm sure you'll find something. Mr. Marvelous there probably left a trail you can follow to get him. Proving he made that tunnel collapse to kill his parents and grandparents will be a little tougher." Powell shook his head in disgust.

"How'd Powell here turn into such a bad character?" the sheriff asked.

"Well, you know, they say Eve talked Adam into eating from the tree. It's her fault." Brock went to the window and waved to the policeman outside.

When Eve came in, David's face was stricken with dread. He yelled, "Oh, no! Monica, is that you? You're married to this punk? Oh," he said, putting his face in his hands.

"I'm sorry, Gramps. Is it all that bad? Can't we work things out?" She went over to the front of the desk and tapped her fingernails.

Brock continued his story. "Monica here met Adam after they graduated from high school. She knew about working for Sturges Lumber, and how all the family members had that opportunity, but she came up with a better idea. She and Adam hatched a plan to get the fifty percent ownership away from Corey Powell. They figured to buy the rest from David and take the place over. Then they could show those other seven great-grandchildren who the smart one was."

David had put his arms and face down on the desk and was mumbling to himself. "Gramps, why are you acting this way?" Eve asked.

Brock came over to her and crossed his arms. "Did you ever wonder why your Gramps didn't buy out his friend, Corey Powell? The man raked in a lot of dough for seventy-five years. Does that seem right?" He leaned down and spoke to David Sturges. "Are you going to tell them, or should I?"

"You tell 'em," David said before he let out a muffled growl.

Brock directed his attention to Adam and Eve. "You folks don't have any kids, do you?"

"No," Adam replied.

"Good. Aren't planning on having any, right?"

"Maybe, who knows?" Eve said, miffed.

"I wouldn't advise it. You see, Mr. Sturges is Adam's great-grandfather too, just like you. He had an affair with Corey's wife, Sharon, and Corey thought the child was his. Sharon was David's Bathsheba. He has spent the last seventy-five years trying to buy back his conscience."

"That's sick," Monica, AKA Eve, spat.

"Adam, I'll tell you what. Sell me your stock for book value, and I'll not tattoo your hind end like you did mine at that gas station. You're going to need all the money you can get to defend yourself in court. Or we can step outside, and I'll break you into little pieces."

Adam Powell looked at Brock sheepishly, and said, "Deal."

MAN'S WORST FRIEND

"Brock, this is your old friend, Charlie White."

"How the heck are you, Charlie?"

"Great. Listen, I'm calling because I've been training an up-and-coming heavyweight who I think has a real shot. His name is Larry Hayes. He's twenty-two years old."

Brock sensed what was coming next. "You know I'm not in the business of buying a piece of a prize fighter."

Charlie responded instantly. "I know that. I want you to do me a favor."

"What's that?"

"He's got a fight in Las Vegas on July Fourth. I want you to spar with him for three days. Ten rounds. Only a thirty-second break between rounds. And try not to hurt him."

"Yeah, right. I'll be thirty-five in August, Charlie."

White chuckled. "You'll be the meanest damn thirty-five around. I wouldn't send the kid your way if you were still twenty-five."

"Okay. He can stay at the house. You heard I got married, didn't you, Charlie?"

"Poor woman. I suppose you didn't tell her your life has been nothing but mayhem."

"I'm still alive, aren't I? And don't you ever tell her anything about my past."

Brock Skinner grew up on a quaint little horse farm near I-75, east of Lexington, on Athens Boonesboro Road. He went to Henry Clay High School, where he played football and dabbled in the decathlon. At six-foot-two and 217 pounds, he developed into a pretty good tight end. The University of Kentucky invited him to walk on to the team, but he turned them down. He didn't want to get hurt and wreck his joints. So, he switched to boxing to stay fit. It was even more dangerous than playing football, so he never actually took any real fights. Instead, he always wore padded gloves, headgear, and a kidney belt, and became the most feared sparring partner in the United States. Brock did that until the investment he'd made in his wife's brother's business began to pay dividends. It wasn't long after that before he became rich. He bought a Lamborghini and turned into the fool who rushed in where angels feared to tread.

~ ~ ~

Over supper, Brock said, "Maude, a friend of mine from Lexington is sending a boxer down here in the morning. He wants me to train with him for a few days."

"Well, that seems harmless enough," she said. Maude had been married to Brock nearly a year, and was painfully aware of his propensity for getting into trouble.

"His name is Scary Larry Hayes. I invited him to stay here at the house."

"I'll run and get another steak before I go to the winery tomorrow," she said.

Larry Hayes drove into Skinner's driveway at ten o'clock the next morning. The humid June day had already begun heating up. Brock came out of the house, excited to meet him. Hayes was a light-skinned Black man with short hair; he looked a little like

Cassius Clay. He introduced himself. "Nice to meet you, Mr. Skinner. Thanks for inviting me down."

"It's Brock. Bring your bags in the house. Let's take our gear and go over to the gym for a workout before lunch."

"Sounds good."

Hayes stood six-foot-three and weighed 222 pounds, which made him roughly the same size as Brock. When they finished sparring, Brock said, "I notice you always move to the right when a punch is coming."

"Yeah, Charlie has been trying to break me of that. He wants me to move left occasionally with a quick right jab to the body."

"We'll work on it. Come on, let's shower off and get some lunch."

The hot and humid weather made them sweat again walking out to the car. The two oversized men shoehorning themselves into a Lamborghini was somewhat of a spectacle in downtown Hazard, Kentucky, especially since one of them was Black. Perry County was 99 percent white, and some of them weren't all that broad-minded. The conspicuous pugilists wheeled into a nearby Asian restaurant where they ordered steamed tofu, rice, and big plates of sautéed vegetables. When they finished eating, Brock suggested, "This afternoon, let's run up the hill to my wife's winery. We can take your car down to the bottom, and we'll go get it after we run up."

Hayes smiled. "I don't want you to hurt yourself now, old man."

"We'll race then, and see who the old man is," Skinner shot back confidently.

When the Lamborghini arrived at Vigneron Winery, Maude watched it park on the back row of the lot. She met Larry and Brock at the door. "I don't see any scratches or bruises. Did you take it easy on him?"

"Ma'am, your husband's a freak. He punches like a piston and never seems to tire out."

"He's a freak, all right. What's the plan for this afternoon?"

"Later, we're going to race up the hill from the main road."

"That's two miles or better," she said.

"Yes, and bright eyes here thinks he can beat me to the top," Brock replied.

The men changed into running gear at the house at three thirty. Larry drove his car around the mountain and stopped at the turnoff to the winery. They stretched for a couple of minutes and started running at a slow pace. Larry said, "Your wife is really nice."

"I know. I don't deserve her. You excited about your upcoming fight?"

"You bet." The hill began to steepen. They picked up the pace.

Suddenly, a large white dog emerged from a grown-over path in the woods and came sprinting at them. Hayes backed away to defend himself. The dog set its sights on Brock, jumping up and biting him. Brock looked to see how badly his arm was bleeding. "Larry, go down the hill and bring your car up. I'll try to keep this beast occupied until you get back. He's hurt. Looks like somebody shot him." There was dried blood all over the animal's rear end. Brock sat down on the edge of the pavement as the dog showed its teeth and growled. By the time Larry arrived in his car, the disoriented animal was shaking. Larry opened the back door of the SUV and Skinner carefully hoisted the dog up onto the floorboard. "Let's take him to the vet in town." Hayes nodded and they started down the hill in a hurry.

The veterinarian came out of the examination room in the back when the dog was brought in. "What happened?"

"We don't know. We found him like this," Brock said.

The vet looked at the back of the dog. "I'm going to have to put him under to dig all that buckshot out of his rear end. Look, leave him here with me, I'll clean him up, keep him overnight, and you can come for him tomorrow afternoon."

"He's not our dog."

"As far as I'm concerned, he is. You want me to fix him up, or not?"

The light went on. "Ah, you want me to pay your bill."

"And it won't be cheap."

"Yes, we'll come get him tomorrow. What kind of dog is it?"

"A German shepherd."

"German shepherd?"

"Very rare markings. I've never seen an all-white one with a red face, neck, and feet. The dog's worth a lot of money. If you need to get a shot for that bite, I'll let you know."

Skinner said, "I'll be fine. Just give me some hydrogen peroxide."

Hayes crossed his arms, shook his head, and said, "Imagine that." The men got back in Larry's vehicle and returned to the bottom of the hill. "You mean you still want to run up after that dog bit you?"

"It's the only chance you'll have to beat me," Brock goaded as he started running again. It took less than twenty minutes for them to scale the hill. Hayes was in tremendous shape, but he let Skinner win out of courtesy. They walked around in the parking lot to cool down, breathing heavily. Brock saw the winery was packed with customers, and said, "I'll go get the pickup truck and we'll fetch your car."

Maude, Brock, and Larry Hayes stood in the lavish kitchen of the Skinner house at six o'clock that evening. The countertops had been redone in veined, beige quartz, and the walls were a newly added splotchy green stucco, in keeping with the motif of an upscale log cabin in the woods. Maude seasoned the steaks on each side, and asked, "Am I imagining things, or are those puncture marks in your arm?"

"Yes. A dog bit me."

"Only you could accomplish something like that, Brock," she commented.

"A stray dog came out of the woods. It had been shot. We took it to the vet."

"What'd it look like?"

"White with brownish-orange fur on its face and neck."

"Think we could train it to scare the varmints out of the vineyard?"

"It's a German shepherd, Maude. They're smart as hell."

"Wonder what happened to it?" Hayes asked.

"Looks to me like the dog was running away from something, and somebody tried to kill it," Brock answered.

The three of them enjoyed a casual dinner on the patio as the sun faded and the air cooled, after which the men stayed up to watch a couple of action movies. Before going to bed, Brock researched white shepherds on the computer and found they weren't allowed to compete in AKC beauty contests, but were prized, nonetheless.

Hayes and Skinner stayed in the gym for nearly three hours the next morning, practicing jabs and good footwork. They showered off after finishing up on the heavy bag. Each of them drank a gallon of club soda with lemon juice in it. Brock said, "Let's get a bite to eat and go check on the dog."

The vet came out leading the alert white shepherd on a frayed leather leash. The dog looked at Skinner and wagged its tail. "That'll be a thousand dollars."

"Is there any cash discount?"

"Sure. I'll take nine hundred cash." Brock handed him the money. "I scanned the dog for a chip. He's registered to a Frank Cushman, who lives at 11538 Hominy Mill Road, northeast of town."

"What's the dog's name?" Larry asked.

"Truman," the vet reported. The dog looked up, panting, when he heard his name. "But there is something odd. The chip number was only posted on the registry last week."

"Why would somebody do that?"

"They may have needed to do it to sell the dog, or maybe there was some other nefarious reason."

"Well, come on, Truman, let's see if your owner will reimburse me for patching you up." They piled into the winery pickup truck, Truman perched between the men, and drove across the North Fork of the Kentucky River, headed for the Cushman place.

At the end of Hominy Mill Road, a narrow gravel lane led a long way up and over a hill through a thick grove of trees into a rugged clearing. A two-story black barn was all they could see on the property ahead. It sat on a limestone escarpment against a sheer wall, and the cliffs that dropped off in the front served as a dry moat two-thirds of the way around the barn. A rusty, iron cattle bridge with big open slits looked to be the only way over to the spit of land. Truman perked up when the truck stopped beside the barn. Brock let the dog jump out untethered.

The two men walked to the back, where they came upon a lean-to that had been added onto the structure. It appeared to be a one-room living quarters with a single door and window and a crude brick chimney in the wall for the fireplace. Nobody was there, and the door was unlocked. The place had no plumbing. Several jugs of distilled water were stacked up in the corner. An electric extension cord came through the wall to power a hot plate, lamp, and radio. A rocking chair, porcelain wash basin, and single bed sat on the rough-plank floor. Through the window, Brock could see the outhouse. The sheer wall behind it had a coal seam. A pick, coal bucket, and shovel were in the shallow cave where the coal was harvested.

At a back corner of the barn stood a big, red, gas-powered generator. Larry pointed at the wall above it and asked, "What are these switches for?"

"I don't know. Let's see if we can fire the thing up." They got it going and started fooling with the levers and buttons. Hearing a humming sound coming from the front of the property, they walked around to see what was making the noise and saw steel beams rising up through the gaps in the cattle bridge. Brock suggested, "Those must be used to keep vehicles from coming and going." They went back and lowered the beams and shut off the generator.

"What's in the barn?" Larry asked, making conversation.

"Let's go see." They rolled open the sliding door to gain entrance and let in some light. Inside were a dozen heavy-duty dog cages on platforms to keep them off the ground. The rest of the stuff lying around implied the place was, or had been, a serious dog breeding operation. Two fireplaces had been built in the back wall to supply heat during the winter, and a set of steps at one end wall led to a mezzanine. They climbed the stairs to find two chairs and a table that had papers on it. The back half of the mezzanine was a large cistern that gathered rain from the roof and supplied pressurized water to the pipes and shower below. Brock looked at Larry and said, "Wonder what happened to Truman?"

"I think I hear him barking." They went back down the stairs and out in the yard to look for the dog. When they found him at the back of the property, he started barking louder and pawing the ground. It looked as though something had been buried there recently. Brock said, "I'll run back up to the barn and get some shovels."

They dug for twenty minutes until the clothing of a person was unearthed. Truman whimpered when he saw the blue jeans and boots on the dead body. Larry threw down his shovel. "What do we do now?" he asked.

Skinner replied, "I'll call the police if I can get a signal out here." He retrieved his phone from his pocket and called the sheriff. "Nathan, it's Brock. We're at 11538 Hominy Mill Road. There's a dead body here."

"Damn it, Skinner. What kind of mess are you in now?"

"We came here to return a stray dog that belonged to the owner. The dog led us over to where the body was buried."

"I'll be there in twenty minutes."

After he hung up, Brock said to Larry, "Come on, let's go back and look through the paperwork we saw on the table upstairs."

"This could be a crime scene. We shouldn't be touching any-thing, should we?"

Truman sat down next to the grave when the two men walked toward the barn.

"Sometimes I bend the rules. If you'd feel better waiting in the truck, I'll go up there myself."

Larry said nothing.

Sheriff Connors and a team of people arrived and worked the scene for several hours. Skinner and Hayes agreed to visit the police station the next morning to give statements. Connors told them to take the dog and get out of there.

When Maude came into the house after work, she saw the white shepherd sitting at Brock's feet. "Hello, boys. And this is?"

"Truman. A regal name, don't you think?"

"What a beautiful dog." She walked over to pet him. Truman stood, as though he knew good manners. "What's going on?"

Hayes offered his narrative. "The vet told us who the owner was and where he lived. We drove out there and Truman led us to a grave. We dug it up and found a dead man. By the way the dog reacted, it must have been his owner, a guy named Frank Cushman."

"Larry, I hope you're going back to Lexington soon. Otherwise, you'll get sucked into who knows what," Maude warned.

"Yes, ma'am. I'll be pulling out tomorrow after we spar one last time. I must say, things certainly are interesting around here." He looked at Brock and grinned.

Brock said, "Maude, the place looked like a dog breeding operation. Frank Cushman just put a chip in Truman last week. Now, why would he do that?"

"See what I mean, Larry? My husband's a magnet for trouble." She glared at Brock, and then the dog.

~ ~ ~

Sheriff Nathan Connors had a perplexed expression on his face as he entered the police station interrogation room at eight fifteen. Hayes and Skinner were sitting there and looking disinterested. "Well, the body had a wallet on it that identified the guy as Frank Cushman. Only problem is, his fingerprints aren't in the system, and I can't find out any information about him. It's like he doesn't exist."

Skinner said, "The dog knew him and liked him. Who owns that property out there?"

"That's even more bedeviling. The deed is in the name of Isaac Marliss. He's a ghost too. Somebody has been sending the property tax payment in once a year, but there's no record of a Marliss around here either."

"What are you going to do?"

"Record it as the death of Frank Cushman. Publish an obit for him and see if anyone comes to claim the body, I guess." The two men gave their statements, but left out one little tidbit—the fact that Brock had gone through the papers in the loft of the barn before the police arrived. He had not shown Larry what he found among the papers, to keep him from being implicated in any wrongdoing.

"He was murdered, though, right?" Brock prodded.

"Yeah, shot in the back of the head at close range with a load of buckshot. Enough to kill him."

~ ~ ~

The last day Brock and Larry worked out together was a good one. After lunch, they went up to the winery so Larry could say bye to Maude. She got his phone number with the intention of texting him congratulations if he won his fight in Las Vegas. He said, "I've really enjoyed my time with you guys. I hope I get a chance to come back again."

"When you do, I won't go so easy on you," Brock said. He faked a gut punch, and then put his hand out to shake. They waved to Hayes as he pulled out of the parking lot and headed down the hill.

Maude stepped in front of her husband and asked seriously, "What are we going to do with Truman?"

"Sell him to the highest bidder."

"You are a heartless human being. Who buys these kinds of dogs?" Brock took a bill of sale out of his pocket and showed it to her. It was the record of the sale a week ago of six German shepherd puppies for $120,000 to Rex and Phoebe Keiper from Pikeville, Kentucky. Maude said, "I suppose you're going over there to see if they want to buy Truman?"

"Yes, but I'm not taking him with me. I want to find out what happened to Frank Cushman if I can."

"Please be careful." She walked away and left him standing alone.

~ ~ ~

Brock decided to take the Lamborghini to Pikeville because the roads over were fun to drive. He put the Keipers' address shown on the bill of sale in the GPS. The house was the last one above a treacherous road that had been cut into the side of a rocky hill. A woman came to the door. "Yes?" She had on an attractive gray pantsuit. Her black hair had been pulled back into a ponytail, and her jewelry looked expensive.

"Are you Phoebe Keiper?"

"Yes," she said, treating him like a door-to-door salesman.

"Is your husband here?"

"What is it you want?"

"I've got a white German shepherd I'm trying to sell."

That piqued her interest. "Come in. Rex, can you come out here?" Rex Keiper appeared in the hallway. He wore khakis and a blue twill Tommy Bahama shirt. "This man says he has a white shepherd to sell."

"Where did you get the dog?"

"Frank Cushman. He sold it to me and told me you bought them. I thought I might try to turn a quick profit."

"What's your name?"

"Brock Skinner. I live in Hazard."

"Mr. Skinner, Frank Cushman sells me all the red and white shepherds bred in this country, and as far as I know, none are unaccounted for. You must be mistaken."

"I don't think so. The dog has a chip in it, and is registered to Cushman as a white shepherd."

"Well, I'll have to contact Frank to confirm that," Rex said.

"Don't bother. He's dead. They found him buried on the property where the dogs were bred."

Keiper raised his brow and put his hand on his forehead. "What happened to him?"

"Your guess is as good as mine. What do you do with the shepherds you buy?"

He hesitated for a few seconds as though searching his thoughts for the right story to tell. "Sell them to buyers in Germany."

Brock figured it was the right time to wear out his welcome. "Ah, I see how this works. You buy six dogs a year for twenty thousand each, sell them for fifty thousand, and make a hundred and eighty thousand a year. Pretty nice living."

Rex Keiper ignored Brock's impertinence. "How much will you take for the dog?"

"Forty thousand."

"That's too much. I'll give you twenty-five. That's five thousand more than I usually pay."

"I'll just keep him then."

"Okay. Give me your number. If I'm willing to pay your price, I'll call you to bring me the dog."

"If you want to buy it, you can drive over to Hazard to pick it up." Brock pulled a sticky note with his phone number on it out of his shirt pocket and handed it to Rex. He nodded to Phoebe and walked out. On the way back to Hazard, Brock kept working his mind to solve three puzzles. Why was Cushman running his operation on land owned by an Isaac Marliss? Why did Cushman put a chip in Truman, and who tried to kill the dog?

~ ~ ~

Brock and Maude's brother, Marcel, were college roommates. They had been business partners for the last fifteen years and had gotten rich together. Marcel had done all the heavy lifting. Brock called him at 7:20 a.m. "Hi Marcel. You going into the office today?"

Marcel sounded like he was in his car. "Yeah, what do you need?"

"Can you have your IT guy see if he can access the birth and marriage records in Perry County for the last fifty years?"

"Fifty years? Are you nuts?"

"No. I'm looking for something specific."

"Like what?"

"I'm trying to find out if a guy named Isaac Marliss had any children, and if so, if any of them got married."

"That's not so bad. Give me the spelling of that last name."

At 7:30, Skinner took Truman for a walk through the grapevines accessible from the back of the log-cabin property. When they returned, he fed the dog while Maude made breakfast for herself. She said, "I sure hope Larry wins his fight."

"He will. He's as good a boxer as I've ever seen, and I've seen a lot."

"Hopefully he'll come visit us afterwards. What are you up to today?"

"Sleuthing," he said. Maude poured a cup of coffee and set it in front of him.

"Sorry I asked. Can you come to the winery this morning and help us build some shelving?"

"I'll head over there right now." He kissed Maude and signaled the dog to follow him.

Brock had finished building shelves when Marcel called back. "What did you find out?"

"Isaac Marliss had two kids, Heather and Cliff. Heather married a fellow by the name of Averil Bond. Is that enough for you?"

"More than enough. I owe you."

"Oh, there's one more thing. Looks like Isaac Marliss died over twenty years ago."

"Thanks, Marcel." Brock went to the winery office to use the computer. Averil and Heather Bond's address was on Messer Branch Road. He drove the pickup truck and parked in their driveway near the main road.

It was a tan brick home with a dirty, low-slope white roof. The chains on a corroded flagpole clanged in the wind. No flag was flying. A van and rusted sedan were parked up against overgrown bushes on the right side of the house. Brock waited for his knock to be answered. A woman opened the door and said nothing. "Hi. My name's Skinner. I'm here to ask about your father's property. May I come in?"

She kicked the door open. A man, presumably Averil, was standing behind her. He said, "What do you want to know?" The couple retreated to their living room. Brock followed.

"The deed is still in the name of Isaac Marliss. He's deceased, I understand, and I'm trying to find out who owns the property now. I'm interested in buying it," Brock stated.

Heather said, "We never had it put in my brother's name. Cliff stays with us sometimes, but he lives on the property most of the time."

"Is he here now?"

"No, he hasn't been around for a week or so. I guess he's out at the property now. The last time he was here, he asked me to register a dog in the name of the man who leases the barn from him. Frank Cushman."

"What exactly is the arrangement with Cushman?" Brock asked.

"For the last several years, he has leased the barn, bred dogs there, and paid my brother, Cliff, to watch and feed them."

"Cliff didn't happen to tell you why he registered the dog, did he?"

Averil said, "He told us one night that he thought Frank was going to sell his last litter of dogs, and then clear out for good. He said he was afraid something bad was going to happen to his favorite dog. I think its name is Truman."

"That's his name," Heather confirmed.

"Did you ever meet Cushman?"

"No. He would come into town, check things out, and pay Cliff in cash. Cliff would bring it to me. You see, my brother's a little slow."

Brock replied, "Seems he was smart enough to figure out something bad was going to happen. Have you been out to the property recently?"

Heather said, "We both went out there a couple of months ago to take him some food. He doesn't drive a car. Cliff walks through the woods from here to his property and back. He can't carry much, so we take him provisions from time to time."

"Do you know about the gas-powered generator that can raise and lower beams to block the bridge?"

"Yeah, Cliff and I rigged that up together last summer. He was worried somebody might come in the night and try to steal the dogs. He also felt more secure sleeping out there."

"Do you think Cliff would be interested in selling the land?"

"If Cushman has cleared out, I'd say he'd consider it," Heather offered.

"I need to find him." Brock sat in the nearest chair and put his elbows on the arms. He looked at the Bonds with some trepidation. "I don't know any easy way to say this, so I'm going to say it straight up. There's a good possibility that Frank Cushman shot and killed your brother a week ago and buried him on the property. Cushman then tried to shoot and kill the dog. I found Truman, and he had buckshot in his rear end."

They both sat down and each put a hand over their eyes. Heather muttered in a broken voice, "How can we find out for sure?"

"Go look at the body. See if it's him. If you want, I can arrange that for you through the sheriff."

"I guess we better." Heather wiped the tears out of her eyes. Averil stood and exhaled audibly.

Brock called Connors. "Nathan, I'm sending a couple down to look at the John Doe corpse. They're the sister and brother-in-law of a man named Cliff Marliss, the son of the man whose name is on the deed of the property. We're afraid the body might be Cliff's."

~ ~ ~

Connors called Skinner the next day and told him to come to the police station. When he arrived, the sheriff ushered him into his office. "How did you find the Bonds?"

"Dumb luck. I located a birth certificate for Heather Marliss. Her father was Isaac Marliss. Then I found her marriage license to Averil Bond."

The sheriff yelled, "Now, how in the hell did you do that?"

"Come on, Nathan. Don't push me."

"What do you mean, don't push you? I'm of a mind to lock you up."

"Do that and you'll have trouble solving the murder," Brock retorted.

"Of all the gall."

"Tell me, what was in the wallet found on the body?"

Nathan was still steaming. "It had a calling card in it that said Frank Cushman, dog breeder. There was a phone number we couldn't trace. So, tell me what you think happened."

"Cliff Marliss found out somehow that Frank Cushman was going to pull out, leaving him without a renter and job. He was also afraid that Cushman was going to kill his favorite dog, Truman."

"Why would he want to do that?"

"To cover his tracks, I suppose. But what Marliss didn't count on was getting killed himself. He put a chip in Truman and registered the dog so that if it was found dead, there'd be a clue leading back to Cushman."

"In your earlier statement, you said you found the dog over by the winery, and that it had buckshot in its rear end. Who shot him?"

Brock gathered his thoughts. "The best I can figure, Cushman did. When Marliss told him he'd registered the dog to protect it, Cushman shot Marliss at close range, and then tried to shoot the dog. Truman was smart enough to hightail it out of there."

"How'd the dog get across the cattle bridge?"

"The only thing I can think of is that Marliss and the dog were in the driveway waiting for Cushman to arrive. Cushman must have taken Cliff's body over the bridge and buried it after he shot him."

The sheriff processed the information, and said, "If that's what happened, we'll be able to find traces of blood somewhere near the driveway leading up to the bridge."

"If it happened that way, one other thing is for sure. Frank Cushman will disappear for good," Brock added.

"I've looked everywhere for him. I checked the DMVs in Kentucky, Tennessee, and Virginia. No hits."

"What about West Virginia?"

"I haven't tried that yet. Let me do it right now." Connors got up and went out to assign the task to one of the staff. Five minutes later, a deputy came in with a photostat of the driver's license for Frank Cushman from Williamson, West Virginia. The license expired two months ago and had not been renewed. The sheriff threw the photostat over to Skinner and said, "Bingo." Brock looked at the picture of the man and pushed the copy of the license back across the desk.

"He won't be there now, that's for sure." Brock stood with the intention of leaving.

Connors said, "You seem to be one step ahead of us. Have any ideas how we can find the man and solve the murder?"

"Not a clue. But if I come up with something, I'll make sure you get the credit."

"How big of you." The sheriff looked out the window as Skinner walked out.

After supper, Brock answered a call on his cell phone. Rex Keiper said, "Okay, Skinner, I'll buy the dog for forty thousand."

"Good. Meet me at the barn at noon on Saturday. I'll have him with me."

"See you then."

"There's one other thing, Keiper. The body they found buried out by the barn wasn't Frank Cushman. It was Cliff Marliss, the man who attended to the dogs. Do you happen to know where I can find Cushman?"

Keiper replied, "If I tell you where he is, will you keep my name out of it?"

"That's a promise. Be there on Saturday." He cut the line and turned to Maude. "What do you say we go to Lexington tomorrow to see Larry Hayes train?"

"I'm in if you'll invite Marcel to join us for dinner."

"Deal. We'll take Truman. He'll want to see Larry."

~ ~ ~

Summer didn't officially start for a few more days, but the weather was already hot and the days long. The heavy Friday traffic on I-75 skirting Lexington began to slow at all the exits into the city. The Skinners made it to their condo downtown by ten thirty. They were in the gym where Larry Hayes trained by eleven. Charlie White saw them come in and approached the couple with great enthusiasm. "You must be Brock's wife."

Brock said, "Charlie, this is Maude."

She offered her hand. White shook, and said, "Pleased to meet you. Who is your furry friend?"

"Oh, this is Truman." The dog went over and sniffed Charlie. "I think he likes you."

"What a beautiful animal. So, what brings you guys in?"

"You asked me for a favor recently, Charlie. Now I need one from you."

"Sure."

"I want you to give Hayes tomorrow off so he can drive down and spend the day with me in Hazard."

White scratched his cheek. "Okay. If you'll train with him today, that is."

"I'd be honored. Larry's a really good guy, and a great boxer."

"What are you up to in Hazard, anyway?"

"Making sure Truman here finds a good home."

Hayes popped out of the locker room and saw the dog. "Hey, fellow, come here." Truman wagged his tail and went over to get a little sugar. "Maude, Brock, what are you guys doing here?"

Charlie said, "They talked me into giving you tomorrow off. But first, Brock says he wants to see if he can knock you down."

Hayes grinned. "You can try. Get your gear on, old man."

Maude watched her husband spar for a half hour. At noon, she left for lunch and called her brother, Marcel, to arrange a dinner date. Brock came into the condo at five o'clock looking a little spent from being punched around for the better part of the day. He said, "It's all set. Larry's going to follow us down in the morning. We'll leave here at seven."

Marcel Sutherland brought a female business associate to dinner. The foursome decided on the Holly Hill Inn in Midway. The girls chatted while Marcel asked about the information his IT guy had sent over. Brock gave an abbreviated version of what was going on. "It's looking like this business leads back to a woman. With any luck, everything will be resolved by tomorrow afternoon."

"What woman?"

"All I can tell you is that she's rough on men, and she's not through with them yet."

"Maude said you found a white German shepherd."

"Larry Hayes and I did. A guy who wants to buy him is coming to Hazard tomorrow."

"You going to sell?"

"Technically, he's not mine. This affair is more about murder and deceit than dogs," Brock said.

"Watch your step," Marcel warned. The two couples enjoyed their meals and parted company in a good mood.

~ ~ ~

Rex Keiper pulled into the Marliss driveway on Hominy Mill Road at five past twelve on Saturday. He had a large dog kennel in the back of the white SUV that rattled every time he hit a bump. There were no cars or trucks in sight, so he rolled down his driver's-side window and circled to park facing the cattle bridge after crossing it. Within five minutes, Keiper began to worry something had gone wrong. Suddenly, the sliding door on the barn began moving. Once the door was open, Skinner appeared with his hands on his hips. He said, "Take the money, Rex, and put it in the grass over there." He pointed toward the back of the property.

"What do you take me for, Skinner, some kind of fool?"

"I thought you wanted to buy the dog. I have him in a cage in here, and when I see the money, I'll put him in your vehicle, and you can be on your way. But first, tell me where I can find Frank Cushman."

"You're a bigger fool than I thought." Rex stepped out from behind the wheel holding a double-barrel shotgun, which he aimed at Brock's head. "I'm not telling you anything, and I'm not giving you forty thousand dollars either. Now, bring the dog out and put him in this cage." Keiper opened the back of the SUV while keeping the gun trained on Skinner.

Behind the barn, the sound of the generator coming to life startled Keiper. Brock stepped out of view and quickly shut the sliding door to the barn from the inside. The ominous hum of the steel beams rising in the bridge distracted Keiper long enough for Larry Hayes to stick a rifle around the corner and yell, "Drop it!"

The barn door cracked open, and the barrels of Skinner's shotgun came into view. "Okay, Rex, if you want to live, you'll throw the gun down."

"You wouldn't shoot me."

"Yes, I would. In the leg. Then I'll turn the dog loose and he'll maul you to death. The bridge is blocked. You ain't going anywhere." Keiper threw down the gun, and Brock hollered to Hayes, "Get it, Larry, and his cell phone." Larry picked up the firearm, shoved Keiper down, and reached in the vehicle for the phone.

"What's going on?" Rex said, panicking as he got up and dusted himself off.

Skinner opened the barn door again. "Now, I'm going to turn Truman loose, so I would suggest you jump up on the hood of your car if you don't want him to tear you apart. Otherwise, Larry Hayes here will use you for a punching bag. He's a prize fighter." Rex didn't think twice. Truman came firing out of the barn, went to the front of the SUV, and started barking, growling, and jumping up. Rex moved carefully away from the edge of the hood, struggling to keep his balance. "If you want to leave here alive, you'll give us some answers. Why'd you kill Cliff Marliss?"

"Who says I did?"

"The dog here." Truman kept clawing the front bumper and growling. "You killed his best friend, and then tried to kill him. Dogs don't forget stuff like that." Skinner poked at Keiper with the gun barrel, causing him to nearly slip and fall off the hood.

"Okay. I'll tell you what you want to know if you'll let me drive out of here."

"Start talking."

"Marliss must have overheard me say that I was going to kill Truman. He told me that he put a chip in him to protect his identity. When I came out a week ago to dispose of the dog, Marliss was on the other side of the bridge, turning him loose. I shot at the dog running away, and then killed Marliss and buried him with one of Cushman's cards I had in the truck."

"Why did you need to kill the dog?"

"Because my wife got a call from one of the people we sold a pup to in Germany. They told her the pup's DNA matched that of the only white shepherd with red markings known to exist. That dog, which we presume is Truman, was stolen six years ago. Cushman must have gotten a hold of him from somebody and started breeding him to all-white females."

"So, you and your wife are trying to get rid of all the evidence. That would include Cushman. Where is he?"

"All I'll say is he's no longer around. Now, open the bridge and let me make a run for it."

Brock put a leash on Truman and said, "Looks like this dog has turned out to be man's worst friend, or yours at least. Larry, go open the bridge for Mr. Keiper. That is, once he hands us forty thousand dollars." Brock pulled Truman back. Keiper got in the SUV and threw the package of money out the window onto the ground. He drove down to the bridge and waited for the beams to be lowered. Brock called the sheriff and said, "He's on his way out. Send a car over for us. I've got his cell phone and the shotgun he used to kill Marliss."

When Hayes returned from shutting off the generator, Brock said, "Nice work."

Larry crossed his arms and grinned. "As I said before, things are pretty interesting around here."

~ ~ ~

Phoebe Keiper pulled open the front door of her house in Pikeville to find Brock Skinner standing there. She was wearing a sleeveless yellow dress and open-toed heels. He said nothing. Finally, she spoke. "Where's my husband? Where's the dog?"

"May I come in?"

"Yes. I was expecting to hear from Rex shortly after noon. He hasn't called." They sat in chairs in the living room.

"Well, I believe he's where you want him," Brock said. "Dead."

"What are you talking about?"

"You didn't get any call from someone in Germany talking about Truman's DNA, now did you?"

"Is that what Rex told you?"

"Yeah, you were just setting him up, weren't you? I saw the picture of Frank Cushman on his expired driver's license."

"What do you mean?" She began squirming in her seat.

"You met Frank Cushman through your husband. You charmed him into killing Rex and taking on your husband's identity. You came up with the story about needing to dispose of Truman. Once he killed the dog, you were going to let him get caught for killing Rex too. But since Frank killed Cliff Marliss, it would be even better if he got sent up for that. You've ruined the lives of two men. Why?"

"Appalachia. Living here is like being in prison. No shops, no restaurants, no clubs. And worst of all, no interesting people."

"Well, I take offense to that. My wife and I love living in the mountains. All you have to do is drive two hours to get all the culture you're looking for. Lots of people in New York have a two-hour commute to work every day."

Two Pikeville police officers walked in the house and cuffed the cold-blooded highbrow, Phoebe Keiper.

~ ~ ~

Larry Hayes pummeled his opponent in Las Vegas on July Fourth, scoring a sixth-round TKO. Maude sent him a text congratulating him on his victory. Brock mailed $40,000 to Charlie White with a note inside that said he'd changed his mind. He wanted to finance a piece of Charlie's prize fighter after all. Truman learned how to scare the varmints out of the vineyard, and he took up residency at the winery. Most times Maude would bring him home with her. She was a softy as opposed to her heartless husband. That fact was lost on Truman.

Ne Plus Ultra

At four o'clock, on a remarkably clear Saturday afternoon in July, the tables scattered around the veranda at Vigneron Winery had been staked out by people waiting to see Joan Brewer and her troupe perform a twenty-minute snippet of *The Importance of Being Earnest* by Oscar Wilde. Joan had once been a meth addict. Brock Skinner helped her get clean, and his wife Maude gave her and her sober friends acting gigs at the winery. In the character of Lady Bracknell, Joan flawlessly delivered one of the play's funnier lines: "To lose one parent, Mr. Worthing, may be regarded as a misfortune; to lose both looks like carelessness." The crowd tee-heed and chattered quietly, enjoying the unusually dry weather and cheerful theatrics while getting mildly pixilated on Vigneron's serviceable wines. The cast bowed dramatically to a warm applause at the conclusion of the vignette. Maude peered at Brock and said with glee, "Isn't she just great?"

"Yes, she is." He seemed a little logy, disinclined to look at her when he spoke.

Maude knew he acted this way when he was bored, so she suggested, "Hey, what do you say we go to Peka Forge for supper? I promised Dewey Prater I'd bring some of our wines over for him to stock at the bar."

"Maude, all they have there are soup beans with lard and cornbread. You up for that?"

"Well, there's not that much lard in it, not enough to hurt you, anyway," she argued. "I'll ask Joan to meet us there."

"Nothing ventured, nothing gained," he remarked.

"Put a mixed case of reds and one of whites in the trunk of your car."

Natural selection, if there was such a thing, and survival of the fittest defined hardscrabble life in Hazard, Kentucky. If your heart couldn't handle saturated pork fat, or stretches of sedentary life tended to plug your arteries, you were a goner. Those who, through generations, had inherited anomalous cardiovascular capacity blithely streamed into Peka Forge for the best soup beans in the universe. Some of the grease was cut by the alcohol consumed before, during, and after a meal, which was the whole idea of the lone, high-fat offering on the menu. Soup beans were low overhead, high margin, simple to fix, and repeatable. People looked forward to a bowl, just as they would an episode of their favorite TV show. Patrons had tried to convince Prater to add clam chowder to his cuisine, but since things weren't broken, he wasn't inclined to fix them.

Dewey's great-great-great-great-grandfather, Earl Prater, came over the mountains in 1844 to the headwaters of the Kentucky River, now called the North Fork. He claimed being of Russian descent, and his intentions were to open a blacksmith operation on the banks of the river. First, he had to construct the shop and comfortable place to live above it. That took him over a year. He opened for business in the spring of 1846, around the time the new post office put Hazard on the map. Prater named the place Peka Forge based on the Russian word for river.

The stone building, designed as a traditional two-story affair, featured a high-pitched gray roof. The kitchen, a small square wing off the back left, had its own doors and windows. There were brick fireplaces in the side walls to supply heat to every room in the building during the winter. The main section of the structure had a centered, arched front door, with two windows trimmed by white shutters on the left, and large white barn doors on the right that opened to the shop. A string of five windows with black shutters ran across the face of the second floor. For security reasons, the access to the living quarters was up the outside stairs on the back wall covered in deciduous vines. Today, the barn doors were gone, replaced by a picture window that let sunlight in the bar. Otherwise, the building looked from the street much like it did when it was built.

Inside, a pantry by the busy kitchen door had small sacks of dry beans and the makings for cornbread stored on high shelves. A tall ladder to access ingredients leaned against the back wall. Booze bottles were kept in a closet behind the bar. Restrooms covered the width of the end wall, one on either side of the now decorative brick fireplace, down the hall farthest away from the kitchen. Twenty cocktail tables with chairs had been strategically placed in open spaces, and a dozen red-leather stools banged up against the brass foot rail of the bar.

Walls in the eating areas had been finished in an ornamental pattern of light gray plaster. The man who rented the apartment upstairs had purportedly created two-foot-square works of art for sale, hanging on the parging, and the pieces, suited for elegant commercial offices, were spectacular, patinated, three-dimensional copper scenes of Appalachia. Eight to ten of them sold each month at $450 a copy, enough to pay the rent and keep the artist fed.

When the Lamborghini geared down as it approached Peka Forge, everybody within a half mile heard the varoom of the engine. As Brock turned in past the pub, he happened to notice the steel bars behind the diaphanous sheers in the upstairs windows. He pulled in next to a black pickup truck with a Peka Forge logo by the door handle. Other beat-up trucks filled the rest of the parking lot, making the Lamborghini look ridiculously out of place.

Joan stood by the entrance with a bright smile on her face. "Thanks for inviting me to tag along. I've wanted to try these soup beans for a long time. You can't call in a carryout order, but I heard the guy who owns the place will let you take a container home if you eat at least one bowl inside. Go figure."

Humid air in the barroom came from steam sweating off pots of beans in the kitchen and the hot air of conversation at the bar. Most tables were occupied, but Maude found a cozy one in the corner that had three chairs. The interesting artwork on the wall behind the table caught Brock's eye for a moment. The rest of the clientele hadn't dressed for opening night at the opera, yet weren't distastefully clad. Reggae music by Lucky Dube beeped faintly out of the overhead speakers, while subdued talk at the tables followed the understated manner of typical mountain men who, on this evening, outnumbered the women two to one.

"Maude, look, I know that girl behind the bar." Joan waved conspicuously. "Portia?"

The girl looked over when she heard her name. "Amanda, is that you?" She had an oval face, naturally blonde hair, and dazzling green eyes.

"Yes. I haven't seen you in at least five years. What are you doing here?"

"What does it look like? Working." She walked up to the table, drying her hands on the way.

"Portia, these are my dear friends, Maude and Brock Skinner."

"Pleased to meet you. I didn't know you lived in Hazard."

"I do, and there's something I need to tell you. The nice people who adopted me when I was a little girl named me Amanda Critchfield, but I've recently learned about my birth parents. Now I'm going by the name my birth mother gave me, which is Joan Brewer."

"Well, I'm still going by Portia Sweeney, and it's good to see you again, Joan. That new name will take some getting used to. What can I get you to drink?"

"I'll take water. I'm on the wagon, but you might talk my friends here into ordering something."

Maude said, "Bring us the beer that goes best with the food."

"You mean the soup beans and cornbread, or the soup beans and cornbread?"

"Might as well bring that with the beer," Brock suggested politely.

"Coming right up," Portia chirped as she moved off toward the kitchen.

"How do you know her?" Brock asked.

"We went to Carson-Newman in Tennessee together. She's a firecracker."

When Portia brought the food and drinks, Brock asked, "Where does this incredible artwork come from?" He stared again at one of the patinated coppers on the wall.

Portia looked up and shot a finger in the air. "From the guy who lives upstairs. Fillmore Breedlove. Dewey calls him Morrie. He makes it and we sell it, for a cut I'm sure. He's an oddball. I guess all good artists are."

"Huh." Brock inspected the piece closest to the table more carefully. He couldn't believe the precision in the detail. Maude took note of his fascination and knew he was headed down a rabbit hole.

The soup beans were so good, Brock nearly had a religious experience. "Man, this stuff is out of this world." He acted like a rube on his first visit to the big city.

"I told you," Maude stated triumphantly.

Portia came by the table and said, "I saw how much you liked the soup beans, so I brought you a cup to take home."

"Thank you," Brock replied sincerely.

Dewey Prater stepped out of the kitchen and spotted the Skinners. He hurried over and asked enthusiastically, "Did you bring me some of your wines?"

"Yes. Muscles, here, will go get it." Maude looked over at Brock. She introduced Joan Brewer and told Dewey that she was a friend of Portia's.

Dewey said tentatively, "If you're anything like her, you'll get a wide berth from me."

Joan stated seriously, "I'm an actress, but drama comes naturally to her."

"Boy, you said it." The four of them had a few laughs and chatted for a while when Brock came back from schlepping the wine. Prater went to the cash register and brought over the money to pay Maude. "Don't be strangers," he said.

On the way home, Brock asked his wife, "Why are there bars on the windows in the apartment above Peka Forge? I mean, nobody can get up there."

"Brock, I can't take you anywhere. You borrow trouble faster than a squirrel in a dog kennel."

"Speaking of dogs, is Truman at the house?"

"Yeah." When they walked in, the white German shepherd danced around, happy to see them. Brock took the container of soup beans out of the bag and put it in the refrigerator.

~ ~ ~

When Monday rolled around, humidity had moved in, along with much warmer air. Brock stood in front of the reception desk at the police station with his hands in his pockets. "Is Sheriff Connors in this morning?"

Connors, down the hall, heard Brock asking for him. "Come on back." They stopped at the coffee pot and went straight into the interrogation room. "Please tell me this is a social visit, or you're collecting for the community chest."

"I have to admit, Nathan, I'm borrowing trouble where there doesn't seem to be any."

"What is it this time?"

"Maude and I went to Peka Forge on Saturday night. I've never eaten there before, but Maude wanted to."

"Oh, no. Heaven help us." Connors spoke like someone had hit his big toe with a hammer.

"What do you mean?"

"I was hoping beyond hope you'd never want to know anything about Prater's operation."

Brock sat up. "Why, what's going on?"

"Morrie Breedlove, that's what's going on."

"You mean the guy who lives in the apartment over the bar? Apparently, he is the artist producing incredible patinated coppers hanging in the barroom. Hell, in New York, those things would sell for three thousand a pop. Why is he letting them go for a fraction of that? And why are there bars on the windows in the apartment?"

"Brock, I don't suppose there's any way I could convince you to forget about Peka Forge, is there?"

"Are you asking me to?"

"Frankly, no."

"Maybe you better tell me what's going on then," Brock urged.

The sheriff stood and walked over to a corner of the room with coffee cup in hand. "Well, first off, Breedlove hasn't produced any of those coppers in the four years he's been here. When he came to town, he brought twenty crates with him."

"Why in the world would he show up in Hazard, Kentucky, to rent an apartment? Where's he from anyway?"

"Chicago. Had an art studio there."

Brock put his arms on the table. "Now I am getting suspicious."

"You're not the only one. About three months ago, two FBI agents showed up here to surveil the mystery man. They watched him night and day for better than two months."

Skinner asked, "What'd they find out?"

"They told me he got zero mail. Walks over to the Dollar General and grocery store across the street every day, but other than that, he is in that apartment alone the rest of the time doing who knows what. Finally, they got a warrant to see what was up there. Mark here in our office went with them."

"What'd he say about it?"

"I'll get him in here." Connors found the deputy and asked him to step in the interrogation room. "So, Mark, when you went into Breedlove's place with the FBI, what did you see?"

The deputy gathered his thoughts. "Nothing unusual, really."

"Describe it for us," Skinner urged.

"Well, the first thing we noticed was the impenetrable door at the top of the steps. I don't think we could have blown it open. The FBI knocked, and it took Breedlove a couple of minutes to answer. We showed him the warrant. He said nothing. Just stepped aside and let us in."

"What does the man look like?" Connors asked.

"Five ten. Slender build. Blue eyes. Fiftyish. Buzz haircut that looks like he does it himself. Fearless-looking."

"He said nothing?"

"Not a single word the whole visit."

"You mean the FBI guys didn't interrogate him?"

"No."

"That's odd. What else?"

"There's a wall to the left of the door that divides the place when you walk in. Behind it is a sitting room, small kitchen, bedroom, and bathroom. In the main room, there are two chairs on wheels, a couple of work tables, and crates of copper artwork. The tables have high-powered lights and magnifying glasses on them with adjustable arms, and sophisticated machines I have never seen before under the tables."

Skinner asked, "Did you see any art supplies?"

"No." The deputy crossed his arms and waited for more questions.

"What else?"

"In the corner to the right, along the back wall of the building, there is a black safe. It was unlocked. Inside were Breedlove's passport, six or seven thousand in cash, and what looked like a bag of tools to work metal."

"Did you find any paperwork of any kind?"

"Not really. Only newspapers and receipts for food and knick-knacks that he'd bought across the street. The FBI agents searched the place for two hours, looking for something, which I guess they didn't find."

Brock turned his attention to the sheriff. "Nathan, did they share why they were interested in him?"

"They shared next to nothing. I asked if he was a fugitive or a fence or something. According to them, there's no way he could be handling merchandise. They watched him when he was shopping, and nobody passed him anything. No packages ever came in or went out."

Brock asked the deputy, "Does he have a computer?"

"Yeah, there's a laptop and printer in the sitting room."

"Did you find anything on it?"

"Only the tax returns he filed electronically for the years he's been here."

"Anything unusual in them?"

"No. He used a Chicago address and reported thirty to forty thousand in income each year from art sales. His expenses were a little more than his income, so he never paid any taxes. There was no evidence of any bank accounts."

The sheriff pivoted and moved to another corner of the room. "What in the hell has he been doing up there for four years? Thanks, Mark." The deputy went back to his office.

"Do you think Dewey Prater knows anything?" Brock asked.

"You'd think so."

The deputy stuck his head back in the interrogation room and said, "Sheriff, we just got a call from one of the men. He's at an apartment where a girl's been dead about six hours. Strangled, apparently. Neighbor who has coffee with her most mornings found her."

"Who is she?"

"ID says Portia Sweeney."

Brock blurted, "Oh, crap."

"What?"

"She waited on us at Peka Forge on Saturday night."

"Pick up Dewey Prater and bring him in. Skinner, I want you behind the glass when I talk to him."

Sheriff Connors questioned Prater for nearly two hours and learned that Portia Sweeney purportedly walked into Peka Forge six months ago and asked for a job. She was persistent, so Prater finally hired her, and soon customers were coming in more frequently just to see her. Prater thought she was good for business. Despite occasional contretemps, he got along with her great, or so he said. She left the bar at eight o'clock on Sunday night, right after closing. He went home at nine.

Four years ago, Dewey Prater lived above Peka Forge. He told the sheriff he'd saved up enough money to buy a nice house and advertised the apartment for rent. Fillmore "Morrie" Breedlove applied, so Prater let him move in. Morrie asked Prater to sell his coppers in the bar. Prater agreed and got a hundred dollars for every one he sold. He claimed he knew little about Breedlove except that the man was quiet and paid the rent on time.

After Dewey Prater left the police station, Connors joined Brock in the room behind the mirror. "Hear anything that bothered you?"

"Yeah, he's lying about Breedlove."

"How do you know that?"

"Because Breedlove put in a safe, fortified the door, and put bars on the windows when he moved in. Prater had to have known why he wanted to do that."

"I suppose you're right. I'll sweat him after I figure out what happened to the Sweeney girl."

By late morning, the sun began to feel like a broiler on high. Brock got in the Lamborghini, cranked up the air-conditioning, and returned home a little before noon. He took the soup beans out of the refrigerator and put them in the microwave. He nuked the cup for a minute, and then stirred the contents. Something hard was in the bottom of the cup. Brock fished the object out with a spoon and washed it off. He couldn't believe his eyes. It was a humongous orange diamond.

~ ~ ~

At three o'clock, Brock sat in the private office of the jeweler he frequently dealt with in Lexington. "Don, hypothetically, if I show you a gemstone, and you suspect it's stolen, how do you handle that?"

"I usually notify the police."

"What if you can't be sure?"

"Then I don't call them."

"Okay, I'm going to show you what I found in a bowl of soup beans, and want you to tell me what you think." Brock reached in his pocket for the velvet bag, uncinched it, and put the diamond in front of the jeweler, who stared at the stone for twenty seconds before picking it up. He inspected it with his loop for the next twenty minutes without saying a word. Brock finally spoke. "Well?"

"Ne plus ultra. The ultimate."

"Come again?"

"The finest vivid orange diamond in the world. This thing is around twenty-eight carats. A thirty-carat stone like it called 'The Sweet Potato' was stolen in Chicago four years ago. If this is the same stone, it has been recut and polished, and whoever did the work is the finest craftsman in the world. I've never seen precision like this."

"How much is it worth?"

"Probably thirty million."

"Don, would you help me pick out a pair of diamond stud earrings my wife would like for her birthday? Send me the bill."

"Sure," the jeweler said with a slight grin on his face. Brock put the diamond back in the velvet bag.

Driving back to Hazard, Skinner called Maude to let her know he'd been out shopping for her birthday gift. He asked if she'd heard about the death of Portia Sweeney. She hadn't, so he explained the circumstances to her, and then said, "I'll be home at seven. Tell Joan about Portia, and ask her to join us for dinner at the house."

"I can't believe she's dead," Joan said when she came through the door. Maude had trotted out a reheated lasagna she made that morning, along with a magnificent antipasto salad.

Brock asked, "Do you know where Portia was from?"

"Chicago."

"I was afraid of that. She could've come to Hazard to do some business with Morrie Breedlove." Brock had a good idea what that business was, but kept it to himself.

Maude stopped eating. "Like what?"

"She must've known what he was doing here, and had a good reason to find him."

"What would that be?"

"Something illegal, by the looks of it. Breedlove might have had a reason to kill Portia, but I just can't figure out how he could have done it. Joan, what else can you tell me about Portia?"

"Not much. She told me once that her dad was an FBI agent."

"Uh-oh," Brock uttered.

"What?"

"Some things are starting to connect up," Brock said.

The three of them finished eating. They played gin for an hour, with the loser of each hand sitting out the following one.

Next morning, Brock called the sheriff to get the names and phone numbers of the two FBI agents who had been in Hazard recently. He heard tapping on a computer keyboard before Connors said, "Jerome Rhyne and Damon Booth, out of Chicago."

"Have you located Portia Sweeney's parents?"

"Only her father, Howard Sweeney. We found his name in an address book in her apartment. He's coming into town later today to claim her body."

"Does he have a Chicago address?"

"Yes."

"I want to talk to him when he gets here."

"Why?"

"I think he works for the FBI. I'd like to get some information from him about Rhyne and Booth."

Howard Sweeney looked badly shaken after seeing his deceased daughter at the morgue. Sheriff Connors brought him to the police station and ushered him into the interrogation room, where he was introduced to Skinner. "I'm sorry for your loss, Mr. Sweeney. What an awful tragedy," Brock said.

"She was so full of life. Why would anyone want to strangle her?" His eyes were searching for answers.

Connors said, "We're pursuing leads, sir. Mr. Skinner has a couple of questions."

"I understand you work for the FBI. Do you know agents Rhyne and Booth?"

"Yes. What about them?"

"They've been watching a man who lives above the bar where your daughter worked. We are trying to find out if he had anything to do with her death."

"You're talking about Morrie Breedlove. Rhyne and Booth suspect him of recutting a stolen diamond from a collector in Chicago. They sent my daughter here to look for it. You see, Portia was also an FBI operative." That came as a bit of a shock to the two Hazard boys in the room.

"How did they get onto Breedlove?"

"He had a studio in Chicago where he made copper artwork. He got into cutting diamonds, and his reputation for design, detail, craftsmanship, and perfection quickly became known among criminals wanting to get stones recut. A week after one of the most valuable diamonds in the world was stolen, Breedlove disappeared. It took the FBI over three years to locate him."

"So, now they're trying to find the diamond and pin the recutting on Breedlove," Brock concluded. "You asked why someone would strangle your daughter, Mr. Sweeney. Maybe she got hold of the stone, and that person killed her for it."

He looked away and closed his eyes tightly. "I guess it doesn't matter much now."

~ ~ ~

Skinner parked in front of Peka Forge at three thirty. He walked around back and climbed up the stairs to the second-floor apartment. He pounded on the heavy door several times before it opened a crack. "What do you want?" Morrie Breedlove's one visible piercing blue eye looked crazed.

"May I come in?"

"Who are you?"

"Brock Skinner. I heard you recut gemstones. I want you to cut one down for me."

"I do copper artwork," he said.

When Breedlove tried to shut the door, Brock stuck his foot in it and pushed it open enough to step in the room. He let the door shut behind him and said, "Now that's better. I'm not here to look for The Sweet Potato, or to cause you any trouble. I just need some information."

Morrie had on black jeans and shoes and a button-down, chalk-blue shirt, not tucked in. His face was gaunt. He wore no glasses, and his short gray-brown hair had been haphazardly cropped. His arms and fingers were long for a man his size. "Leave or I'll call the police."

"Oh, really? You've been a recluse in this apartment, and you're going to call the police? I don't think so."

"Let's get this over with." Morrie resigned himself to having to cooperate.

"What have you been doing in here for four years? It certainly wouldn't take you anywhere near that long to recut one thirty-carat diamond." Brock scanned the main room to take in the safe, work tables, machinery, and crates of artwork.

"Copper scenes."

"You haven't produced a single copper since you've been here. I know what your problem is. You've now become obsessed with cutting diamonds just like you were with making patinated coppers."

"I don't know what you're talking about. Please get out."

"Oh, I will. Before I go though, just tell me why you killed Portia Sweeney."

"Who's that?"

"The girl who worked downstairs at the bar."

"She's dead? How could I have killed her? I've never been farther than across the street in this town since I've been here. You'd better look somewhere else for the killer. Now get out!" he yelled.

Brock reopened the door and looked Morrie up and down. "Losing that big diamond has made you pretty darn cranky." Breedlove started to say something, but thought better of it.

Skinner walked into Peka Forge in search of Dewey Prater. He checked the kitchen, and then asked the man at the bar where Prater had gone. "He just left for the police station. Probably something to do with Portia's death. What a shock." The man finished drying a martini glass and put it on the shelf.

Connors was sitting across from Prater when Brock came into the room. "Dewey."

"Brock."

The sheriff started his line of questioning. "Let's go back to the beginning. Breedlove, out of the blue, called you and wanted to rent the apartment?"

"Yes."

"Okay. Why the bank-vault door, safe, and bars on the windows?"

"He said he had some valuable artwork and didn't want to take a chance on somebody breaking in and stealing it."

Brock said, "Come on, Dewey, don't lie to us. There's more to it than that."

"Yes. He said he'd give me ten thousand over what it cost to fortify the place if I'd make the improvements."

"Ah, the money," Connors said sarcastically.

"So, you worked a deal with him to peddle his copper landscapes. Why'd he sell them so cheap?"

"The man had to eat," Prater retorted. "Not too many people walk into a bar in Hazard, Kentucky, willing to pay north of five hundred for a piece of art."

Brock asked, "How many of the coppers did he bring with him, and how many have you sold?"

"Oh, I'd say he brought five hundred, and we've sold over four hundred."

"He's not making more. What do you think he's doing with his time?"

"Honestly, I have no clue."

The sheriff went in another direction. "So, just like Breedlove, Portia Sweeney shows up out of the blue."

"She did." Prater began to get weary.

"Why did you hire her?"

"Personality. She had a wild one."

"Have any ideas who might have killed her?"

"Well, it wasn't Breedlove, and it wasn't me. It had to have been one of the men customers she flirts with all the time. Maybe he got jealous."

They let Dewey Prater go after going through the events of the day Portia was killed. Brock said, "His story just doesn't hang together for me. He knows damn well what Prater is doing up there."

"If he's lying about that, then he could be lying about everything."

~ ~ ~

Dew glistened on the grass of Skinner's yard early Wednesday morning. Brock stood on the patio, drinking coffee at seven o'clock, before the heat of the day began ramping up. A hazy mist over the vineyard was just starting to evaporate. He went back into the house and saw Maude fixing an English muffin. Truman was eating the dog food she had gotten him, fit for a king. Brock refreshed the coffee in his cup and sat down at the computer. The information available on the theft of The Sweet Potato was limited. A wealthy anonymous collector had reported it stolen, but nothing about the gemstone had turned up since.

Brock rapped on the glass at Peka Forge with his car key a little before eight o'clock. Dewey Prater, wearing an apron, unlocked and opened the front door. "Mr. Skinner. Want to help with the cooking?"

"The only thing I know how to do is grill meat."

"Well, you can keep me company then." Prater went back in the kitchen to tend to the large pots of beans. Several black cast-iron skillets for making cornbread were stacked up on the back of the stove. A big container of bacon grease had spoon marks in it where dollops had been extracted. "I sort of have an idea what you're going to ask me."

"I'll ask it, then. Can you think of any men who came in that were particularly fond of Portia?"

"Oh, there were a half dozen. None of them seemed overly serious about pursuing her." Prater stepped in the pantry and got on the ladder to pull down a few small burlap bags of pinto beans. He pushed aside a couple that had red stitching. "Frankly, Brock, I don't think her death had anything to do with us here."

"What about Morrie Breedlove upstairs? Did he ever meet her?"

"I don't think so." Prater emptied the bags of beans in a pot of water to soak. He moved down the line to stir the ones almost ready to eat.

Brock changed the subject. "I have to tell you, Dewey, these soup beans sent me over when I had them on Saturday night. What makes them so good?"

"Everything. The pureed mirepoix, type of garlic and other spices, brand of bacon grease, water, stock, and quality of the beans, of course."

"I thought a bean was a bean." He moved closer to the batch that just went in to soak.

"I'm afraid not. Mine are from Venezuela," Prater revealed. Brock looked at the name on the burlap bag: Galaz Foods, Inc., Chicago, IL.

"I've heard you don't allow takeout orders."

"I'll give someone a cup to take home if they eat here, but I'm afraid if I start doing carryout, there'll be people standing around disrupting everything, and besides, if we got a run of orders, there might not be enough to feed the customers who come in to eat."

"You've got a point. Well, next time I come in, I'll let you send me home with a cup, and some of that delicious cornbread. I'm going to head out. Let me know if you hear anything related to Portia's death."

"I will." Prater relocked the front door after Brock walked out.

Maude was at the winery when the Lamborghini pulled in. She went to meet Brock at the entrance to give him a big kiss. "What are you up to?"

"Oh, about six feet two," he said.

"Hah, hah."

"I came by to see your pretty face, and jump on the computer in your office for a minute."

"I should have known you had something other than me in mind." Maude left him and headed for the flower bed by the winery sign out by the road.

Galaz Foods out of Chicago, where Peka Forge got its beans, distributed specialty dry foods from around the world in the United States. The owner of the business, Labin Galaz, was originally from Venezuela. Brock Googled his name and began reading all the references that came up. One posting reported that he had been the successful bidder on "The Blue Torpedo" at a recent auction. The gemstone was a thirty-three-carat blue baguette diamond. He paid $11.35 million for it.

Brock shut the computer down and called the sheriff. "Nathan, I just ran across something that might be significant."

"What's that?"

"If you'll remember, Howard Sweeney said that Morrie Breedlove got into cutting and polishing gems. That's what he's been doing in that apartment the last four years. Sweeney also said that Breedlove disappeared right after one of the most valuable diamonds in the world was stolen. I've got a hunch the owner of the gem was a man named Labin Galaz."

"Who's he?"

"His company distributes food. Prater buys pinto beans from him."

"There's some connection?"

"My guess is that Galaz used to buy patinated coppers from Breedlove, and when he found out that Morrie had switched obsessions to cutting and polishing gems, he made a deal with him to disappear. Galaz had a big customer in Hazard, Kentucky, and figured that would be the ideal place for Breedlove to hide out."

"For what purpose?"

"I think he gave the valuable diamond he claimed was stolen to Breedlove to be recut, and somehow he's pushing other gems through there."

"If that's what's going on, Dewey Prater is up to his neck in it."

"Exactly," Brock said.

"I won't be able to get a warrant to search his place until in the morning."

"Hopefully, by then, we'll have the rest of this puzzle figured out."

Brock went to the gym after lunch to work out. When he got home, he tried to call Jerome Rhyne of the FBI, but he didn't pick up. Damon Booth did answer when he called. "Mr. Booth, this is Brock Skinner down in Hazard, Kentucky. I'm working with the police, and I met Howard Sweeney when he came to identify the body of his daughter."

"Yes, what can I do for you?"

"I'm trying to get a little background information. Who exactly decided to send Portia here to pursue Morrie Breedlove?"

"Agent Rhyne and myself. We discussed the case and Miss Sweeney said she knew that part of the country and would enjoy going back there for a few months."

"Did she ever say she found anything?"

"She reported that every week or so, suspicious-looking people would come in, eat lunch, and ask for beans to go. Prater, the owner of the place, would go over and chat with them for a second, and then bring over a cup. She thought that's how the diamonds cut by Breedlove were going out."

"But you guys couldn't figure out how they were coming in."

"Right. We went to Hazard to watch his every move for a couple of months, and finally searched his apartment to look for diamonds. We found nothing."

"The police here in Hazard are thinking she found out how the diamonds were getting in, and got killed for it."

"Have you found a tape recorder in her apartment?" Booth asked.

"What are you talking about?"

"We gave her one that fits in a lamp. It loops every seventy-two hours."

"Thanks, we'll look for it." Brock hung up and called the sheriff. "Nathan, tell me Portia Sweeney's address. Meet me there as soon as you can."

"What's up?"

"Just meet me there."

At Portia's apartment, Brock told Connors what Agent Booth had told him. Connors looked in the bottom of the lamp by the sofa. There it was. He carefully pulled the wire for the microphone down and extracted the little recorder. "I'll take it to the station and let one of the techs review it. Might take him the rest of the day to listen to the whole thing."

Skinner returned home and spent the evening racking his brain. By midnight, he had it all put together.

~ ~ ~

The digital clock by the bed read three thirteen on Thursday morning when Brock awakened to Truman's low growl. Maude appeared to be sleeping soundly. He slipped on his clothes, which had been lying nearby, and reached in the nightstand drawer for the loaded pistol. He pulled the bedroom door shut after the dog came out. Truman went to the windows on the side of the house and started barking at a shadowy figure in the yard. Upon hearing the dog, the prowler ran back out to the main road and jumped in a pickup truck.

Brock went to the kitchen to get the keys to the Lamborghini and then ran out the back door toward the detached garage. The sports car would have no trouble catching a pickup truck, except for one minor detail. There were two forks in the road. Brock chose a direction at the first one and sped down the road at high speed. After about three miles, he backtracked and took the other fork. At the next split, he stayed on the road going into town. He turned toward Peka Forge to see if the pickup truck there had a warm engine.

Approaching the bar, Brock saw a hooded person key open the entrance door and step in. He stopped his car, jumped out, and ran to see if the door was open. It was locked. After retrieving tools from the glove box of the Lamborghini, Brock picked the lock and searched for the light switches inside. "Anybody here?" he yelled. The place was still. He went to the pantry, climbed the ladder, and slid open the ceiling panel. Several small boxes with side doors were attached to the bottom of a steel plate. He closed the ceiling and grabbed one of the soup-bean bags with red stitching on it.

When he got home and climbed back into bed after four o'clock, Maude asked, "What was that all about?"

"Truman saw a prowler."

"Hum." She fell asleep again.

At eight o'clock, Brock shaved and put on a dark green shirt and khakis, tucking the big orange diamond in his right-front pants pocket. He arrived at the police station by eight thirty. Connors had hauled Dewey Prater and Morrie Breedlove in for questioning, and they were both seated next to each other in the interrogation room. The sheriff sat on the other side of the table.

Brock, holding a sack of pinto beans, sat down beside Connors and asked, "Was there anything on the tape?"

"We'll get to that," the sheriff said. "Brock, why don't you tell us what you think has been going on over at Peka Forge, since you seem to be so smart."

"Okay. Labin Galaz from Galaz Foods in Chicago got into diamonds several years ago. He found out about Breedlove becoming obsessed with cutting and polishing stones, and made a deal with him to go hide out here in Hazard. I don't know what he did to induce Breedlove to do such a thing. Maybe he'll tell us. Nonetheless, Galaz knew Dewey Prater because he sold beans to him. He cut him in on the diamond laundering scheme and asked him to fortify a spot where Morrie could crank out recut diamonds in peace."

"How did the gems go in and out of there?"

"That's the clever part of the operation. It was so good that the FBI couldn't figure it out. Last night, it dawned on me that the pantry by the kitchen at Peka Forge is directly under the safe in Breedlove's apartment. The ceiling in the pantry slides open, and the safe has a false bottom in it." Brock threw the bag of beans on the table and asked the sheriff, "Do you have a knife on you?" Connors pulled one out of his pocket. Brock cut open the bag of beans. Inside, there was a paper packet with diamonds in it. "The beans that came in with red stitching on the bag were the ones with stones inside. Dewey must have put them in the little boxes on the false bottom of the safe, where Morrie could retrieve them."

"How'd the recut stones go back out?" Connors asked.

"The mule would come in the bar and eat a bowl of beans. Then he'd ask to talk to Prater. If the man spoke the right code words, Dewey would make up a carryout order of soup beans and drop the outgoing diamonds in it."

"How do you know that?"

"Because Portia Sweeney, either by accident or on purpose, brought me over a cup of beans to go. This was in it." He reached in his pocket for the velvet bag containing the vivid orange diamond, took it out of the bag, and set it on the table. Breedlove looked stunned, and Prater was mad as hell. "The mule who was supposed to pick it up must have come back Sunday to ask Prater where it was. I found out this morning how Breedlove gets in and out without being seen. He goes through the bottom of the safe onto the ladder in the pantry and then out the side door, where the pickup is parked. Prater here must have given him a key to the truck."

"So, you think Morrie went to Sweeney's looking for the diamond?"

"Good possibility," Brock said.

"The recording from her apartment will clear that up." Connors pushed the play button.

There were rustling sounds of someone breaking in, and Portia could be heard saying, "What do you want?"

A male voice spoke. "Where's the diamond?"

"I don't know what you're talking about."

"You dumb bitch." Then came sounds of a struggle, coughing by Portia being choked, and the thud of her body hitting the floor. The man who murdered her spent another fifteen minutes turning the place upside down, looking for the stone she had put in Brock's soup beans.

"That's the voice of Dewey Prater. Now, all you have to do is prove it's his," Brock lamented.

The sheriff called for the deputy to take Portia's killer and put him in a jail cell. On the way out, Prater spat at Brock, "Tell your wife her wines suck."

"That might be, but your soup beans are still to die for." Brock looked at Breedlove after Prater was gone. "Morrie, you're the ne plus ultra of diamond cutters. Why'd you get messed up in this thing?"

All the emotion had drained out of the man. He said, "Because I love it. Galaz told me if I'd stay in Hazard for five years, he'd buy me the one diamond in the world I hoped to possess. The Blue Torpedo. He bought it and sent me a note in one of the incoming shipments to tell me that it would be mine in less than a year."

Connors said, "It's not going to work that way, Morrie. You're going to help us convict Labin Galaz."

Breedlove leaned back in his chair and shook his head in frustration.

Lucky at Bridge, Unlucky at Bats

Like Sherman through Georgia, the late afternoon heat began overwhelming the undersized air conditioner pumping tepid air into Vigneron Winery. The temperature reached seventy-six degrees inside, yet it still felt relatively comfortable. The lot out front had no more empty spaces for cars. Visitors parked in the shade, on the side of the road coming up the hill. Patrons formed a line in the tasting room to keep cool, and eventually bellied up to the bar to sample wines made by Maude Skinner, who wiped her forehead with her sleeve as she tried to keep all the plates spinning. Her husband, Brock, had inopportunely gone to the pistol range for an hour of target practice. He was expected back any minute.

Maude saw Deborah Michaels come through the door wearing a yellow tennis outfit. Her hair was tied back in a short ponytail. Deb waved with a quick wiggle of the hand and worked her way over to the side of the bar. Maude said, "Hi there. I've got your wine in the back. I'll run and get it." One of the Michaels would come in once a month to get a few bottles of Vigneron's better brands, to restock their cellar at home. Brock knew Deb's husband, Eric, because he was one of the lawyers involved in the sale of Sturges Lumber, a local company Brock had recently purchased.

"Boy, you're doing a land-office business today," Deb commented.

Brock had returned from the gun range and was standing in the door leading to the barrel room. He picked up the six-bottle tote and gave it to Deb. "Here you go."

"Thanks. Hey, I wanted to ask you guys if you could join us on our houseboat tomorrow afternoon. We're docked at Duffs Bay Marina on Buckhorn Lake. Two other couples are coming along. The weather is going to be great."

Maude looked at Brock. He raised his eyebrows and grinned, signaling he was in favor of the idea. "Sure. What time should we meet you there?" she asked.

"Boat leaves at one o'clock sharp. You don't need to bring anything."

"Okay. We'll see you tomorrow."

Vigneron opened at noon on Sunday. Joan Brewer worked that day to cover for Maude. The Skinners swung by the winery on the way to the lake to make sure Joan had everything under control. On the way out, they grabbed a bottle of the best red wine in stock.

The roads over to the marina were winding and treacherous, and the people who lived in the area would run you down if your tires weren't squealing on every curve. Brock's Lamborghini had no trouble negotiating the foothills of Appalachia over to the uncomfortably hot asphalt lot at Duffs Bay Marina. A slight breeze blew from the west, providing little relief from the direct sunlight or heat radiating up from the pavement. Maude wore a straw hat and sundress over a one-piece swimsuit. The wine she brought along was in the bag over her shoulder. Brock had on a foppish pair of striped red trunks, manufactured by his brother-in-law's clothing company, to go with the light gray Hawaiian shirt he'd bought off the rack.

Eric rushed to the front of the houseboat to greet the Skinners as they came near. "Stand back!" he yelled. "Landlubbers approaching. Watch your step. Don't fall in the lake."

Brock fired back, "Did you put the plug in this tub? I don't want to have to swim back." The houseboat, mostly white, had decorative teal and orange stripes running diagonally on the sides of the cabin.

"All fitted out, sir. Nothing to worry about."

Deb spoke from the top deck: "Come on up. I want to introduce you to our friends." After climbing the stairs, the Skinners walked over to the two couples standing aft. "Maude and Brock, this is Cara and Andy Copeland, and Sadie and Kevin Stancati."

"Pleased to meet you." The seven of them stood around making small talk while Eric untied the vessel. The twin outboards in the back were already idling. The engines snapped in reverse and the houseboat began to back away from the dock.

Over the noise of the engines, Brock said, "Thanks for inviting us. Maude and I haven't been on the water since we got married."

Lake people were a special breed, social and fun-loving for the most part. Many were world-class drinkers, but you'd never know it because their personalities didn't change much when they got soused. Angry drunks never got invited back. Eric shifted into drive and pointed the houseboat south. Soon, the women began talking among themselves, and the men congregated around the captain's chair. Brock asked Kevin Stancati, "What business you in?"

"CPA. Andy here is one of my clients. How about you?"

"I'm involved in two companies; one sells tailored clothing, the other lumber. Maude owns and runs Vigneron Winery."

"Right. Eric told me that," Kevin said.

Andy Copeland added, "I have a business that improves habitats for wildlife. We eliminate things in nature that kill birds, fish, and animals."

"Interesting. How do you folks know each other?"

"We formed a bridge group after getting acquainted playing in a tournament in Lexington. The card games haven't lasted, but our friendships have."

"Bridge groups are usually eight people. What happened to the other couple?" Brock asked.

The three men looked at each other grimly. Kevin Stancati said, "The guy's wife left him."

Eric pulled the boat close to shore and opened a well in the floor to retrieve the black anchor tethered by a yellow-and-black nylon cord tied through a scupper. Andy Copeland cranked up Delbert McClinton on the CD player, and everyone went overboard and floated on life jackets for a good half hour to get relief from the hot sun. Buckhorn Lake, water impounded by the Corps of Engineers from the Middle Fork of the Kentucky River, was relatively narrow and deep. Hills shot into the lake at sharp angles, with lush trees growing right down to the water's edge.

Once back on deck and dried off, the gang of eight went in the air-conditioned cabin for refreshments. Maude said, "Deb, would you mind opening that bottle of wine we brought? I want everyone to try a sip. I think it's the best we've ever made."

"Alcohol's not allowed on the water," Deb said facetiously. "But a bottle of wine divided among the eight of us is more like a taste test than bona fide drinking. Coming right up." She poured a little in a clear plastic cup for each person. "Hey, since we're all in here, let's play a hand or two of bridge. Men at that table, ladies over here." While the card games were going on, each person commented on how they liked the red wine, which made Maude very happy.

Brock couldn't help himself. He had to ask. "You mentioned the other couple in your bridge group split up. What happened?"

Eric said, "Ladies, which one of you wants to take that one?"

Cara Copeland volunteered. "Nicole Parker told us she couldn't stand living around here anymore. Said the trees and mountains were driving her crazy."

Kevin offered, "Dion, her husband, is an interesting fellow. We invited them into the group because he had a reputation for being the best bridge player in town."

Each table finished a rubber, leaving the winners to face off in a championship game. Deb and Sadie beat Andy and Kevin in the end by way of a small slam. Eric weighed anchor, and at a brisk pace, set a course farther south. Another houseboat came into view, starboard side, running north. Brock pointed at it and asked, "What's on the side of the cabin?"

Eric replied, "That, my friend, is a straight-on view of a Virginia big-eared bat. Dion Parker, formerly of our bridge group, is standing in front of it. I guess we'd better swing around and say hi."

Dion spoke first. "Eric. Andy. Kevin." He had on floral-patterned swim trunks and no shirt. His red-brown tan suggested Cherokee blood. The coal-black hair and stubble on his face reminded Brock of Brutus on Popeye.

"Dion, how's it going?" Kevin asked. Eric threw the boat in reverse to keep from drifting by. The lake was a little choppy in the middle, causing both houseboats to sway slightly.

"Pretty good. Nice to see you guys again."

"Catch any fish?"

"A couple of large mouth," he said.

"Enough for a meal?"

"I'll pan fry them in corn-flake batter."

The girls stepped out of the cabin and waved to him.

Andy said, "Enjoy. Be safe." Eric put the boat in gear and headed north. Dion gave a thumbs-up as they pulled away and went back to the helm of his craft. He ran toward the eastern shore, turning north after the Michaels' houseboat had gotten a half mile ahead.

Brock asked Eric, "What's with the bat?"

"He's got several caves on his property where bats hibernate. Some of them are endangered species."

"No wonder his wife left him."

"Yeah," Eric agreed.

At five thirty, the sun had fallen to the west enough to drop anchor again in the shade of the shoreline. Deb said, "Eric, fire up the grill. I'll get the asparagus and steaks ready." They ate inside on the bridge tables, talking and laughing throughout the delicious meal. By seven o'clock, the houseboat had docked again at Duffs Bay Marina.

Maude said, "We had a great time. Thanks again for inviting us out."

Deb watched them step onto the dock. "Maybe we can get together again soon for another hand of bridge."

"Yes. At our house would be great," Maude offered. The Skinners chatted with the Copelands and Stancatis on the way up to their expensive European SUVs in the parking lot.

Brock cranked up the air conditioner in the Lamborghini. He looked over at Maude and said, "I want to know the real reason Nicole Parker left her husband."

"I figured as much," she replied earnestly.

~ ~ ~

Maude left for the winery early on Monday morning. Brock went for a short jog with Truman, their German shepherd, tagging along. He took a shower afterward, had a heavy breakfast, and sat at the computer. Dion Parker's place was listed on a dead-end road east of town.

Skinner took the winery truck back into Rocky Hollow, checking the addresses on the mailboxes as he went. The wide concrete driveway leading to Dion Parker's house, partway up the hill, made it easy to park by the front entrance. He got out and knocked on the varnished oak door.

Parker appeared and asked, "Yes? Can I help you?"

"My name's Brock Skinner. I saw you yesterday out on Buckhorn Lake. I was with Eric, Andy, and Kevin."

"Yeah, I remember." He had shaved and was well dressed.

"They told me you had several bat caves up here. My curiosity got the best of me."

"Come on in." The inside of the house had a low ceiling and was rather dark, making it look like a bat cave. A gigantic amber ashtray, on a side table next to the lounger, held a stubbed-out cigar butt. The black leather furniture looked expensive. "What did you want to know?"

"Well, it's more what I'd like to see. Could you show me what a bat cave looks like?"

"Sure. Let's go out the back." They walked up the hill about a quarter of a mile to an uneven plateau, with a craggy rock wall dotted with a series of limestone caves of varying sizes and shapes. "You can peek in there, but don't go too far. You'll spook the bats and send them flying all over the place." Brock walked in far enough to see dozens of bats hanging upside down on the walls and ceiling.

"What got you interested in these creatures?"

"I studied biology when I was at Transy. That's where I met my wife, Nicole. You know, there are over fourteen hundred different kinds of bats. They are one-fifth of all mammal species, and the only ones who can fly."

"I wasn't aware of that."

"Bats eat insects. They save the agricultural industry twenty-five billion a year in crop damage. Kentucky has sixteen different types. Three of them are endangered."

"Is that because of man disturbing their habitat?"

"Partly. Mostly it's white-nose syndrome—a fungus that kills bats by the thousands."

"Can anything be done to stop it?"

"Yes. I think we've found the solution."

"Best of luck on that." They went back through the house toward the front door. Brock turned and said, "The guys on the boat yesterday told me you were a good bridge player, but you had to quit the group because you and your wife separated. Sorry to hear that."

"Well, the good news is she hasn't asked me for a divorce yet. Maybe we can reconcile and get back to playing bridge again. Oh, and if you want to help save the bats, you can donate to the Bats for the Future Fund."

"I'll look it up. Nice meeting you."

"You as well." Dion Parker had turned into a convivial salesman all of a sudden. Brock coasted down the hill, out of Rocky Hollow, troubled by a number of things.

~ ~ ~

Nathan Connors looked out the window of his office, deep in thought, and saw Brock Skinner high stepping up the stairs in front of the police station. The sheriff went out to greet him. "It's been a couple of weeks since you've been in. I was wondering if you'd left town or something."

"I'm still here."

"What can I do for you?"

"I want you to look up the marriage license of Dion Parker." Brock had helped Connors solve several cases, enhancing his reputation in the law-enforcement community.

"Who is he?"

"A really good bridge player. I'm trying to find his wife."

"Did he hire you to do that?"

"No." They went into the sheriff's office and sat down.

"Then what do you want with her?"

"Just to make sure she's north of the dirt. You needn't worry about anything."

"You should talk. Dion Parker, you say?" Connors typed away at the keyboard of his computer, looked at the screen, and recited, "Married on July Fourth four years ago to Nicole Peterson of Lexington." Connors read off the address of Nicole's parents shown on the marriage application. Brock got up, thanked the sheriff, and abruptly walked out. Connors yelled after him, "Stay in touch."

The law practice of Eric Michaels was in a smutty-looking, gray, stucco, two-story office building with cobalt-blue soffits and fascia. The cloud cover of the day made the place look dingy and foreboding. Skinner entered and asked if Michaels would see him. In a few minutes, Eric came out smiling, offering his hand. Brock shook it and asked, "Got a minute?"

"Sure. Come in my office." After pleasantries, Michaels asked, "What can I do for you?"

"What can you tell me about Dion Parker?"

"Why are you interested?"

"I went up to his place this morning, introduced myself, and asked him to show me a bat cave. After I saw the bat on his houseboat, I wanted to see what the critters looked like firsthand."

"Did you see them?"

"Yes. He said they were getting wiped out by something called white-nose syndrome."

"Yes. He got a grant from a charity to test a solution to the problem."

"How do you know that?" Brock asked, shifting in his seat.

"Because he hired me to prepare a proposal for the funding. It was an elaborate form that required a detailed explanation of how the grant money was to be spent. Andy's company completed the fieldwork, and Kevin did the accounting paperwork that had to be submitted."

"Well, he claims he's got the answer."

Eric confirmed, "Yes, he told me that."

"He also said his wife hadn't asked for a divorce yet. What do you know about her?"

"Kind of a serious woman. Never seemed happy to me. Conservative bridge player."

Brock probed further. "I take it Dion is more aggressive?"

"I'll say. He figured out that the genteel bridge scoring system from a hundred years ago favors taking risks, which in the old days was considered bad form."

"Do you know where his wife went?"

"Probably back to Lexington where she's from," Eric suggested.

"When was the last time you saw or heard from her?"

"Last Friday. She called into the switchboard and asked to speak to me. She wanted me to recommend a good divorce lawyer. I told her that would be a conflict of interest."

"What do you think's the real reason she's leaving him?"

"Probably the typical thing. Found another man more to her liking," Michaels said.

Skinner gave his thoughts. "I'm guessing she fears for her life."

"Who would want to kill her?"

"Dion Parker."

~ ~ ~

The Skinners arrived at their condo in Lexington right before noon on Tuesday. The August heat had subsided, and low humidity coupled with broken clouds made it bearable to walk outside. Maude had made sandwiches for lunch before they left Hazard. She said, "What's got you all wound up about this Nicole Parker?"

"You don't leave your husband because of mountains and trees."

"So, she lied to the other women. What's the big deal?"

"Maybe nothing. I intend to find out." They ate lunch at the kitchen table. Brock cleaned up the dishes and declared he was going to visit Nicole's parents. Maude planned to do a little shopping downtown.

The Petersons looked to be in their early sixties. Both were thin, attractive, and well-groomed, with heavy Kentucky accents. They invited Brock in after he explained he was trying to reach Nicole on behalf of a lawyer she wanted to hire, which was not exactly true. The painted-brick house had traditional colonial furnishings, big divided-light windows, and cream-colored walls.

"When was the last time you heard from Nicole?"

Mr. Peterson said, "Oh, it must have been three weeks ago. She called to ask if she could come and stay with us for a spell."

Mrs. Peterson said, "Nicole told us she was going to leave her husband." She had a defeated expression on her face.

"Did she say why?"

"He was doing experiments on bats. She was afraid of being bitten by one that had a deadly virus."

"Wonder where your daughter is now?"

"We don't have any idea."

"I'm thinking you should file a missing person's report with the police. Do you have a recent picture of her that I can take?" Brock asked.

Mr. Peterson left the room to find one. He returned with a five-by-seven color shot and handed it to Brock. "We probably should have called the police a week ago."

Nicole's eyes were dark. There were thin lines in her forehead and around her mouth. She looked a lot like Sadie Stancati. "Do you have a phone number for her?"

"Yes. We've tried to call it for the last week or so. No answer."

On the way out, Skinner told the Petersons he would contact them if he learned any news about their daughter.

That evening, Maude's brother brought terribly spicy Chinese food to the condo for supper. "Dang, Marcel, this stuff is five-star hot. You can dial it back a couple of stars next time," Brock suggested.

Marcel ignored the comment. "So, what are you doing to keep busy?"

"I'm trying to find a woman who has disappeared."

"What happened to her?"

"She left her husband because he was raising bats. From what I can surmise off the Internet, she's afraid of getting the Nipah virus from one of them, which is deadly to humans."

"I've never heard of such a thing," Marcel said.

"I'm learning more about bats than I care to know." Brock frowned, took a big drink of water to put the fire out in his mouth, and scratched his forehead absentmindedly. After Marcel left, the Skinners decided to drive back to Hazard that evening.

~ ~ ~

Brock tracked Andy Copeland down the next morning to ask him about the fieldwork he had done. "So, Andy, I heard from Eric that you conducted some experiments for Dion Parker on cures for white-nose syndrome in bats."

"Yes," Andy replied, "he hired my company to determine if polyethylene glycol and blacklight detection could eradicate a fungus that turns bats' noses white, making them use up stored food reserves during torpor and eventually causing them to die."

"Does it work?"

"Apparently. The fungus on the bats we watched cleared up and they lived."

"How much did he pay you?"

"Two million, two hundred thirty thousand dollars."

Brock looked at Andy in disbelief. "You're kidding."

"No. It took us an army of people over a year to collect the data from multiple sites, and then verify the results. Kevin did the accounting on it. We made less than ten percent profit."

When he got back home, Brock placed a call to Kevin Stancati to discuss the bat experiments. He asked him where all the money had gone.

"Andy paid two dozen people for better than a year. The costs of equipment, chemicals, light fixtures, travel, and report writing were massive. I had to detail the information for the charity that funded the research."

"Was it the Bats for the Future Fund?"

"Yes, it was. By the time I charged Andy for my time, he didn't end up making much on the deal."

"Thanks, Kevin." Brock rang off, climbed in the pickup truck, and drove over to Rocky Hollow again to find Dion Parker. When he located him near the bat caves, he asked, "Dion, have you heard from your wife recently?"

"As a matter of fact, I have. She called this morning and told me she was living in Key West, working at a hotel on Duval Street."

"Did she give the name of it?"

"No. She sounded like she wasn't coming back anytime soon."

"That's a shame. Are you going to make any money off the cure you came up with for white-nose syndrome?"

"Maybe. I'll get some notoriety for testing it, and if it works on a large scale, the Bats for the Future Fund may send me a reward. Who knows? We'll see."

"One more thing. Can you catch the Nipah virus from bats?"

"I suppose if one bit you, and it got in your bloodstream. Bats aren't vampires. I've never heard of that happening."

Skinner called the Petersons on the way back to the winery to report what he had heard about Nicole. When Maude saw the pickup truck, she went out to meet Brock and see what he'd been doing. "I went up to visit with Parker again. He reported that Nicole has taken a job in a hotel on Key West."

"I know what's coming next," she said. "We're going to Florida for a quick vacation."

"How'd you guess?"

"Because you're like a bulldog on a meat wagon. We're flying. I'm not driving all that way."

Brock said, "I'll get the tickets." He booked flights and a rental car for the next day, and made a reservation for a penthouse room at the Marriott.

The strong wind blowing from the southwest took the edge off the heat and humidity, and it was five degrees cooler in Key West than in Hazard. The island almost seemed deserted in the dead of summer. Maude stepped onto the penthouse porch to take in the view of the gulf to the north. The bright aquamarine water mesmerized her. "Brock, let's take a boat ride and go snorkeling this afternoon."

"Sounds great."

They joined a group of divers and rode out about two miles to an area where there were plenty of fish to see. After a couple of hours in the water, they were exhausted, in a good way, and returned to the room to shower off and get ready for a fresh seafood meal at a downtown restaurant. As they approached the older section of town in the rental car, a place to park opened up near Truman Avenue.

There were less than a dozen hotels on Duval Street proper, so the Skinners hit a few of them before dinner, asking for Nicole Parker. They had no luck. They chose a fancy spot to eat that featured lobster and crab. The clanging, banging, and loud talk coming from the kitchen detracted somewhat from the intimacy of the place. Brock said, "I can't explain why I've gotten so hung up on trying to find the woman, but you have to admit, looking for her has its fringe benefits."

"I'll say," Maude replied.

They resumed their search for Nicole after a light dessert and decaf coffee. The front desk clerk at the biggest hotel in the area said he'd met Nicole Parker two days ago. She'd started working there, but had quit and walked out less than two hours ago. Brock showed him the picture. He couldn't be sure.

Maude said, "Let's head back to our hotel and relax."

"I'm for that."

They slept in the next morning, ordering room service at nine thirty. The wind had died down considerably. Brock finished his coffee and said, "Somebody has gone to a lot of trouble to contrive a Nicole Parker sighting. Eric Michaels told me she called him last Friday, which means she was certainly alive then. Dion Parker said she was here in Key West. I don't trust him. If she isn't actually here, he'd be the one who staged it to cover his tracks, I suppose. I think he killed her."

"Why?"

"She must have had something on him worth killing her for."

"You'll never be able to prove he did it. He's too smart for that," she said.

"Brock Skinner doesn't think in terms of never," he said.

"Well, you arrogant shit. I can't wait to see how you pull this rabbit out of a hat."

"Meanwhile," he interrupted, "let's spend the weekend doing Key West, one end to the other."

"You do have some redeeming qualities." Maude got him in a headlock and rubbed his short hair.

~ ~ ~

When the Skinners landed in Cincinnati on Monday morning, Maude took the Lamborghini to their condo in Lexington while Brock caught a flight to Washington, DC. Late in the day, he walked into the offices of the National Fish and Wildlife Federation. It looked like a typical bureaucracy. The person in charge of the Bats for the Future Fund wouldn't be in until the next morning. Brock returned then and got an audience with the man in charge. "I'm interested in hearing about the research done on polyethylene glycol and bats."

"We've awarded several grants to see if the chemical can thwart white-nose syndrome. A reduction of the bat population will cost our country billions of dollars, you know," the man reported.

"Which of the studies seems to be the most conclusive?" Brock asked.

"The one from Hazard, Kentucky, by Dion Parker, is very extensive. He's got the most complete data. Numbers and species of bats, locations of roosts, et cetera."

"Would it be possible for me to see the report?"

"I guess so. You can look at it on the computer. I can't let you take notes or print anything out. I'll set you up in the room next door."

Brock spent over three hours reading the impressive report. He thanked the head man and handed him a $500 donation check for the fund.

He flew back to Cincinnati and hailed a limo on Tuesday afternoon to drive him to Lexington. When Maude saw him come in, she asked, "Find out anything interesting?"

"Maybe. I'll know when we get back home. You don't mind if we make good on the promise you made to host a bridge party at our house, do you?"

"When are you thinking?"

"Saturday night, if we can get everybody to show up on short notice," he said.

"Sure. Let's leave for Hazard now," Maude urged.

Brock took the rest of the bags from the Key West trip out to the car. The wheels in his head were spinning as the Lamborghini left downtown Lexington.

The Skinners arrived at Vigneron Winery an hour before closing time. Maude made the rounds, verifying that everything had gone smoothly while she'd been away, and Brock asked her to take Truman home in the pickup truck. He wanted to take care of some urgent business with Dion Parker.

When Parker opened the front door of his house, he noticed Brock's Lamborghini parked on the driveway facing downhill. "Look at that machine," he said. "I'm surprised some hill jack hasn't beaten you up and taken that thing away from you."

"Oh, it's been tried more than once."

"What brings you up here this time?"

"My wife and I are planning to have some people over for bridge. I would like you to join us. Since I don't have your cell number, I'm inviting you in person."

"Do you have the date yet?"

"We're thinking Saturday, but need to arrange it with the others. Give me your number. I'll call to confirm." Brock punched it in his phone when Parker gave it to him.

"Who will my partner be?"

"Me. You might as well tell me now how you play, and what conventions you use. I'll want to brush up on them."

Dion spent the next half hour lecturing him on how to win at bridge. Brock went home and spent the rest of the evening studying many complicated bidding strategies.

~ ~ ~

The Hazard police station had plenty of activity for a damp Wednesday morning. Sprinkles of rain blew onto the streaked windows of the waiting room, making unsettling snapping noises. Being around unpredictable lawbreakers was stressful enough. Brock finally got in to see the sheriff twenty minutes later.

Connors asked, "Did you find the woman you were looking for?"

"No. I think I know where she is, though."

"What is it you need from me now?"

"Three things, actually, Sheriff."

"Let's hear it."

"First, can you get me Dion Parker's phone records for the last year?" Brock read off his number.

"I probably can, but I'll need a good reason." Skinner laid out the other two things he wanted from the sheriff, and tied them back to the phone records. "You know, Skinner, how is it you find all this trouble and suck everybody else into it? If I don't find anything, who's going to pay for this goose chase?"

"I will. You always get the credit for solving the cases that fall in my lap. What are you complaining about?"

"Well, you've outdone yourself this time. Getting those phone records will take at least two hours."

"I'll come back later this morning." Brock got in his car and started looking for bat roosts he remembered from the Parker report. The rainclouds had moved out, turning the atmosphere into a hot, wet soup. After he'd made a big loop around Perry County, Skinner pulled over, put his head back, and turned the fan in his car to MAX AC. Something even more sinister than he had thought was afoot.

Brock picked up the several pages of Parker's phone records from the police station before returning home. The list included lots of calls to Eric Michaels, Andy Copeland, and Kevin Stancati. There were also a dozen calls to a business by the name of Mountain Gold Exchange in Whitesburg. Brock was standing in their vestibule in less than an hour.

The one-inch-thick, bulletproof glass separating the business from its customers left a pall of illegitimacy on the establishment. There were four cluttered desks in the narrow room behind the glass, and a bank-vault-style safe on the back wall with its door open. A morose, middle-aged man stepped to the microphone, asking how he could help. Skinner said, "I'm interested in buying some gold. Dion Parker recommended you to me."

"We only sell gold coins. How many do you want?" he asked.

"It depends on the price."

"I'll tell you what I told Parker. On a thousand coins or more, the cheapest I'll go is one percent over spot."

"That's nearly a two-million-dollar transaction. You'll make twenty thousand in five minutes."

"What's your point?"

"Did Parker buy that much?" Brock asked.

"None of your business. Now, get the hell out of here." The man was wearing a pistol for personal protection, which did him no good behind the bulletproof glass. It probably served to scare away the tire kickers, Brock thought.

Truman was standing between the first two rows of grapevines, panting, when he saw the Lamborghini pull in at the winery. The dog sprinted over to greet his owner, who said, "Happy to see me? Come on, let's go inside." They headed for Maude's office without saying hello to anyone. Brock called Eric, Andy, and Kevin to invite them and their wives over on Saturday night for dinner and a bridge game. The Skinners were becoming known as the wealthiest and most influential couple in Hazard—turning down an invitation from them posed a social and political risk not worth taking for any local. The three couples said yes to the bridge party within an hour. Brock called Dion Parker to let him know to arrive at six thirty, after dinner.

Maude Skinner was a big woman and strikingly beautiful, particularly when made up and smartly dressed in the green-and-blue silk outfit she was wearing on Saturday night. A man in a white cotton jacket tended the bar in the corner of her opulent kitchen. Couples arrived promptly at five thirty. After drinks, Maude ushered guests through the upscale buffet of salad, filet mignon, green beans, and side of pasta. While everyone was eating, Eric Michaels decided to poke fun at Brock. "Maude, with your talent and beauty, why did you ever agree to marry that husband of yours? You could have done a lot better."

"Huh. He says he could have done a lot better than me. I guess what I like most about him is his propensity for delusion."

"Well, that explains it." Everyone laughed. Brock kept quiet. He'd have plenty to say later in the evening.

Maude put coffee and tea out next to the chocolate and cookies in the card room. Andy Copeland asked, "Are we going to draw for partners?"

"No, actually," Brock said, "Maude has agreed to let me replace her in the group with a ringer. I want to see just how good Dion Parker is. He's going to be my partner. He should be here any minute."

Sadie Stancati piped up, "Cara and I believe, as partners, we can beat anyone. Right, Cara?"

"Yes. We're the best bridge players in town. No offense to our husbands."

Kevin and Andy said in unison, "None taken."

Loud chimes went off, startling the group. Maude opened the front door, introduced herself to Dion Parker, and invited him in to where the card tables were set up.

There was an awkward moment among the seven old friends. Eric finally said, "Dion, this is a surprise."

Parker went for a cup of coffee and cookie. "For me, too. It's been a few weeks since we've played."

"I say we get started," Cara said. "Sadie and I think we can take you, Dion."

"I'd be disappointed if you didn't think that," he replied. Maude went back in the kitchen to quietly clean up. The man tending bar had taken a seat in the dining room. The two tables of players made and dealt the cards simultaneously, all eight of them deadly serious as the auctions began. Sadie opened with a Jacoby 2NT. Cara went to 3NT. The girls captured five tricks, winning the first game. The first hand in the second game, the Parker-Skinner team got a leg on. They added to it the next hand, and surpassed a hundred points below the line to even the match.

Entering the third game tied, it was time for a little chatter. Dion said, "You know how I play, Sadie. If you want to get a contract, you're going to have to bid it up."

"Speed kills, Dion. Let's see how the cards fall."

Cara and Sadie had most of the points on the deal of the first hand of the third game. Dion wouldn't let them win the bid, so he took the contract. Parker-Skinner went down two tricks. Copeland-Stancati bid four clubs and made five the next hand. On the third deal, Brock bid 2NT. Parker bid a four-club Puppet Stayman, which led them to a contract of four hearts. They made four to cut the Copeland-Stancati leg off, win the rubber, and match.

At the other table, the Copeland-Stancati men won the first rubber over the Michaels couple, but lost the second and third. The championship would be a one-rubber match. Parker-Skinner didn't get the cards, yet managed to slog through to victory. Dion said to Deb and Eric afterward, "That was a close one." Then he turned to Cara and Sadie, who were watching, and said, "Brock and I were getting good cards against you guys. I hope we get a chance to play again when the cards fall more evenly." Parker addressed Skinner last, saying, "You're an excellent bridge player. Thanks for inviting me to be your partner."

"I'm pretty good at other stuff too." Brock said.

"Such as?" Eric asked.

"Figuring out things that don't make any sense."

"Like what?"

"Why Dion's wife left him."

"We told you. Living in the mountains was getting to her," Sadie said.

"That was the first tip-off something wasn't right. The fact you'd offer that lame story with such conviction and expect me to believe it."

"What difference does it make? She took off, and it doesn't look like she'll be coming back," Parker said.

Brock kept pushing his train of thought. "The 'why' she left is what I couldn't let go of."

Andy Copeland got up from the table and walked over to Brock. "So, what's your answer to that question?"

"Nicole Parker's parents told me she was afraid of getting a virus from a bat."

"Okay. What's the big deal?"

"My guess is that Nicole found out something Dion had done that she couldn't go along with. Dion's answer to the problem was to let a bat bite her, which is how I think she died."

"Skinner, you're pretty good at bridge, but bad at detecting," Dion replied. "Eric talked to Nicole a couple of weeks ago, after she left me, and I heard from her myself early last week. She took a job in Key West. That can be checked out."

"We'll get back to that in a minute. The next thing I wondered about was exactly what Dion had done."

"And what was that?" Kevin asked.

"He falsified a report on research pertaining to polyethylene glycol and bats."

"No, he didn't. Andy, Eric, and I all worked on that report. It's legit," Kevin retorted.

"You might have been able to stick to that story if I hadn't read the report. Twenty of the sites referenced in the study as locations for the bats don't exist. Andy, you had to know that." Brock stared at him. "What's the matter? Cat got your tongue? And Kevin, you had to cook the books to cover for those expenses that weren't real."

Eric said indignantly, "Surely you're not going to suggest I had anything to do with this fantasy."

"That's rich, Eric. I'll get to you later." Eric suddenly looked like the defense lawyer whose client just got the death penalty.

"So, what exactly is the crime here? Nicole is still alive and the report we filed is valid." Dion set his coffee cup down and crossed his arms.

"Now we're getting to the nut of it. Best I can figure, you're the one that discovered polyethylene glycol could cure bats of white-nose syndrome. You knew that other people were about to make the same discovery. The only way you could figure to make any money from it was through a grant."

Deb chimed in, "And you think all of this nonsense is about money?"

"Oh, yes. And so do you. Before Nicole was killed, she told you ladies that she wouldn't go along with stealing grant money."

"What money?" Kevin asked.

"Why don't you explain it to us, Kevin? Andy's company spent about two hundred thousand validating the research done on Parker's property, but you made up fake invoices from vendors who never received any of the two million dollars that was left."

Eric sat down at the card table, trying to figure a way out of this mess. He asked, "So, where did the money go?"

"Dion went to Whitesburg and bought two million in gold with it. A half million in coins will fit in a large cigar box. Each of you men got a box full. I'm sure that's the deal Dion had to make to get everybody on board."

Cara said, "What makes you think we women knew anything about this?"

Brock addressed Sadie. "You know, you look a lot like Nicole Parker. I'm guessing Dion gave you her passport and driver's license and told you to go to Key West and find a job in a hotel for a couple of days. Maude and I went to that hotel. You had just left a couple of hours before we got there."

"So, let me get this straight. You're worried about the accounting on some grant, and you think my wife is dead? Where's her body? You've got nothing, Skinner," Parker stated with confidence.

Brock got down to business. "Okay, let's see if you guys stick together or start giving each other up. Eric, I know you're part of this because you claimed to have spoken to Nicole after she was already dead. And there's another reason that will become clear to you in a moment."

"The body, Skinner?" Dion pressed.

"Ah, and the biggest mistake you made, Dion, was being predictable. You're a fisherman. What is one of the things you need to know to catch fish?"

"Where they are, I suppose."

"Yes, and how deep the water is. If you were going to drop a body in a lake, you'd want to do it in the deepest part. You fish Buckhorn Lake, and know where that is."

In a loud, stentorian voice, Andy Copeland said, "I've heard enough! Let's get out of here."

Brock replied, "I wouldn't try it. There are two police cruisers outside blocking your cars." The man in the white jacket who tended the bar came into the room. "And this is Sheriff Nathan Connors. He mixes a pretty good drink. I asked him to drag the deepest part of the lake, and he found Nicole Parker's body. She was bound by a yellow-and-black nylon rope and black anchor, which was the spare off your boat, Eric. If you want to claim that Parker had already killed her before bringing her body to the boat, now's the time to do it."

"I'm not admitting to anything," he said.

"Bosh. That's the lawyer in you. Anybody else want to speak up and spend less time in jail?" None of them did. Skinner turned to the sheriff. "Well, Nathan, with seven to work with, I'm sure you'll get all the facts to come out." Connors slapped cuffs on them and the deputies put the whole gang in the cruisers.

Once everybody had gone, Maude poured herself a glass of red wine and plopped down on one of the card-table chairs. Brock sat next to her. "I think, not too long ago, you called me an arrogant shit."

"Yes, I did, you arrogant shit."

GAME OF DRONES

The second Thursday in September was one of those breezy days that lifts people's spirits, making them forget life's never-ending problems. It wasn't, however, all that uplifting for Valerie Goddard, the foremost expert in the country on the existence of extraterrestrial life. She found herself stuck in a shallow indentation, on the side of a serrated limestone cliff, in south Perry County, Kentucky. Miraculously, the phone in her pocket had two bars, so she was able to call for help. Arrangements were made to send out a drone to track her weak signal. The medical helicopter landed below in the only clear spot for two miles in any direction, and the men who hiked over and climbed up to retrieve her were less than happy. One of them said, "How in the world did you get back here? What are you doing?"

"Oh, thank you for rescuing me. I was afraid I'd be here until somebody came along."

"Uh, ma'am, that would be never."

"Yes, I suppose you're right," she admitted in a downtrodden voice. Valerie had dropped her backpack full of camping and climbing gear to the base of the cliff, fifty feet below, before realizing her predicament. That had been her undoing. One of the men hauled the backpack to the helicopter for her so she wouldn't fall down and hurt herself.

Sheriff Nathan Connors, in a pensive mood, stood next to his cruiser and waited for the helicopter to land on the tarmac behind the hospital. After the rotors stopped whirling, he marched over to meet the girl who had been airlifted out. Without introduction, he asked pointedly, "What's your name, miss? Where are you from?"

"Valerie Goddard. Roswell, New Mexico." She looked rather bookish. Her frizzy brown hair swirled around like pampas grass in a storm.

"You'll have to pay them for getting you out of there, you know. Thirty-five hundred dollars."

"I don't have that kind of money."

"Do you have a car?" Nathan asked.

"Yes, a rental from Cincinnati. I parked it at the end of Garman Branch Road."

"You hiked from there over the mountains to where they found you?"

Valerie put her head down, scratching the ground with her right shoe. "I did."

"Why, pray tell?"

She rose up and said, "To find the obelisk."

"What obelisk?"

"The one at these coordinates." She showed him the crosshairs on her phone that marked the spot.

"How did you know it was there?"

"Somebody posted a drone flyover on YouTube, so I found it on Google Earth. It appeared about a week ago. I traveled here to locate it."

"Get your gear. I'll take you to your car." Connors was on the verge of losing his cool. Valerie started to get in the back seat like a perp, but the sheriff stopped her. "No, sit up front." They drove away, and after a couple of minutes of silence, he asked, "Why do you want to find this obelisk?"

"To see if it's from outer space."

"Oh, really? I can assure you, it's not."

"How do you know?"

"Because there is no extraterrestrial life, just like there's no extra-sensory perception."

Valerie Goddard had confronted doubters her whole life. She knew when to let it go. "You could be right," she said. "Just so you know, I won't be the only one coming."

"What do you mean?"

"As long as that video is on YouTube, people like me will be looking for the obelisk."

Connors knew when to let it go as well. "Did you find it?" he asked.

"I got to where it once stood, but it was gone." She glared at the sheriff as though he was the one who made the obelisk vanish. He instructed her to follow him back to the police station.

Once they were in the interrogation room, Connors said, "Let me see your driver's license." He read the address on it. "Is this where you live?"

"Yes."

The sheriff went into the next room to make a copy of her information. Upon returning, he said, "You'll be getting a bill from the hospital. I'm going to let you go if you promise to drive to Cincinnati and fly out of here. Before you leave, I want you to pull up that YouTube video." He handed her the wireless keypad and mouse that worked the monitor mounted on the wall.

The video was forty-eight seconds long. A drone dropped down from overhead, circled a few times, came closer, and then flew up and away. The obelisk was four-sided, tapered, mirrored stainless steel, with a tiny pyramid on top. It looked about seven feet tall. "One more thing. Give me the coordinates for it." She wrote them on a foolscap tablet, grabbed her gear, and left the police station.

The USA Drone Port near Hazard, Kentucky, was in what was called Class G, noncontrolled airspace, which meant drones could fly around unabated. The US government research facility had plenty of the little machines, and used the most sophisticated computer technology available, known as Internet 2, to fly them. The proximity of the so-called obelisk to the government out-post, ostensibly, was the reason Valerie Goddard thought aliens were snooping around the area. The sheriff figured some knuck-lehead who worked there had the temerity to cut a one-minute snippet out of a government tape and post it on YouTube. Reaper drones fitted with Hellfire missiles could fly right into the leaker's kitchen and blow him and his house to South Carolina. That didn't seem to deter whoever was behind the obelisk farce.

Connors called the government facility and demanded the video be taken down and the person posting it be disciplined. In addi-tion, he insisted a drone go out the next day to fly over the site where the obelisk had been, to see what the hell was going on atop that isolated mountain.

A government employee called the sheriff on Friday afternoon to report the video had been posted by a private citizen, Trowbridge Banks, and since it wasn't taken with a government camera, there was no legal basis to force him to take it down. Making matters worse, the small drone sent to surveil the former location of the obelisk was blown out of the sky with a shotgun by someone sit-ting up there sporting a Richard Nixon mask.

~ ~ ~

Brock Skinner heard Truman, the white German shepherd he'd recently adopted, barking at something, so he put his lukewarm coffee and folded-open *Wall Street Journal* down on the kitchen counter and went out in the yard to see what the fuss was about. A small gray drone with a black camera mounted on it was hovering under the big tree by the driveway. "Come on, Truman. Let's go in. Maybe it'll go away." The dog reluctantly trotted over to its master, following him back into the house.

After they entered the kitchen together, a humming noise could be heard through the window behind the table. The drone had repositioned itself as close to the glass as possible. That persisted for five minutes. Brock went to the garage, opened his gun case, took out a shotgun, and went around the side of the house to confront the unwanted visitor. He said, "Move along now. You're beginning to annoy me." The drone flew in closer. Brock started walking away from the house, toward the vineyard. When he heard the whining machine following closely behind, he spun around suddenly and blasted it out of the sky, and spent the next fifteen minutes picking up the strewn pieces, tossing them in a garbage can.

Maude Skinner stood in the cellar of her winery counting white wine, comparing the total to the inventory on the computer in her hand. She heard footsteps and turned to see her husband approaching. "Hi. What are you doing today?"

He replied, "Don't know yet. Did you hear a shotgun blast a while ago?"

"I did."

"I shot a drone out of the sky that was pestering Truman."

"Its owner recorded the event, I presume?"

"I suppose so."

"Better check YouTube to see if it's been uploaded yet."

"I don't look at those things. Waste of time."

Maude started walking in the direction of the tasting room. "Did you happen to shoot it when the camera was on Truman?"

"No. It was on me," Brock said.

She gave him a rotten look. "Great."

~ ~ ~

Sheriff Connors pulled up the Trowbridge Banks YouTube channel and saw that another video had just been posted. He hit play and witnessed the business end of Brock Skinner's shotgun discharging a mere one-third of a second before the video went black. He couldn't believe his eyes. Next, he brought up the posting of the silver obelisk, to study the object in greater detail. Connors noticed the four sides were not seamed at the corners. He began to think flat panels were just hooked onto a lightweight quadripod. If the frame could be folded, and the four sides were just flat plates, it was possible the parts to build the obelisk were carried up the mountain by one person. It could also be disassembled and carried back down. He clicked the channel off. The sheriff's anger welled up inside of him as he thought of Skinner being involved. He exited the police station, got in his cruiser, and headed for the Drone Port.

One of the government technicians escorted Connors outside to a white, open-sided tent where there were people working at music stands with computer tablets on them. The tech logged in on one and brought up the video of the government drone. It had been sweeping the mountaintop until running across someone sitting on a rock under a tree, holding a shotgun, wearing a Richard Nixon mask. The person remained perfectly still for a few seconds, and then raised the gun and shot the drone. The tech said, "The only interesting thing we saw on here is the watch the shooter was wearing. It's a limited-edition Bell & Ross V2 model. I'm sure we'll be able to trace it. Might lead us to the culprit."

"Thanks for letting me see what happened." The sheriff knew who wore that watch, but wasn't sharing any information yet. He called Brock on the way back to the police station. "Am I going to have to arrest you for shooting down drones?"

"How'd you hear about that?"

"It's on a YouTube channel named Trowbridge Banks."

"Maude warned me that might happen."

"Brock, there's something else. A government drone was shot down on a mountain beyond Garman Branch yesterday by somebody wearing a Richard Nixon mask."

"What's that got to do with me?" Brock asked.

"He had on a Bell & Ross watch, exactly like the one I've seen on you."

"So, you think someone's trying to set me up?"

"Well, you've been recorded shooting down one drone. Why not more?"

Skinner's mind raced. "I guess I better find out who's behind this."

"I was afraid you were going to say that. Come on down and I'll give you the back story."

After Brock walked into the police station, the sheriff told him about the encounter with Valerie Goddard, handing him a copy of her driver's license and the coordinates for the location of the obelisk.

~ ~ ~

Sunday at noon, Skinner met his brother-in-law, Marcel Sutherland, in a little hippie coffee shop off Broadway Street in Lexington. Overhead, black clouds were setting up for a hot rain. Marcel asked, "So, what's this kooky story about aliens?"

"Darndest thing. A silver obelisk appeared on a mountaintop near the secret US government drone facility in Hazard. It disappeared a few days later. When the government flew a camera up there to check things out, the drone got blown out of the sky by Richard Nixon with a shotgun. When someone leaked it to the press, the newspapers suggested, tongue in cheek, the shooter was an alien. Now, every outer-space nut will come looking for the obelisk and gunman."

"Who owns the mountain?"

"A coal company here in town."

"So, the owner's not involved?"

"No, but I am. The Trowbridge Banks YouTube channel that posted the video of the obelisk also posted one of me blasting a drone out of the sky that was buzzing my house and bothering the dog."

"Are the two events related?"

"Yes, the government will eventually think I'm the one who shot down their drone. My Bell & Ross wristwatch is in both shooting videos."

A sour look appeared on Marcel's face. He set his coffee cup down, rubbed his eyes, and said, "Marvelous. Where'd you get the watch?"

"Maude gave it to me for my birthday. I've got to find out who owns that YouTube channel. Is there any way to trace it?"

"Well, you have to get the IP address and track it back to the computer it's on."

"Can your IT guy do that?" Brock asked.

"I don't know. I'll call him. You said the name on the channel was Trowbridge Banks?"

"Yes."

The clouds finally broke. Big raindrops smacked the ground, sparingly at first before building up to a short-lived deluge. After the rain subsided, steam began rising off the pavement. The two men headed downtown to watch a little football on TV. Marcel called his IT guy at home, asking him to chase down the computer of Trowbridge Banks.

Brock said, "I'm also going to have to find out who shot down the government drone. That won't be easy unless it's the person who owns the YouTube channel."

"Are you going up the mountain to look for evidence?"

"I guess I'll have to."

"Who found the obelisk in the first place?"

"Some girl from Roswell, New Mexico."

"She have any part in this?"

"Probably not," Skinner replied. "She's just one of the tinfoil-hat crowd."

Brock got back to Hazard after dark on Sunday night. The romantic comedy Maude was watching ended as he ambled in the door, exhausted from the trip. "How's Marcel?" she asked. Truman glanced up from his slumber, falling back asleep in two seconds.

"Good. He told me we had to trace the IP address of the fellow who posted the videos so we could find out who and where he is."

Maude moved off the couch and went into the kitchen. Brock followed. She said, "I've been trying to figure out what this character is doing."

"Seems obvious to me," he said. "Somebody's trying to frame me for shooting down the government drone."

Maude put a cartridge of decaf in the Keurig and pressed brew. "But why?"

"I guess to get me to come up the mountain to clear my name."

"That's what I thought," she said. "Now, tie that in with the obelisk."

"I'm not following you."

"It disappeared into outer space, and so will you if you go up that mountain alone." She gave him an ominous look. The coffeemaker finished its job with a flourish. Maude sipped from the cup, returning to the family room to watch another movie.

He trailed behind. "You think someone's trying to kill me?"

"And make an outer space hero out of you," she said.

Brock was dumbstruck. "That would certainly get bruited about as a possibility, if I get killed. I guess I shouldn't have shot down that drone."

"Shoot now and ask questions later. That's your style."

"Uh-huh." He headed for the refrigerator to find something to snack on.

~ ~ ~

"Hello."

"Is this Valerie Goddard?"

"Yes?"

"My name's Brock Skinner. I live in Hazard, Kentucky."

"I've been there recently."

"I know. Sheriff Connors shared that with me."

"What can I do for you?"

"I was wondering how you came across the video of the obelisk on the mountain around here."

Valerie sighed. "Well, I got an email from somebody with a link to it. The note said the obelisk had suddenly appeared near a secret government drone facility. I took an interest in finding it."

Brock asked, "Do you know who the email was from?"

"No. The sender encrypted it."

"Did you find anything on the mountain where the obelisk had been?"

"I did. I saw a small piece of sheet metal nailed to a tree that had words etched on it."

"What did it say?"

"We are taking a man from here and will be taking a woman from a nearby location soon."

Brock laughed inside. Connors had warned him that Goddard was a true believer. "That's interesting."

"Yes, it is."

"If another obelisk pops up nearby, you're welcome to stay at our house with my wife and me. If you decide to chase after it, that is. We own a winery you might like to visit while you're here."

Valerie liked Brock a lot; the sound of his voice and what he said. "That's very nice of you. Most people think I'm a kook, and they steer clear of me."

"Sheriff Connors told me you were very nice. If I can help you with anything, please let me know."

"Thank you. I will." Valerie ended the call. She spun her chair around to look out the window at the tantalizing morning sky. Too damn bad he was married, she thought.

Just as Brock hung up with Valerie, the UPS man rang the doorbell, leaving a box on the porch. It contained his order for an Autel EVO II drone, which had a range of four miles and flight time of thirty minutes. Brock read the instructions carefully, figuring out how to charge the battery and sync up the controller and camera to his computer tablet. Learning to fly the thing was a bit more challenging, but he got the hang of it pretty quickly.

Skinner printed out a detailed topography map of the land beyond Garman Branch Road and put an X where the obelisk was found, determining the sensible path someone would use to hike to it. The drone, when folded up, came in a surprisingly small case. Brock threw it, a shotgun, and pistol in the cab of the winery pickup truck. He checked the gas gauge as he pulled away slowly from the garage behind his house.

Garman Branch Road ran along the side of a rocky hill until the pavement gave way to coarse gravel that had been there for decades. The last house on the road was more than two miles back. Deciduous trees hadn't started turning colors yet, and plenty were clustered at the base of the mountains ahead.

Brock parked the pickup, lowered its banged-up tailgate, and got the drone ready for flight. Once it was powered up, he hit record, took the whining machine straight up, and steered it over the valley between two mountain ridges, in the direction of the spot where the obelisk once stood. Referring to the map, he piloted the drone on a direct route, surveying the area, looking for anything suspicious. The former location of the obelisk, on top of a high mountain with cliffs all around it, came into view nearly two miles from the drone's takeoff point.

Brock heard something to his left. Another drone, three hundred yards away, came out of the trees, barreling toward him, full tilt. He ran around and pulled open the pickup's passenger door to grab the shotgun and pistol before crawling under the truck.

When the noise of the drone got louder, he peeked out to see where it was hovering. A gun was mounted to the bottom of the flying death trap, so he rolled out in the open, aimed the shotgun, and fired. The armed machine broke apart and fell lifelessly to the ground. Skinner went to the back of the vehicle in time to see his own drone on the tablet screen being blown out of the sky by another craft on the mountaintop. He clutched the computer and controller, slammed the tailgate shut, threw the guns in the cab of the truck, and jumped in. Someone wearing a Richard Nixon mask was now running in his direction, and carrying a long rifle with a scope. Brock wheeled the pickup around, swerved to miss the drone he had shot down, and sped off as fast as the truck would take him. Just when he thought he was clear, the back window of the pickup exploded. Pebbles of glass pounded his back, neck, and head. The bullet went on through the front windshield without shattering it. He looked back and saw where the person had lowered the rifle and stopped running. Blood began trickling down his neck, and spots of red formed on his cotton camouflage shirt.

Brock rinsed the blood out of his shirt in the shower when he got home. A couple of places on the lower part of his neck were still bleeding. He stuck Band-Aids on the wounds and put on a collared shirt to hide them. Then he relocked his guns, cleaned the broken glass out of the pickup, and wiped the bloodstains off the seat. The place downtown where he dropped the truck off to get the windows replaced was two blocks from the police station.

The sheriff saw Brock approaching and said, "You're on foot. That's never a good sign." Skinner summarized the events of the day, starting with the call to Valerie Goddard. Connors added his theory of someone being able to carry the folded pieces of the obelisk up on the mountain. "The shooter has probably cleared out by now. He made an attempt to kill you, and since it failed, he'll likely give up on that enterprise," Connors said.

"Why do you think that?"

"Because this whole charade seems to have simply been a way to bump you off and make it look like aliens took you into outer space."

"Why not just kill me and dump my body where no one could find it?"

"There must be some reason why Richard Nixon wanted to put closure on your disappearance. There may be more to come from this clown. I'd watch my back."

"Yeah. Maude's not going to be happy when she hears about this. Can I bum a ride home from one of your men?"

"I'll take you." On the way, the sheriff said, "A government officer at the drone facility is trying to chase down the Bell & Ross watch in the video. He knows you have one and I gave him your address. He asked me to tell you he'd be coming by your house at six thirty this evening."

Brock was right. Maude was not happy.

Colonel Harkie Nelson, wearing a tan military uniform, took a seat in the family room at Maude's urging. She said, "Can I get you something to drink?"

"No, thank you. Did the sheriff tell you why I wanted to come by?"

"He did," Brock replied.

"Before you tell me about the watch, do you have any sense as to what's going on here?"

"I do," he said.

"Let's hear it."

"The person behind this had an elaborate plan to kill me. First, he found a piece of property at the end of a road that nobody lives on. He hiked in quite a way to a mountaintop carrying a knocked-down obelisk, and constructed it in a place easy to see from overhead. He filmed the thing with a drone and put it on YouTube."

"Why did he go so far off the beaten path?"

"To keep anybody from hiking over to it, but that's where things took a wrong turn. The culprit sent a link to the YouTube video of the obelisk to an extraterrestrial expert in Roswell, New Mexico. He knew she could find where the object was, and expected her to call the police about it. Instead, she came to Hazard and hiked over to the thing herself. When she got there, it had already been disassembled and taken off the mountain."

"Where do you come in?"

"The would-be killer sent a drone to my house to aggravate me, counting on the fact that I'd shoot it out of the sky while wearing the watch Maude gave me for my birthday. The video of me was then posted on the Trowbridge Banks YouTube channel. He knew a government drone would be sent up to see what happened to the obelisk, so he waited for it, wearing a watch just like mine, intending to make it look like I was the one who shot it down."

"But why?"

"To lure me up on the mountain. He wanted to kill me and get rid of my body. Eventually, someone would find the metal plaque nailed to a tree up there that said 'we are taking a man from here and will be taking a woman from a nearby location soon.' I'd be gone forever, in outer space somewhere."

"This whole story is ridiculous. What does killing you do for anybody?" the colonel asked.

"That, sir, I have not figured out yet." Brock leaned back on the couch with a confused expression.

"Let's get back to the watch." Nelson turned to Maude. "Where did you buy it?"

"At Horton Jewelers in Campton. I grew up there and went to Wolfe County High School. Debbie Horton and I are friends from school. I trust her."

"Did she order it, or was it in stock?"

"Heavens no. The thing cost a bloody fortune. She ordered it for me."

Colonel Nelson said, "The shooter had to get the same watch somewhere, unless, of course, you are lying to me and shot down our drone yourself."

"Colonel, you're not too hot at winning friends and influencing people," Brock said sarcastically.

"How do you think I got to be a colonel?"

Maude shifted on the couch and said, "If I were you, sir, I'd chase after Richard Nixon and Trowbridge Banks."

After the colonel had unceremoniously driven away, Maude asked her husband, "Why does somebody want to kill you?"

"It's my sparkling personality, I'm sure."

~ ~ ~

Two weeks later, Valerie Goddard got an encrypted email with a link to another video on Trowbridge Banks YouTube channel. The email said the obelisk had been spotted at Red River Gorge in Kentucky. She went to Google Earth again and searched until she found it perched on the edge of a cliff. The leaves had started to turn colors, which made the scenery around the obelisk a picture postcard. She looked in her phone for the number the man from Hazard had called her on, pressing it to reach him. "This is Valerie Goddard. Do you remember me?"

"Yes, of course. How are you?"

"Fine. The obelisk has resurfaced. I was wondering if your offer to put me up at your house still stands?"

"Certainly."

"I'll be there tonight. What's your address?" He gave it to her and went to tell Maude the woman from Roswell was on her way.

It was nine thirty when Goddard's rental car pulled in the driveway. Maude answered the door, and showed her to the guest room. After Valerie got situated, she came into the family room. "This is some kind of log cabin. I'm not used to such luxury." Seeing Brock for the first time only served to heighten her attraction to him.

"Make yourself at home. Can we get you something to eat?" Brock asked.

"No, thanks. I got something on the way."

"You told me people think you're a kook. You don't look like one to me," he said.

"You haven't heard me talk yet. You'll change your opinion."

Maude said, "Oh, I doubt that. We say, live and let live. So, what's your plan?"

"I want to hike over to the obelisk and inspect it. See if it's from outer space."

Brock sat up and struck a serious chord. "Well, it might be more complicated than that." For the next twenty minutes, he chronicled the events leading up to his near-death experience at the hands of a would-be killer.

"What are we going to do?"

"I say we fly a drone over to it."

"I guess that's better than nothing."

Brock said, "Frankly, I'm afraid the person behind this thing is still trying to kill me for some reason, and you might be in some danger if you hike over to the obelisk."

"That's disappointing," Valerie replied.

"I bought two drones last week and know how to fly them. Let's go over to the gorge tomorrow morning and do a flyby. You have the coordinates for the location?"

"I do."

"Have you checked Google Earth to make sure it's still there?"

"I have. It is."

"Good. We'll see you in the morning." Once in the bedroom, Brock commented to Maude, "I'd like to know if Nelson found anybody else who bought a watch the last couple of months like the one you gave me."

"If he did, he'll not be telling us about it."

"I'm just trying to figure out how someone could have seen me wearing a new watch, and be able to run out and buy one just like it. Maybe Marcel's IT guy could hack Bell & Ross and get a list of recent buyers. I wonder how he's doing trying to find the IP address of Trowbridge Banks?"

"If I were you, I'd worry more about getting shot at the gorge tomorrow. Whoever this guy is, he's probably growing more desperate and will be taking more chances."

"Whatever happens, I've got to find him and put an end to this. Valerie is the wild card. She's unpredictable. I'll have to watch her every move."

"Are you going to tell Connors what you're planning?"

"No."

"I'm not sure that's such a good idea."

The girls were talking the next morning when Brock came out of the bedroom; he was dressed in camouflage again for the trip to Red River Gorge. The hazy sun, shining through the trees, shot a glare across the tall kitchen windows. The smell of eggs, bacon, and strong coffee brightened his mood. Valerie wore a loose-fitting, gray-brown hiking outfit that was not particularly flattering to her nice figure. Maude said, "Are you guys going in one vehicle?"

Brock looked at Valerie, and said, "I think we should take your rental car. It's less recognizable."

"Okay, but I want you to drive."

"Fine. Let me have the keys and I'll load up the two drones after breakfast." All three of them left the house at eight forty-five. Maude went to the winery, and the other two struck out to the north.

Ten minutes up the road, Valerie said awkwardly, "You know, Maude's lucky to have a husband like you."

"How so?"

"Well, you're a real man. Not a pusillanimous character like the ones that try to date me."

"Yeah, a real man who damn near got killed a couple of weeks ago. Actually, I'm the lucky one. She has to put up with a lot."

"I've been mulling over the story you told last night. Your wife is a beautiful woman. I'm thinking somebody's trying to kill you to clear the way to her." Brock gave Valerie a twisted stare, but said nothing.

They crossed over Mountain Parkway and took a secluded road that followed the top of a rocky ridge out to a turnaround in the middle of the gorge. The immense chasm kept expanding on both sides of them, and the colors, just beginning to come forth, were beyond words. Valerie looked to the west and pointed. "There it is!"

"I'll rig up one of the machines. We'll fly over there and take a look." He sent the drone out about twenty feet. Suddenly, a terrible feeling came over him and he yelled, "Valerie, this is a trap!"

"What are you talking about?"

"The killer put the obelisk over there knowing we'd come up this road. It's a dead end. When we try to drive out of here, he'll pick us off like shooting fish in a barrel."

"You mean he'll kill us both?"

"Yes. I guarantee you he's nailed a plaque to a tree over there that says something like, 'we took a man and woman from here.' He'll get rid of our bodies and remove the obelisk in the dead of night."

"What are we going to do?"

"Take cover and fly back up the road to find him." Brock landed the drone, went to the trunk of the car, and put two pistols and extra clips of bullets in his pockets. "Here, carry the controller and tablet for the drone. Let's go over the hill and find a place where we can defend ourselves."

They located a sandstone crevice underneath the dry promontory at the end of the road. Brock took the controller back from Valerie, reorienting himself to the levers, and flew the drone up the road until a black pickup truck in the woods came on the screen, parked on dirt hardpack, ready to drive out. He circled behind the vehicle and began descending. When the drone hovered over the cab and started panning around, out of nowhere, Richard Nixon popped into view, five feet away. One shot from his pistol broke the camera and disabled Skinner's craft.

Soon after that, a drone could be heard whining somewhere near the crevice where the two of them were hiding. When the noise moved closer and stabilized on the right, Brock took the safety off one of the pistols, jumped out, found the invader, and shot right through the lens of its camera, returning the favor. He fired at the machine three or four more times until it fell out of the air and tumbled down the hill, then unhooked the controller for his downed craft and threw it in the direction of the drone he had just blasted out of the sky. He turned back to Valerie and asked, "Do you know how to use a pistol?"

"Yes."

He handed the second gun to her along with a clip. "Here's the safety. I'll be back later this afternoon to pick you up. I'm going to try to end this thing now. You should be able to protect yourself in here until I get back." He took the second drone, still in the case, and his computer tablet with him when he climbed the hill to get in the rental car.

Brock's plan was simple: rip by Richard Nixon at high speed, hoping not to get shot up. The only thing wrong with the plan was the ex-president had already left or moved to another spot. His solution for that was to step on the accelerator and roar out to the main road without wrecking the car. It worked. There was no sign of the black pickup. He pulled over onto a wide gravel berm, out in the open, after traveling east for a quarter of a mile. Valerie answered his call. "Yes. I'm still here," she said.

"I'm coming back to get you."

"Don't do it. I'm heading for the obelisk. You go do your business and come back later." She hung up.

Brock looked at his phone in disgust. He placed another call. "Marcel, was your IT guy able to trace that IP address?"

"Funny you should call. This morning he said it was on a computer in a call center in India. Just a couple of minutes ago, he told me he was able to hack the IP address renewal database. One thread that was supposed to be blocked led back to someone by the name of Alfred Cross."

"Where's his computer?"

"In Campton."

"Really?"

"Yes, at 9947 Wilgus Tolson. I remember that road from when our family lived near the high school. I think the house overlooks the Mountain Parkway."

"Marcel, you're a miracle worker. And, by the by, I've found the woman for you."

"What woman?"

"I'll tell you later." Brock put Alfred Cross's address in his GPS and slammed the car into gear. In fifteen minutes, he was driving past the gray brick house with black shingles, built at least fifty years ago, on the lower side of the road. The back porch overlooked the interstate highway, and a white dormer with a triple window projected out over the front porch held up by two tapered white columns.

A separate detached garage, built much later, almost as big as the house, was to the left. Skinner parked at the end of the road and started back on foot, gun in hand. He ducked out of sight when a man emerged from the house and strode to the garage. The overhead door went up, exposing the black pickup truck and a small blue BMW. The man, Alfred Cross or Trowbridge Banks, drove the car up the hill onto the main road and turned west toward town as the garage door went down automatically.

The lock took a minute to jimmy open. A small table, right inside the door, facing the front wall, held a large computer screen. The place was clean, neat, and sparsely furnished. In the master bedroom closet, the long gun with a scope was tucked in the corner behind the hanging clothes. A dark oak chest of drawers contained neatly folded garments, and the Richard Nixon mask was hidden under a stack of T-shirts in the bottom, right-hand drawer. There was a two-drawer file cabinet sitting on the chest of drawers with hanging files and folders in them. Brock rifled through some of the contents and found a sepia-tone picture from the 1800s of a jeweler named Trowbridge Banks, who may have been part of Cross's family heritage.

There was a big bathroom and single door off to the side at the top of the stairs. Brock pushed the door open and felt adrenaline surge through his body. The walls were covered with enlarged pictures of Maude, spanning from about age fifteen until now. The most recent photo featured her standing behind the tasting bar at the winery, smiling, talking to a customer. He took his phone out of his pocket and called her. "Maude, do you know somebody by the name of Alfred Cross?"

"Is he involved in this?"

"Yes, up to his neck. He's the guy that's been trying to kill me."

"I know him. He was obsessed with me in high school. When I went off to college, I had to get a restraining order against him. He kind of disappeared after that."

"Well, he's back."

"Be careful, Brock."

The next call he made was to Sheriff Connors. "Nathan, I've found the guy who shot down the government drone."

"Where are you?"

"Campton. The nut job lives here."

"What do you need?"

"Call Colonel Nelson and ask him to haul his ass up here in a hurry. Tell him to bring some handcuffs. Have him meet me at Horton Jewelers in downtown Campton in an hour or less. Then call the Wolfe County sheriff and ask him to get a search warrant for 9947 Wilgus Tolson Road. Alfred Cross lives there. They'll find the Richard Nixon mask, firearms, and a room full of pictures of Maude."

"Should I send a man over to the winery to watch her?"

"No. I'm pretty sure Cross is here in Campton."

Finally, Brock tried to call Valerie Goddard again. No answer.

Horton Jewelers was in a small strip center on Main Street, with rings, bracelets, and watches displayed prominently in its large window. Brock saw the blue BMW parked in the gravel lot out front. He drove around the building, noticing the store had a rear door. He decided to go up the street and get a meal at McDonald's to kill time. Upon returning, Brock parked the rental within two inches of the back door of the jewelry store and walked the long way around to the front of the building, where he stood at the corner, watching for Colonel Nelson. When he arrived, Skinner waved him over. He was in civilian clothes. They entered Horton Jewelers together.

"Hello. Are you Debbie Horton?" Brock asked.

"I am." She was a pleasant-looking, heavy-set woman who had on a red, frilly top.

"I'm Brock Skinner, Maude's husband, and this is Harkie Nelson." The colonel nodded to her.

"Oh, so nice to meet you. Maude thinks you hung the moon."

"That's good to hear. Say, is Alfred Cross here?"

"You're lucky. He is. He works odd hours."

"What does he do here?" Brock asked.

"He's my jeweler."

"Would you ask him to come out here, ma'am?" Nelson requested.

Debbie pushed open the door to the back and said, "Alfie, step out here for a minute."

Alfred Cross eased through the door, looked at the two men, froze for a second, and then hurriedly retreated. Nelson and Skinner pushed Debbie aside and followed him. Cross tried to escape out the back, but the door was blocked by the rental car. Colonel Nelson shut the door to the backroom from the inside, and things got dicey for Alfred Cross for the next few minutes. The colonel brought him out in handcuffs, put him in the car, and drove off.

Debbie was visibly rattled. Brock said, "It was nice meeting you. Sorry for all the commotion."

"But what about my jeweler?"

"You'll probably need to hire a new one."

Brock rushed into Red River Gorge to search for Valerie Goddard. When he looked over to where the obelisk once stood, he found that it was gone. He got out the drone and flew it across the breathtaking gorge to circle the area. No Valerie. And the obelisk had been disassembled and was in a pile. For a fleeting moment, he considered the possibility that she had actually been taken, but he dismissed the thought. When Brock climbed down to look in the crevice where the two of them had hidden earlier in the day, there she was. She said, "What? The thing was a fake! You told me to be here when you got back." He laughed heartily.

When Valerie and Brock were on the way back to Hazard, Connors called to report that Alfred Cross was in custody, and a search warrant was being issued. He asked, "How did you know he would be at Horton Jewelers?"

"The watch. Cross must have been there when Maude came in to order it. I figured he had to work there and must have run to another jewelry store to get one like it. Nobody else could have acted so fast. That's when he hatched the plan to kill me and get a chance to court Maude again."

"Wonder why he got Valerie Goddard involved?"

"He must have done some research and determined she would be the one person who could plausibly be taken by aliens." Brock looked over at Valerie and smiled.

~ ~ ~

At five thirty that evening, Marcel Sutherland stood in the log cabin's kitchen, holding a glass of Vigneron wine and talking to his sister. Brock was on the back porch firing up the grill. When he stepped back in the house, he needled Marcel, saying, "I warned her to never visit one of your clothing booths. It wouldn't be appropriate for you to know her measurements. I also told her that you were a real man. She likes real men, so act like one."

"I'll try."

Valerie Goddard came into the room wearing the best clothes she'd brought with her from New Mexico. Her hair had been fixed with the help of Maude's hair styling tools. Brock said, "Valerie, this is my brother-in-law, Marcel Sutherland."

Marcel bowed slightly. "Pleased to meet you. You look out of this world."

Maude chimed in, "Was that supposed to be a pun, Marcel?"

Year of the Terrible Sevens

The Union and Confederacy, both in need of salt to preserve meat during the war, knew the importance of the salt works at Cornettsville, which in 1862 produced 250 bushels a week. Kentucky claimed neutrality in the Civil War, promoting the idea that the center of the universe was somewhere in the state. Battalions for both sides were plentiful in the Appalachian Mountains to the southeast. Sons of an owner of the salt operation joined the Confederacy, signaling the South had already laid claim to the enterprise, though some workers were sympathetic to the North, eventually causing the Battle of Leatherwood.

Cornettsville, at the mouth of Leatherwood township, on the southwest edge of Perry County, was where the battle was reenacted every year on the fourth weekend in October. The fall colors were at their peak then, as they were this year, and the mild weather made the event tolerable for the frontier women and overweight men clad in wool throwback uniforms.

Vigneron Winery had a booth rigged up beside a burrito stand, away from the period buildings and youngsters milling around. Occasionally, a peckish customer wandered in for a pick-me-up. A proper woman, conspicuous by her finishing-school posture, looking completely out of place, stepped in the booth, smiling. Brock Skinner acknowledged her. He and his wife, Maude, were bored out of their gourds, and hoped she might be in favor of some interesting conversation.

The woman spoke first. "Hello. I'd like a glass of white wine."

"Sure." Maude retrieved a cold bottle of her brand from the cooler and poured some in a clear plastic cup. "There you go. That'll be five dollars."

The woman reached in her purse for the money. "Is Vigneron Winery near here?" she asked.

"Yes. In Hazard. I make and sell wines there."

"That's a nice profession."

"Keeps me busy. My name's Maude Skinner. This is my husband, Brock."

"Pleased to meet both of you. I'm Virginia Purdy, from Cincinnati."

"What brings you down for the reenactment?" Brock asked.

"Oh, I'm interested in buying property around here. I want to build a cabin in the woods, on a mountaintop, not too far off the interstate."

"You have anywhere specific in mind?"

Virginia pointed across the way, as she took a sip of wine, to a hill at the end of the open field. "Over there."

Brock found the spot with his eyes. "Putting a road in will cost you more than the cabin." He could vaguely see a deer stand at the edge of the trees.

"I hope I have the budget for it."

The shooting was about to start. Men were taking their positions. Back in the day, Major Blankenship from Harlan and his Union soldiers camped at the Lewis farm nearby, intending to contact the men at the salt works who wanted to join the North. Captain David Caudill brought his Confederate soldiers over from Whitesburg to guard the place. They were out stealing watermelons from a deaf and dumb man's patch when the Union men caught them, and started shooting. Captain Caudill got shot in the ass and could no longer stay in the saddle. The Confederates ran. The raid by the Union force netted them several barrels of salt and a fifty-pound pone of corn.

Not long after, Colonel Ben Caudill, Captain David's younger brother, took five hundred men into Harlan and got back most of what had been taken in the ambush. Colonel Ben Caudill was a tireless, ardent Christian evangelist and peacemaker, before and after the war. He wasn't, however, a conscientious objector during it.

"What's your interest in that piece of property? There are more picturesque settings for a cabin in the woods up near our winery in Hazard. The amount of road you'd have to put in would be a lot less too," Maude suggested.

"Some of my relatives lived here during the Civil War. This area has sentimental value to me."

"That's nice. Do you know who owns the property you want?"

"No. That's the reason I'm here. I'm trying to find out."

Brock said, "I can help you with that."

Maude added, "If you don't have overnight accommodations, you're welcome to stay with us. We have a fancy place right behind our winery."

"I wouldn't want to impose," Virginia replied. "I certainly like your white wine." She peered at the half-empty plastic cup.

Brock offered, "Tell you what. Why don't you come to our house for supper? If you don't want to stay over, I'll make arrangements for you at the best hotel in town." The Skinners were starved for a stimulating dinner party with an out-of-town guest.

"Deal. I'll follow you when we leave here."

Virginia Purdy wasn't what you'd call good-looking, nor would she make a train take a dirt road, either. She had Grace Kelly's high-society demeanor, and looked vaguely like her, except every one of her features was a little off. Compared to Maude she was a plain Jane. "What a beautiful home."

"Thank you. Do you have any dietary requirements?" Maude asked.

"No. Thanks for asking. I encourage my clients to ask that of their dinner guests. I also tell dinner guests to eat what's served if they can."

"What is your business, if I may ask?" Brock was sniffing out a good learning opportunity.

"I'm a manners consultant."

"Hot dog. I could use some improvement in that area," he said. "Could you give me a few free pointers on how to behave?"

"Well, you haven't asked me to pay for my meal yet, so in a way, my advice wouldn't be free."

"True."

"I'll start with the basics. A man should never offer to shake a woman's hand. If she wants to shake, she'll stick her hand out. Never touch other people's children unless specifically directed to by the parents. Listen to people like you want to be heard when you speak, and don't talk loudly, or too much."

"What about women?" Maude interjected.

"Don't be surprised if a man tries to paw you when you're wearing provocative clothes. RSVP immediately to invitations. Don't stall and wait to see if something better comes along. Unless one is teaching English class, one should not correct the English of another person. Never boast about your money or possessions."

Maude browned boneless chicken thighs rubbed with red chile paste. She sweated onions in sesame oil in the same pan and added a can of coconut milk and the rest of the red chile paste left in the jar. The thighs went back in, and the dish was brought to a boil before going in the oven for twenty minutes. The chicken was served with basmati rice, cilantro, and lightly cooked asparagus on the side. After the meal, each of them had a decaf espresso. Virginia commented, "I can't remember food that good, and company so enjoyable."

"It was a delight having you join us," Brock said. "Maude is a wonderful cook, and vintner as well." He gazed out the tall patio door at the grapevines beyond the backyard. Streaky shadows began to form past them as the day's sun weakened. "Shall we play a few hands of gin? If we do, you'll have to take us up on our offer to stay here. Can I show you your accommodations?"

"Since I'm convinced neither of you are ax murderers, I'll say yes to your offer." Her expression momentarily turned to stone. "And that was an example of bad manners. Many things are better left unsaid. Just let your yes be yes and your no be no."

"I need to hang around you for a couple of weeks," Brock said.

"Watch what you wish for. With your help, I'm going to contact the owner of the property I want to buy and make an offer on it. I might end up getting the better end of the deal before it's over."

Maude said, "As a courtesy, I'm going to warn you about Brock. He can find trouble where there isn't any."

"I'll keep that in mind."

~ ~ ~

Plats of land in Perry County had been scanned and put on the computer, making it easier to find a particular piece of property. Virginia scrolled through the sections until she found the lot she was interested in. "Here it is." The dimensions were 210 feet of road frontage going back 5,250 feet, catching the top of the mountain and a little of the downslope on the back side. Basically, the twenty-five-acre parcel was an acre wide and mile deep.

Brock peeked over Virginia's shoulder and said, "Write down the legal description."

"Then what do we do?"

"See who it's deeded to. After that, I'll get a title company to take a quick look."

The deed indicated the property had been bought by Horace Leland a year ago from a man named Gino Carnahan. Brock made a call to the title company and gave them the address. He asked for a rush job, offering a spiff. "You don't have to ask," he said to Virginia. "I know what you want next. How do we find Horace Leland, right?"

"I was thinking we might try to find Gino Carnahan first, to see why he sold, and why Leland wanted to buy."

"Good thought. Let's walk over to the police station. Maybe we'll get lucky."

Sheriff Connors was surprised to see Brock Skinner escorting a woman other than his wife into headquarters. "Mr. Skinner, nice to see you again. And you are, ma'am?" The sheriff stuck out his hand.

Brock scolded him. "Pull that hand back. Don't you know if a woman wants to shake, she'll offer her hand?"

Connors let his hand fall to his side.

"My name's Virginia Purdy. And this is a good opportunity to discuss handshakes. In some cases, the woman will just go ahead and shake a person's hand and not make a fuss about it. On other occasions, it's best she look away as if she didn't see the gesture from the man, and move off to avoid embarrassing him."

"What in the world are you two talking about?"

Brock replied, "Never mind. Miss Purdy is a manners consultant. It's not important. Maude and I met her yesterday at the Battle of Leatherwood. We're helping her locate the owner and former owner of property in Cornettsville she wants to make an offer on."

"And who might they be?"

"Gino Carnahan and Horace Leland."

The sheriff said, "I'm not sure about Horace Leland, but I do know Gino Carnahan. He buys property, keeps the mineral rights, and sells the surface rights, usually as hunting land. He often ends up owning the mineral rights for next to nothing. Then he goes to energy companies and sells those rights to them for a nifty profit."

Brock said, "Sounds like a smart operator."

"Do you happen to know where we could find him?" Virginia asked.

"He has lunch at the Hazard Country Club every day it's open, and then plays eighteen holes of golf, weather permitting."

"Is he any good?" Brock asked.

"I've heard he is. I must be crazy telling you this, Skinner."

"Why?"

"Because you tend to find trouble. Were you aware of that, Miss Purdy?"

"Yes, his wife alerted me to the fact."

Brock changed the subject. "Nathan, we're going up to the winery for lunch. Care to join us?"

"Thanks for the offer, but I've got too much going on," he replied.

Virginia stuck out her hand to shake and said, "It was nice meeting you." The sheriff looked at his hand comically after they left the police station.

Brock and Virginia were in separate cars and met up again at the winery. The air was still, a little cool, and the sun shone brightly overhead. Maude saw them come in and suggested they eat outside, against the building, in the warm sunshine. The three of them sat and gazed at the majestic mountains across the ravine, out over the county. Joan Brewer approached, carrying menus that listed a limited lunch offering. She smiled, dropped them off, and said nothing. Maude remarked, "Joan's only been with us a few months. She puts on theatrical events on the weekends. I wish she'd find a boyfriend."

"Give her this tip," Virginia offered. "Do you know how to judge the measure of a man?"

Brock said, "Yeah, by how he keeps the inside of his car."

"That is one way. I prefer looking at his shoes. Steer clear of a man whose shoes are dirty, scuffed, dilapidated, down at the heel. If he can't keep his shoes right, he's unlikely to keep much else in his life in good order."

Maude, being amused, retorted, "So, what you're saying is a good-looking lover boy with bad shoes is a quandary for a woman."

Brock piped up, "Not really. She should just get him a new pair. I'm kidding." He threw up his hands. The three of them had a pleasant lunch, and the conversation turned to Horace Leland and how to locate him. Brock decided to dial up his brother-in-law. "Marcel, maybe you can help us. We're trying to find a guy who owns a piece of property in Perry County."

"IT's plugged into several databases. We can look there for his name. What is it?"

"Horace Leland."

"Give me a few hours. I'll see if he pops up."

"Thanks. The weather tomorrow is looking pretty good. Why don't you drive down in the morning, and we'll play eighteen holes of golf after lunch?"

"Sounds like a plan."

Brock put the phone down and spoke to Virginia. "Tell us about the Purdy family."

"We've been here ten generations. Robert Purdy, from Northern Ireland, jumped on a pirate ship in seventeen seventy-six. The vessel sank off the coast of North Carolina, and Robert swam ashore with a heavy bag full of five-hundred Spanish gold escudos. The rest of the crew chased him inland until he finally shook them when he got deep into the mountains of Kentucky."

"Let me guess, he wintered over on the land in Cornettsville you're interested in."

"He did, but in seventeen seventy-seven, the year of the terrible sevens, the Indian tribes in the area, working together, tried to kill or run off every white man in the state. Robert went back to North Carolina, found a wife, and started farming. He died in seventy seventy-nine, when his son Joseph was only a year old."

"What happened to the gold coins?"

"Robert, out of fear of being captured, buried them in Kentucky, and his great-grandson, Warren, went back there and dug them up right before the Civil War."

"How do you know all this?" Maude asked.

"Papers passed down through generations. My father was the first Purdy who didn't have a male heir, so he gave me all the family information."

"Did Warren Purdy follow a map to find the coins, or were there directions that told him where to dig?"

"Robert described the unusual rock formation on top of the mountain, and then recorded how many paces east and north to go to find the spot to dig."

"Well, how in the world would Warren Purdy know where to find the right mountain?"

"Robert noted it was about a mile north of a heavy salt deposit. Warren only had to ask around."

Maude said, "I presume you still have the papers."

"And others."

"What do they say?"

"One letter says in the summer of 1860, Warren took the Spanish escudos he dug up to New Orleans and used them to buy four-hundred United States gold double eagles minted there and dated that year. That was the last mention of gold in any correspondence."

Brock mused, "So, there's a possibility he reburied the gold in the same place when the Civil War broke out."

"Possibly. He was killed in the Battle of Leatherwood, leaving a wife and seven-year-old son behind. I think they made their way to Cincinnati, where the Purdy's have been ever since the Civil War."

Brock's phone rang. He recognized the number of the title company, answering the call and pressing the speaker-phone button. "What'd you dig up?"

"The property was cut out of a farm and deeded to a Warren Purdy in eighteen fifty-nine. His son Raphael sold the parcel back to the original owner in eighteen seventy-seven. The family who's owned the farm for over one-hundred forty years sold the twenty-five acres to Gino Carnahan two years ago. And finally, Carnahan sold the surface rights to Horace Leland last October. He still owns the mineral rights."

"Thanks, Marguerite. Great job, as usual. Send over your charges." He ended the call.

Virginia said, "Please give me the bill when you get it. Thanks for helping me on this." She stood, saying, "I'm going to drive on home. I'll be back Wednesday morning. Here's my phone number. If you find out anything important, please call. I'll see both of you in a couple of days, and thanks again for your hospitality."

They watched Virginia elegantly stroll to her car and drive slowly down the hill. The lunch crowd on the veranda also dissipated, heading for the parking lot. Clouds formed, blocking the sun intermittently, causing a disquieting breeze to whip up each time the sun disappeared. Maude, feeling unsettled, wagged her finger at Brock. "Don't say it. You smell a rat."

"How did you know?"

"Because you have no faith in mankind."

"That's right. Ever since Adam ate from the tree," he said. Brock picked up the dishes and followed Maude into the winery.

Marcel called Brock at five o'clock to report that Horace Leland, from Cincinnati, had fallen out of a tree stand on his hunting property in Cornettsville the second week of January, and broke his neck.

"That figures. Thanks, Marcel, for running him down." He hung up, placed a call to Hazard Country Club, and got a tee time for 1:10. "You can put us with Gino Carnahan if he's looking for a game."

~ ~ ~

The last days of October were often the best of the year for playing golf. The idea put Brock in a good mood on Tuesday morning. He called Virginia Purdy to give her an update. "Good morning. I trust your trip home yesterday was uneventful."

"Yes, actually it was quite pleasant."

"Good to hear. I have a couple of things to report. I'm playing golf with Gino Carnahan this afternoon. What would you like me to say to him?"

"Tell him you have a friend who's interested in making an offer for the twenty-five acres. Ask him how Leland came to buy the surface rights from him a year ago, and whether he would consider selling the mineral rights. Don't mention my name or anything about my family."

"Okay. The other news I have is that Horace Leland fell out of the deer stand on the property while hunting in January, broke his neck, and died. He lived in Cincinnati."

Virginia said nothing for several seconds. "Well, as we saw yesterday, the property hasn't been deeded to anybody yet, which means it's probably still in probate. I'll see if I can find the court records. Maybe they're taking offers for the land."

"So, what's my good manners tip of the day?"

"When is the only time a man goes through a door before a woman?"

"When he's the king of Prussia?"

"No. Into an elevator. It's his responsibility to press the buttons and make sure the elevator is in good working order."

"I don't know about that one, Virginia. I think my wife would smack me if I tried that."

"See? This is a good example of how a man's brain works. In general, men are poor communicators. All you have to do is explain why you're going ahead of her."

"Gee. That never occurred to me."

Marcel rolled into Hazard at eleven o'clock dressed for golf. He and Brock decided to grab an early lunch before going to the country club, and on the way, Brock filled him in on the Purdy saga. "Tell me again exactly what she said about New Orleans and the gold coins."

"She said that Warren Purdy traded the escudos for four-hundred double eagles minted there and dated that year."

"Ah. Now we know what this business is about."

"What?"

"If memory serves me, the New Orleans mint only made sixty-six hundred of those coins. Today, they're worth fifty thousand in almost uncirculated condition, and a hundred grand if uncirculated."

"A piece?"

"Yeah. We're talking twenty to forty million dollars' worth of gold coins," Marcel confirmed.

Brock said, "At least, there's one good thing. I can report to your sister that you found trouble where there wasn't any instead of me."

"She won't be surprised."

The Hazard Country Club course didn't have any par fives, which meant eighteen holes carried a par of 68. Marcell was practicing chipping, and Brock putting when Gino Carnahan brought his golf cart to a stop on the path leading to the first tee. He got out carrying his putter, and walked up to Brock. "I'm Gino." His hands were enormous. He had a face like Steve McQueen, and short, dark hair.

Brock looked at his shoes, first thing. They were pristine. "My name's Brock. This is Marcel." He pointed and Marcel nodded. "Shall we make it three-way match play for, say, a hundred bucks a game?"

"I had a feeling I was going to like you guys," Gino sang out.

Marcel took a big turn and pounded the ball down the middle of the fairway. Carnahan's short backswing and tremendous acceleration through the ball kept it low, bouncing with overspin in the direction of the green. Brock's easy swing left him short and to the right of the other two drives. All three were on the green in two, each putting for birdie. Brock missed his putt and settled for par. Marcel and Gino both made theirs. Game on.

At the fifth hole, Brock said, "Gino, I've got a little business to discuss with you."

Carnahan stepped out of his cart and shot Skinner an untrusting glance. "What?"

"An acquaintance of mine, who wishes to remain anonymous, is interested in buying a piece of property you own the mineral rights on in Cornettsville."

"Which one?" He stepped up to the tee and punched the ball down the left side.

"The mile deep, twenty-five-acre lot."

"Anything's for sale, Brock, for a price. I sold the surface rights to a hunter a year ago."

"How did you come to buy the property in the first place?" Brock asked. Marcel hit a long ball near the trees on the right. It became obvious why Carnahan kept his ball left.

"The same way I buy all property. I go to the courthouse, find who owns the land, contact them, and make an offer."

Brock was swinging the club harder now. He crushed a drive deep to the left-center of the fairway. "How did Horace Leland get involved?"

"He called me up and said he was looking for some hunting property. I like those deals because the buyers don't really care if I keep the mineral rights." The three of them moved to their balls for the second shot. Before Gino hit, he said, "I'm about to get the surface rights back, too. I have the right of first refusal on them from Leland's estate. He fell out of his deer stand and died in January."

"I heard that. Why haven't you sold out to an energy company? After all, that's why you bought the land in the first place, isn't it?"

"It was. I don't need the money, and just haven't gotten around to it. You know what Mark Twain said: they ain't making any more of it." Once again, all three balls landed on the green in regulation. This time Brock made his birdie putt, and the other two missed theirs. Gino and Marcel were one under, and Brock even par.

They moved to the sixth tee. Brock jumped out of his cart, and asked. "What will you sell the property for once you get the surface rights back?"

"I'll have to think on it," Gino said. "I'm in no hurry to sell." The rat Skinner had been smelling began to stink to high heaven.

Brock shot a one-under 67. Gino had a 70 and Marcel 71. Gino spoke to Marcel, "Pay him what you owe me." He turned to Skinner and said, "That's the first time I've been beaten this year." Marcel dug in his pocket for two one-hundred-dollar bills and handed them to Brock.

When the two of them got in the car, Brock gave the money back to Marcel. "Thanks for driving over. I got more than two-hundred dollars' worth of information out of him."

"I hate to lose." That characteristic in Marcel's personality was why he and Brock were rich.

Brock said, "I know you do."

~ ~ ~

Wednesday morning began overcast, windy, and cool. The lumpy white clouds were not the kind that held rain. When Sheriff Connors got to his office, wearing a light-tan jacket with police patches on it, there sat Skinner. The sheriff took off his jacket, hung it on the hook on the back of his office door, and said, "Do you want some coffee?"

"Yes, thanks. Black." A few seconds later, Brock started in. "I'm surprised at you, Nathan. I would've thought you'd have remembered the name of the fellow who fell out of his tree stand and broke his neck in your county."

"You're talking about the guy in Cornettsville last winter? What was his name?"

"Horace Leland. One of the men I asked you about the other day."

Connors leaned forward on his desk and wove his hands. "Yeah, now I remember. So, he owned the land your lady friend is trying to buy?"

"Yes, and like you said, Carnahan kept the mineral rights when he sold the surface rights to Leland. Carnahan is getting the surface rights back from Leland's estate."

"Okay, Brock, aren't you wondering why I haven't asked you what sort of trouble you've found now?"

"I was kind of wondering why you hadn't blasted me already."

"I'm getting ready to. What the hell is going on?"

"I think Carnahan killed Leland. Broke his neck and threw him off that deer stand."

The sheriff stood, threw his arms out to the side, and pronounced loudly, "And there it is, folks, another Brock Skinner special."

"Why is it you get the credit for solving the crimes that go on in your county, and all I get is a tongue lashing?"

Connors dropped his arms. "Because if you didn't live in this town, there wouldn't be any crime. Kapish?"

Brock twisted in his seat, somewhat angrily. "Whatever. Would you just get the file and tell me what it says?"

The sheriff turned gentle as a lamb. "Why, sure. I'll be right back." When he returned, he started reading. "Another hunter found Leland face down below his deer stand at five in the afternoon. The guard rail on the landing had given way. The time of death was estimated to be around eleven in the morning."

"That's all there is?"

"No. The only thing he had in his pockets were car keys. His car was parked at the front of the property, by the road. His wallet was in the glove box, and there was a shovel in the trunk."

"Sounds like he was planning on doing some digging," Brock surmised. "Does it say whether there was any dirt on the shovel?"

"No. Did you ever consider the ground is frozen in January? Here you go again. Borrowing trouble where there isn't any."

"What trouble? I'm just helping a lady make an offer on a piece of property." He got up from his chair, stood over Connors with his hands in his pockets, and said, "All you have to do is build a fire over the spot where you plan to dig to thaw the ground."

Brock entered the empty boxing gym up the street in a bad mood, and with each punch of the heavy bag, went from one scenario to the next in his mind, laying out what might have happened the day Horace Leland met his demise. He figured he'd have to test each theory, starting with the one that made the most sense. The three-legged stool he concocted asked: How did Leland know where to dig? Did he dig? What did he find?

Truman, the white German shepherd working pest duty between the rows of grapevines, heard his master drive into the winery parking lot, and ran to greet him. Brock saw the dog's dirty paws, and in canine baby talk, said, "Where's your mom, Truman, huh?"

Maude heard the car too, looked out the window, and waved. Brock got as far as the door before he heard another vehicle pulling into a spot near the building. He turned to see Virginia Purdy step out into the parking lot. She was wearing black slacks and a dark-green wool sweater that had a thick, high collar. As she was coming closer, Brock yelled out, "So, what's my tip of the day?"

"Don't drink directly from the milk carton or juice container. You never know when you'll have to offer refreshments to a guest. And please wash your hands with soap and warm water when in the restroom. You may like your germs, but it's discourteous to spread them to others."

"What do you think we are, Virginia, heathens?"

"I prefer not to answer that," she replied softly, with a sniff. "Now *you* can give *me* some advice. I found out that Gino Carnahan will be buying back the surface rights of the property from Leland's estate. How can I get him to sell to me?"

"Honestly, it depends on whether those gold coins are still in the ground or not. I want you to be straight with me. You don't care a fig about that land, do you? You just want to dig up the gold, right?"

"Well, to be frank with you, yes."

"Ah, now we're getting somewhere. I think Horace Leland already dug it up, and Carnahan killed him and took it."

Virginia's eyes opened wide and she staggered back a little. "That would be a terrible calamity."

"There's only one way to find out."

"How?" She acted as though she hadn't fully recovered from the possible bad news.

"I'm going to go out there and do some digging."

"What if you get caught?"

"I'll worry about that if it happens. Now, tell me how to find the spot where to dig." Virginia explained what the rock formation looked like, which was the benchmark for walking to the location. She told him to use a compass to go thirty-one paces due east, and then sixteen paces straight north. Brock said to her, "Follow me over to the house. I'll have to change clothes and get some things. After that, I'll need you to drop me off at the property. I'll call when I want you to come and get me." He put a pistol in his belt and grabbed a compass and shovel.

Virginia Purdy dropped him off at the property thirty minutes later. After she drove away, he noticed a mailbox on the other side of the road. A few letters addressed to Gino Carnahan were in it. He closed the box door, put the shovel over his shoulder, and walked in the direction of the deer stand.

The wind had died down by the time Skinner found the place to dig on the mountain. In less than five minutes, he broke a sweat. Two feet down, he hit the wooden lid of a small trunk. It took another fifteen minutes to dig around the edge of the box enough to lift it out of the ground. It was certainly heavy enough to be a stash of gold coins. He raised the lid, finding a load of rocks and a note on top of them that read: *Contents Removed in 1877.* Brock stuck the note in his pocket, reburied the box, and called Virginia. "No luck. The buried trunk had rocks in it. You can come and get me." While he was waiting to be picked up, Brock thought to himself, *Eighteen seventy-seven was the year of the terrible sevens for Virginia Purdy instead of 1777.*

On the ride back to Hazard, Virginia said, "It's been nice meeting you and your wife. I hope our paths cross again. It sure is disappointing that someone else got to the gold before I did."

"So, I guess you won't be building a cabin in the woods after all."

"No. Look at me. Do I look like I fit in around here?"

"Frankly, no. But if you'd found gold, people would have overlooked certain things."

When the two of them got back to the Skinner log cabin, Virginia handed Brock four one-hundred-dollar bills. "Here; this is to pay the title people. Thanks again, and tell your wife bye for me. I'm heading out."

"Okay, but before you go, how about a few more quick tips?"

She said robotically, "Look a person in the eye when you talk to them. Be on time. It's never too late for an apology. Be sure to thank people who do good things. And finally, look for good deeds to do yourself. People with class are not selfish." She got in her car, rolled down the window, and waved as she drove away.

As she rolled out of sight, Brock was thinking, *I'm a good deed doer.* He called Connors. "Nathan, this one's more complicated than I thought. I want you to help me figure it out."

"Well, that's a switch. You need my brain instead of my brawn this time."

"Can you meet me at the winery?"

"Why not? I'll be there in half an hour."

Brock gave the sheriff some background on the Purdy family and the buried gold coins. He explained how Virginia Purdy had gone through family papers and determined the gold might still be in the ground on the property in Cornettsville. "I still think Horace Leland found out where the gold was buried and dug it up. Gino Carnahan must have known about the gold too, but didn't know where it was, so he waited for Leland to dig it up, and then he took it and killed him."

The sheriff stuck out his chin and blinked several times. "Brock, as an experienced detective, and in my humble opinion, you've got some serious holes in your theory. First, how did Horace Leland find out about the gold and where to dig? Answer: he had to be in cahoots with somebody who knew. Second, how would Gino Carnahan know about the gold? Answer: if he did know about it, he'd have bulldozed every square inch of that property looking for it before Leland could turn a spade. Remember, he owned the mineral rights and could dig anywhere he wanted. And third, if Gino Carnahan was trying to make the killing look like an accident, why would he have left a shovel in the trunk of Leland's car? Answer: no way he would have."

"Nathan, you're one smart cookie. Would you trace Virginia's phone number for me to get her address?"

The sheriff called back an hour later. Her number was an anonymous phone bought with cash from a store in Cincinnati. Brock went into Maude's office and put in the security tape that showed Purdy's car in the lot. He got the license plate number off it and called Connors again, asking him to run it. Fifteen minutes later, the sheriff reported the vehicle was a rental, and it had been turned in a couple of hours ago.

Brock called Marcel. "Hey, could you do me another favor? I need to find the descendants of Raphael Purdy, born around 1855."

"That should be pretty easy. Did Gino Carnahan end up with the gold coins?"

"Not if he was set up for the killing of Horace Leland."

"Are you telling me Virginia Purdy has them?"

"I'm working on it."

Marcel Sutherland called back in a few hours and reported that Raphael Purdy's line had petered out. Dexter Purdy, who died nearly two years ago, was the only son of the descendants, and he had never gotten married or had any children. Brock felt a sinking feeling in his stomach. It took him a week to find out what happened to Dexter's personal property after he died. Everything had been auctioned off to satisfy the claims of debtors.

Brock called the auction house that sold Dexter's personal effects, fishing for information. "Ma'am, your firm sold the property of a deceased man almost two years ago by the name of Dexter Purdy. Would you be able to look at your records and tell me who bought some of the things?"

"Well, sir, I've got the list of auctioned items up on the screen, and there were several buyers."

"Do you see a listing for any kind of papers?"

"Yes. There is one item listed as an accordion file of old papers."

"How much did it sell for?"

"Eight dollars."

"Who was the buyer?"

"Paula Leland."

"Do you have an address for her?"

"Sure, it's 9603 Howell Avenue, Cincinnati."

"Thank you, ma'am, for your help." Brock searched the computer until he found the obituary for Horace Leland. He had a sister by the name of Paula.

Howell Avenue, on the northeast side of Cincinnati, cut through an old part of town. The narrow three-story marked 9603 had a stone base with a glass-block window in the front. The flight of five steps up to the porch was light gray, leading to a big, natural-wood oak door with sidelights and a transom. The red-orange brick had been broken up by a band of limestone at the floor line of the third story. The roof had two steep peaks with brick dental work running across where the slope of the roofs began. Brock went around back and banged on the door where the people inside couldn't see who was there. Paula Leland pulled open the door and tried to shut it when she saw who it was. Brock put his foot in and said, "Now, where's your manners, Virginia, or should I call you Paula?"

She turned her back and let him follow her inside the house. "I thought you'd drop this whole business," she said.

"Not my nature. Do you care to explain yourself?"

Paula Leland looked defeated. "Not really."

"How about I start. Almost two years ago, you went to an auction house and happened to sift through the property of Dexter Purdy that was going to be sold. You came across a bunch of old papers that seemed to point to the possibility of some gold coins being buried in Kentucky, and you bought the papers at auction for eight dollars. Then you went to Hazard and found out the property belonged to Gino Carnahan. You told your brother what was going on and asked him to buy the surface rights for the land, which he did. Horace took a few months to build a high deer stand to make it look like he was actually going to do some hunting. How am I doing so far?"

"I'm not admitting to anything." She crossed her arms and looked out the front window.

"Well, you'd better start, or I'll have you hauled in for killing your brother."

She spun around and whined, "What? You're nuts."

"You sent him down there with a note that read *Contents Removed in 1877* to put in the trunk when he found the gold. I'm going to tell the police you went there with him in separate cars and waited in the deer stand for him to build a fire, put it out, and dig up the coins. He brought the shovel and bag of coins back to the deer stand, climbing up to show you what he'd found. You pushed him through the guardrail at the top of the steps, and he fell and broke his neck. You took the shovel and put it back in his trunk and drove off with the gold. That's where you made your mistake. You should have put the shovel in your car."

Paula Leland switched into a talking mood. "You've got it wrong. I sent him down there by himself. He was going to build a fire just as the sun came up. When he didn't call by noon, I began to worry that something had gone wrong, or that he had taken off with the gold, leaving me out. When I heard he'd fallen out of the deer stand, I began to think he hadn't gotten a chance to dig for the coins."

"What about the shovel in his trunk? He would have taken it with him to the deer stand."

"He probably did. He had two shovels with him and most likely only carried one over to the mountain."

"Were the two shovels identical?"

"Yes, we bought them new right before he headed out."

Brock stuck out his elbows and raised his fists. "That's it! Hey, look, you need to give me the old Purdy papers. If you do, I'll try to keep you out of trouble with the law." She went down the hall, returning quickly with the accordion file. "Are there any more tips on manners you want to give me?" Brock asked.

With a cruel expression, she said, "Yeah, just one. Never lie."

"You didn't follow your own advice when you became Virginia Purdy, a woman who never existed. I have to admit, you had me fooled." He unlocked the front door, walked out, and left Paula Leland standing in the middle of the main room of her house.

When Brock got in his car, he called the sheriff. "Nathan, I was right. There were two shovels. Get a search warrant. See what you can find."

~ ~ ~

At ten after noon the next day, Connors and Skinner entered the restaurant at the Hazard Country Club. Carnahan saw them approaching and said, "It's a little cool for golf, but I'm game. I want to win my money back."

"We've got other business, Gino."

Carnahan squinted his eyes and looked at Connors. "Sheriff. What brings you around?"

Brock took the lead. "Murder. You may have been unlucky at golf when we played, but you were damned lucky back in January when you went to Cornettsville to pick up your mail."

"How so?"

"You saw a car parked there and went to see who it was. You noticed a gun propped on the stairs of the deer stand, and found Horace Leland with a shovel in his hand and a sack full of gold. You must have grabbed his gun and told him at gunpoint to drop everything and climb the stairs. You followed him up, pushed him through the handrail, left the gun, and went back to your car with the shovel and gold."

Carnahan stood and blurted, "You're out of your mind."

Connors added, "We found the shovel and gold coins at your house."

"Those are my coins. You had no right to search my house."

"We checked your mineral rights contract. It doesn't include buried items. Leland was alive when he dug up the coins, and since he owned the land, they belonged to him when you killed him," Brock said. "So, they belong to his heir, his sister Paula Leland."

"Carnahan, you're under arrest for the murder of Horace Leland."
Connors cuffed him and led him out of the Hazard Country Club.

184

THE UNHAPPY HAPPY HAP QUILTER

The Gregorian calendar, used by North Americans since the sixteenth century, has been viewed by superstitious Appalachians as a journey through weather patterns, mimicking the various stages of human life. The average person, by the grace of God, who survived the gauntlet of immeasurable mortal afflictions hoped to live in the mountains until the ripe old age of ninety-six, which in terms of the calendar meant each month represented about eight years of existence. Many hardy souls were still taking nourishment at ninety, but making it past ninety-six was considered a daunting task.

Weather in the months of January and February paralleled the beginning of life, snowy and inert, as the brain developed from zero to sixteen. The chaotic weather of March ushered in sex, drugs, and rock and roll for young adults seventeen to twenty-four. April, and its conspicuous Easter celebration, was a time, twenty five to thirty-two, for answering key questions about life: *Where did I come from? Why am I here?* and *Where am I going?* In early May, at thirty-three, people stood tall, full grown, at their physical and mental peak, and were who they'd be for the rest of their lives.

May through August, and their hot weather, from thirty-four to sixty-four, were considered the work and family years, often frittered away as though old age would surely never come and plenty of time was still left. Labor Day rolled around in early September, at sixty-five or sixty-six. It should have been called the End of Labor Day because it actually signaled the beginning of redundancy. Oh, but then came the most beautiful time of the year (life), the end of September and month of October, ages seventy to eighty. As trees turned and green things ran to brown, the satisfaction of a life well-lived was on full display weatherwise.

Thanksgiving, at eighty-six, as advertised, was the season to give thanks for untold blessings and making it that far in life. The next four weeks, right through the holidays, weather got its revenge. Immortality came into focus once again at Christmas, giving mere mortals one more kick at the cat in their nineties. The dead time—maybe it should have been called dying time—between Christmas and the new year was when life on this earth came to an end, according to a Gregorian calendar, and the next life (year) began, provided a person saw things in that way. Maude Skinner did, in fact, and at age thirty-two, she relished where she happened to be on the timeline of her own life, mainly due to what her mother and father, now living in Florida, had done right and wrong, thanks to her older brother Marcel's money.

Maude's mother was a dour woman, wholly unpleasant, as affectionate as the vacuum cleaner. She'd been angry at God since the terrible misfortunes her family experienced years ago. They lost their farm to the bank when she was a young girl, and the shame of it had blackened her worldview for evermore. She happened to be, however, an incredible cook. Maude was introduced to the wonderful world of spices by her mother and became a brilliant chef in her own right. Marcel learned what misery was like from his folks, driving him to achieve great things, proving that life in the crucible, perversely, had extraordinary benefits.

Maude's faith journey had been an act of defiance. Her mom and dad never set foot in a Christian church, and living in Campton, Kentucky, saw no reason to avail their children to an organization they felt offered nothing substantive, especially since patrons were expected to drop money in the plate, which the Sutherland family had little of. As a sophomore in high school, Maude saw a report in the newspaper about a break-in at the church near her home. *Who would have the courage to do such a thing?* she wondered. A week or so later, parishioners began to suspect an insider of staging the robbery, particularly since twenty-three thousand dollars in the church strongbox had disappeared. The preacher retired, left town, and hadn't been seen or heard from since. The flock figured he needed a retirement nest egg, so they didn't pursue getting the money back.

Maude found herself in the pews of that very same church a few weeks later, working out her own faith. She joined the quilters, and got a full dose of stitching and how mature women behaved. These days, she occasionally shared what she had learned back then with her husband, but scarcely anyone else. Make no mistake, she knew right from wrong, and spoke her mind on the subject when the opportunity presented itself, which is what made her the correct match for the bigger-than-life Brock Skinner.

8:30 a.m., THANKSGIVING DAY

Brock had purchased the log cabin he and his wife lived in more than a year ago, right before they got married. He spent a fortune refurbishing the place, gutting and reconfiguring the inside. The first thing he did was rebuild the fireplace to make absolutely sure it drew properly, which meant tearing out what was there and doing it right. He didn't want any damned smoke smell ruining the cozy atmosphere of a crackling wood fire. The weather was forecasted to be calm, cold, and clear that Thanksgiving Day, so he stacked white-oak logs on the limestone hearth, on each side of the firebox. He anticipated that dinner guests would be huddled there later in the day, sated by Maude's delicious, hearty meal.

~ ~ ~

Marcel Sutherland nervously stood in the lobby of the downtown Hilton Hotel in Lexington, waiting for Valerie Goddard to come down from her room and join him on the ride to Hazard. She had gotten in late the night before from Roswell, New Mexico. Marcel made a bit of play for her a couple of months ago when she was in the Hazard area chasing after extraterrestrial beings. After she found out he was big-time rich, her interest in a common earthling increased considerably. Valerie was tough, very cute, and sweet, and out there somewhere. She harbored no illusions about her own personality and what people thought of her. Marcel found all those qualities in her to be rather charming.

She stepped out of the elevator and said, "Hello, Marcel. Wonderful to see you again. It's great to be back in Kentucky." She gave him a big hug and patted him on the back.

"Center of the universe," he confirmed. "You're looking positively radiant." He looked her up and down, and felt something good in the pit of his stomach.

Valerie had on a pumpkin-tone satin blouse, gray wool slacks, and black denim jacket with the sleeves turned up. "Well, this time, I brought some fancy clothes. Who all's going to be there today?"

"Brock and Maude, you and me, Sheriff Connors and Joan Brewer. She's the nice girl who works at Maude's winery. Her mother, the only family she has left, is on a cruise in Europe, so my sister invited her over."

"I can't wait to see everybody. Let's get on the road." Marcel formally escorted Valerie to his bright red Mercedes, tucked her in the passenger seat, got in the driver's side, and pulled out into light traffic.

~ ~ ~

Sheriff Connors, intending to take the afternoon off, sat behind his desk at the Hazard police station, making sure any trouble in the community was being properly attended to. He reviewed the roster of deputies for the day to confirm adequate coverage, and then filed the papers stacked in his out basket. He only hoped Typhoid Mary, AKA Brock Skinner, wouldn't conjure up some calamity during the day requiring his attention. After scarfing down Maude's spectacular cooking, he intended to kick back, watch football, and engage in friendly conversation with Joan Brewer. She was a little younger than he was, yet seemed to get prettier every time he saw her. While Connors was having pleasant thoughts, he remembered the Happy Hap Quilters were going to distribute lap quilts to the infirm and shut-ins around noon. The sheriff heard that Maude was participating. He thought, *Nothing could go wrong, right?*

~ ~ ~

Maude got a wild hair and decided to prepare an Indian Thanksgiving meal. Real Indian food from India, that is, not the Native American kind: tandoori turkey, xawaash rice, sauteed vegetables, and chaat masala potatoes. She intended to throw in a few traditional American side dishes as well. The spiced-up turkey had gone in the oven after she'd finished prepping everything else that morning. The hard work would come between one and two, as the meal was set for two thirty. Maude expected to be back from delivering the quilt she'd made by twelve thirty, allowing plenty of time to tee up the spread. She hollered to Brock in the family room, "Do you want to go with me when I take the quilt?"

"If Marcel and Valerie have arrived. Nathan and Joan aren't expected until about one thirty."

"I don't want to leave until a quarter till twelve. They'll be here by then."

"Okay. I'll drive."

11:00 a.m., THANKSGIVING DAY

Valerie came through the front door of the Skinner house ahead of Marcel, and called out, "Yuh-huh. Anybody here?"

Brock responded, "Just us aliens. Come on in."

Maude dried her hands, came out of the kitchen, and said, "How are you? It's so good to see you again. I want you to know that it took me a long time to find some good alien recipes. I hope you'll like them."

Valerie smelled the savory turkey in the oven and played along. "Don't you know outer space people don't have to eat? They're much too advanced for that. I'm not, though. What's this?"

The quilt Maude had made was draped over the back of the big leather chair facing the fireplace in the family room. Its pattern consisted of dainty floral strips of red, yellow, and black cloth sewn together somewhat randomly. "I'm a proud member of the Happy Hap Quilters of Perry County. We're handing out lap throws today to those in need."

Marcel asked his sister, "What's a hap?"

"Coverlet, bedspread, blanket, counterpane, that sort of thing."

"Ah, I remember after I went off to college, you were learning how to quilt over at the church."

"Just one of my many talents."

"And she has plenty," Brock added.

"How exactly do you make a quilt?" Valerie took a moment to inspect the stitching and edging of the coverlet more closely.

"When I learned fifteen years ago, Jelly Rolls had just come on the market. It takes one roll of cloth with forty strips, forty-two inches long to make a small, fifty-by-sixty quilt top. Basically, you sandwich the decorative layer with batting and backing, and then stitch it all together."

"Jelly Roll?"

"They call them that because the forty layers of material rolled up and tied look like a jelly roll. They're usually complementary patterns in different colors. Something interesting about Hazard is the tourist trail of forty quilts painted on different things all over the county. Those patterns were done by the real pros."

"Who are you taking this one to?"

"An elderly man who lives in a shack in the woods. We got his address from a guy at the grocery store where he gets food delivered from occasionally. I don't know what the man's name is."

Marcel warned, "I hope Brock's going with you. He'd better take a shotgun along."

"Really, now, I was told he's harmless."

Brock said, "Marcel's just worried you won't be back in time to trot out the meal."

The four of them chatted for another half hour before Brock loaded up the winery pickup. Truman, Skinner's white German shepherd, jumped in the truck and sat in the middle, and the three of them set off.

Noon, THANKSGIVING DAY

The weather at midday was so calm, it attracted no attention. Brock found the road to the hollow, off Bulldog Lane, leading to the little house atop the hill. The old structure had horizontal, wavey, shiplap siding, stained dark brown. The windows were covered with curtains inside that were probably once white, but had turned an amber color. The six-panel, hollow-metal front door was painted a scuffed and chipping dark green. Brock let Truman jump out before he tucked the pistol in his belt. Maude had the folded quilt under her arm when her husband rapped on the door.

"Come on in."

Truman marched through the door, scanned the room, and lay down in the middle of it. The wizened man, with two days of stubble on his face, sitting in a black rocking chair, looked to be in his eighties. He wore dirty khakis, dull-brown boots, and a patterned flannel shirt. At least the place had electricity and a bathroom. The baseboard heat was working a little too well. "Oh, such a pretty dog. What can I do for you folks?"

"I'm Maude Skinner. This is my husband, Brock. We've brought you a lap quilt to keep warm this winter." The pistol in Brock's belt was in plain sight.

When the man stood, Brock noticed his eyes were bruised, and the nasty cut on his lip had scabbed over. He asked, "What happened to you, sir?"

The man carefully touched his face and hesitated before responding. "Oh, I fell down outside." He walked over to the front window to see what kind of vehicle was out in the yard. Brock noticed the tattered Bible on the table next to the rocking chair and flipped open the cover to see if anything was written there. He shut the book as the man turned to speak to Maude. "The quilt is beautifully done. Did you make it?"

"I did. The quilters of Perry County are out distributing them to people in need. Is there anything we can do for you? Are you doing okay?"

"Never better." A friendly grin formed on his battered face.

Brock asked, "How long have you had this place?"

"Oh, most of my life. I've lived here full time since I quit working."

"How long has that been?"

"I can't quite remember."

"What kind of work did you do?"

"I've forgotten that too." He took the quilt out of Maude's hands and hung it on one of the arms of the rocking chair. "Thank you. I really appreciate the gift."

Maude offered, "Would you care to join us at our Thanksgiving table? We'd be more than happy to drive you over to our house and back."

"Not necessary. Besides, the four of us could scarcely get in the cab of your pickup. No, my nephew is bringing me a big meal in an hour or so."

"Well, that's good to hear," Maude said cheerfully. "We'll be running along. By the way, what's your name?"

"I'm ashamed to say it, but I don't remember that, either."

When they got back in the car, Maude seemed sad. "What is it, honey?" Brock asked.

"There but for the grace of God go I."

"You don't believe that malarky about not remembering anything, do you?"

"You don't?"

"Absolutely not. The man's been beaten by somebody who wants something he has or knows about. My guess is he's been hiding here for a while, and the people after him just found him recently, and will be back again. He's faking memory loss, hoping they'll leave him alone."

"What are we going to do?"

"I don't know yet, but I'm damn sure not going to tell Connors about him until after we've eaten."

1:30 p.m., THANKSGIVING DAY

Joan Brewer and Nathan Connors arrived at the Skinner house promptly, in separate cars. She was dolled up in black jeans and an off-white cotton top with rivets and piping on the seams. The sheriff had changed into civilian clothes, washed-out blue jeans and a collared brown v-neck sweater over a black t-shirt. He wore thick-soled, oxford hush puppies that were out of character for a lawman. Brock saw the guests park and met them at the door. "Something smells good," Connors said.

"It's my new cologne," Brock replied in jest. "I put it on when I go hunting. Attracts the game. Hello, Joan." He gave her a warm smile and took their coats.

"That's cheating," said the sheriff.

Everyone except Maude mingled in the family room, leaving her in the kitchen to work magic. Joan said, "Nice to see you, Valerie. I love your outfit."

"Thank you. How's life been treating you?"

"Pretty good. Can't complain."

Connors took the opportunity to engage Joan in conversation while Brock wadded newspaper, put it under the grate, and made a teepee out of kindling. Marcel asked, "What time do the Lions and Cowboys come on?"

"Four o'clock."

2:30 p.m., THANKSGIVING DAY

Brock offered a nice prayer and everyone took a seat at the table. He said, "I just want to say thank you to my beautiful wife for preparing this incredible meal, and speaking for the men, we want to thank Joan and Valerie for being here." Nathan and Marcel raised their glasses, nodded, and smiled.

The way to a man's heart was through his stomach. The men raved nonstop about how good the food tasted. After everybody had their fill, Maude got up to speak. "Now it's my turn to thank my brother, Marcel, for all the things he's done for Brock and me. We love you."

A tear welled up in Marcel's eye, and he took out his handkerchief but said nothing. Maude touched his shoulder and sat again.

The sheriff, feeling a little uncomfortable, changed the subject. "Maude, who was the person you delivered a quilt to this morning?"

"An old man in a small house off Bulldog Lane."

"What was his name?"

"He didn't tell us."

"That's kind of peculiar, isn't it?"

Brock interjected, "His name is Linus Montalvo."

"How do you know that?" Maude asked.

"I opened his bible, and his name was written there."

The sheriff said, "I don't think I know him."

"Well, here comes the bad news, Nathan. He's been beaten by somebody recently. He had two black eyes and a split lip."

Connors thought, *Damn it, Skinner's done it again! Just stay out of it.*

Brock went on. "I say we try to figure out what's going on with him without leaving the house here." It was all the sheriff could do to keep his mouth shut.

Marcel said, "Go light the fire, Brock. Maude, why don't you ladies go into the family room and let us clean up?"

"Gladly."

When Skinner rejoined the men in the kitchen, he said to Marcel, "Can you get into the files at the company through my computer?"

"Sure."

"Let's do that after we're finished here."

Connors finally spoke. "Is there going to be some kind of hacking I shouldn't know about?"

"*Au contraire,* you should know about it. Just don't watch too closely how the sausage is made."

"I guess as long as we don't leave this house, I don't care what we do," he replied.

"Buckle up, then."

Marcel worked the keyboard for several minutes before giving a report. "Linus Montalvo, eighty-six years old, originally from Harlan, bought a small piece of property off Bulldog Lane in Perry County forty-three years ago, and built a little house on it. He took a job as the pastor of a church in Harlan about the same time. He left there and took a pastorship at a church in Campton twenty-five years ago. Hey, wait a minute, that's the church Maude went to before leaving for college." Marcel looked up, perplexed.

"Where's he finding all this?" Connors looked at Brock.

"Don't ask that question, Nathan."

Marcel continued: "It seems he left there and dropped out of sight fifteen years ago."

The three men went back into the family room, made casual conversation, and found places to sit. Brock added two large logs to the waning fire. Marcel asked, "Maude, do you know anything about the pastor who left the church in Campton you went to right before you started going there?"

"As I remember, he was accused of staging a break-in and stealing some money. That's all I heard about it."

Brock suggested, "Why don't we all take a few minutes and call our relatives. I'll go into the kitchen and put on some coffee. Joan, I know your mother is traveling in Europe, but we consider ourselves your family." She came over to him seeking a hug, and got one.

Marcel asked Maude, "Do you know who we could call to get some details about the pastor leaving?"

The sheriff and Joan were having their own conversation again. He was trying to stay out of it. Valerie came over and stood by Marcel, suddenly taking an interest in what he was talking about.

"Well, there were about eight ladies in my quilting group, and they knew pretty much everything that went on. That was fifteen years ago. Many of them are probably dead by now."

Brock said to Marcel, "Go on the church's website and see if they have a directory of members."

In a few minutes, Marcel handed Maude a printed list of names and phone numbers. "Do you remember any of these people?"

She scanned it, stopped on a name, and said, "Carol Pickens. I'm sure she'd remember me."

"Call her," Brock said.

"You mean now?"

"Yeah, I'm sure she's bored to death and would love to hear from you."

Valerie said, "That's probably true. Go ahead, Maude, give her a call. I'm starting to get curious as to what's going on here."

"Okay." She got her cell phone from the kitchen and tried the number. "Is this Carol Pickens? This is Maude Sutherland calling. Do you remember me from the quilting group at church several years ago?" She put the call on speakerphone.

"Of course I do, honey. What a nice surprise to hear from you."

"I'm not interrupting anything, am I?"

"Are you kidding? The family left an hour ago, and I'm just sitting here doing a little knitting."

"Carol, I'm married now and live down in Hazard. It's possible that we may have run into Pastor Montalvo, and I wanted to ask if you knew the details of him leaving the church in Campton."

"Well, it's been a while, but I can tell you what I remember. We went to church one Sunday, and the pastor announced the building had been broken into. After the service, the elders got all of the details. Somebody had stolen twenty-three thousand dollars out of the strongbox, and left a note in it that didn't make much sense."

"What did it say?"

"When we come again, you'd better tell us where the ten thousand is if you want to live."

"Who wrote the note?"

"Nobody's quite sure. After a few days, the elders began thinking Pastor Montalvo had stolen the money and put the note in there to cover his tracks. He was at retirement age, you know."

"Where did the twenty-three thousand come from?"

"Dianne Newkirk, who was in our quilting group, donated all of her possessions to the church before she died. She got cancer and when she was in hospice asked us ladies to get everything out of her house before her relatives could ransack the place. The twenty-three thousand was among her things."

"I take it she didn't like her kinfolks."

"They were all on her deceased husband's side. Her husband's first wife died some years back, and then he was killed in a hunting accident after he married Dianne. She was an old maid, and married him late in life."

"Did you know her husband?"

"I did. The man acted like a scared cat. Seemed to be hiding something."

Maude looked around the room to signal she intended to conclude the conversation. "Thanks, Carol, for the information."

"If you see Pastor Montalvo, tell him I was asking about him. Always liked him. He gave a good message."

Valerie walked over to the window by the fireplace. The weather was changing. Low clouds had moved in and a slight breeze had kicked up. The temperature dropped, and it was cold enough now for snow. She turned to Marcel and asked, "How old is this fellow?"

"Eighty-six."

Valerie looked out the window again, saying ominously, "I should have figured as much. Today's his weather day. Something bad is going to happen to him."

"What are you talking about?" Brock asked.

"Oh, never mind. You'd call me a kook if I explained it to you."

"Try me."

"Every day of a Gregorian calendar coincides with a person's age. Each year, people who believe in this sort of thing check the weather on that day to see how it lines up with what's going on in their lives. Bad weather is considered a bad omen."

Sheriff Connors overheard the comment. "Well, let's hope that's not the case for Linus Montalvo." He was hoping against hope the rest of the day would be uneventful.

Marcel offered, "I'm going to see if I can find out anything about Dianne Newkirk's deceased husband and his family."

"One thing's for sure, that note in the strongbox doesn't make much sense," Brock commented.

"I'm not so sure about that," Valerie replied. "We might be able to figure it out." Her mind drifted off and she headed for the kitchen to get a cup of coffee.

Brock and Nathan followed Marcel back to the computer and waited for him to work his magic. "Okay. Cedric Newkirk married a woman by the name of Baby Girl Bloom in 1971."

Connors leaned over the computer screen in disbelief. "Baby Girl? What kind of name is that?"

"Pretty classy one," Brock said. "I wonder if she went by Baby or Girl, or both?"

"Cedric took a job at the Cincinnati Federal Reserve Bank in 1972. The United States went off the gold standard in 1973. Later that year, the Federal Reserve reported ten thousand had been stolen while gold was being transferred out of the bank one day. Cedric worked there for many years until his death."

The sheriff said to Marcel, "You mean somebody stole ten thousand in gold? At today's prices, it would be worth nearly a million dollars. If that's the ten thousand the note in the strongbox was referring to, no wonder somebody's looking for it."

"It doesn't say exactly what got stolen. The Newkirks had two boys one year apart. They would be almost fifty years old by now. Their mother, Baby Girl, died about twenty-five years ago, and their father remarried this Dianne woman. He must have gotten religion then, because he started going to church with her. Wonder if he got himself right with God before he died?"

"Were the sons out hunting with dear old dad when he had his accident?"

"Give me a minute to find the obituary."

Brock asked, "What were the boys' names?"

"Paul and Silas."

"Huh. Biblical," Connors uttered.

"The obit doesn't give any details on how Cedric Newkirk died."

"Anything out there on the boys?"

"They own a business, Newkirk Welding in Rousseau, Kentucky. Where's that?" Marcel asked.

The sheriff replied, "Northeast of Jackson."

4:00 p.m., THANKSGIVING DAY

The falling snowflakes were huge and wet, and they seemed to take forever to hit the ground. Once they did, they melted right away. Marcel stood by the fireplace, looking out, mesmerized by what reminded him of cascading white parachutes. Valerie came out of the kitchen with a troubled look and said, "I think we need to check on Pastor Montalvo. I'm afraid something bad is happening to him."

Brock walked over to Connors. "Nathan, do you think you could send a deputy over there to check on him. His place is at the end of Bulldog Lane, 7820."

"Yeah, I'll call it in." The sheriff went into the hallway by the front door for a few minutes to use the phone.

Detroit kicked off to the Cowboys. The game announcers were annoying, talking too much, so Maude cut the volume in half. She said, "So what do we know about our friend, the pastor?"

Brock told what he thought he knew. "As near as I can tell, Cedric Newkirk stole ten thousand something in 1973 from the Federal Reserve Bank in Cincinnati where he worked, and got away with it. His two boys, Paul and Silas, found out years later he'd done it, so they threatened to kill him if he didn't tell them where the money was. Looks like he didn't tell, and they killed him. He must have left everything to his second wife, Dianne, which likely enraged the sons. When they found out Dianne was dying from cancer, they couldn't believe their luck, and planned to go through her house when she was in the hospital, hoping to find what they'd been looking for. Dianne double crossed them and gave everything to the church before they could ransack her house. They broke in, took the twenty-three thousand from the church, and left a note threatening Pastor Montalvo, believing he might know where the other ten thousand was."

"I take it you think Montalvo went into hiding, fearing for his life, and Paul and Silas Newkirk are the ones who recently found him and beat him up?" Maude asked.

"That's about the size of it."

"Where do these Newkirk boys live?"

"Rousseau. They have a welding business there."

Joan Brewer stood with a start. "Newkirk Welding? They're drug dealers."

"How do you know that?" the sheriff asked.

"Some of my old friends told me. Ones I don't hang around with anymore."

The Cowboys' drive stalled, and they settled for a field goal.

Marcel said, "Here's what baffles me. Paul and Silas got twenty-three thousand, and they were hell-bent on getting another ten. Still are. Something's wrong."

"I believe Cedric put the ten thousand, or whatever it is, in a lockbox somewhere. If it is gold, it'll be worth a lot now. I'm thinking the Newkirk boys are looking for the key to the box," Valerie surmised.

Connors said, "I'm not sure that holds water. Somebody would have to pay rent on the box every year, and I see that as unlikely."

"Unless Newkirk paid for twenty years of rental in advance. That doesn't make much sense either."

Maude chimed in, "Is it realistic to believe a key in Dianne's house would make it over to the church with the rest of her belongings, and if it did, would anybody pay attention to it? How would Pastor Montalvo know what it was for?"

Valerie advanced another theory. "Maybe Dianne told him on her deathbed."

"I'm not sure I like that idea much. Montalvo would have already cleaned the box out," said the sheriff.

Brock replied, "Maybe he did."

"Then why's he living in squalor in a broken-down shack?" Maude challenged.

The Detroit Lions drove the length of the field and scored a touchdown before the end of the first quarter. The snow had stopped falling. The clouds began breaking up.

"Maude, do you have a room in the house where you make quilts?" Joan asked.

"I do. Want to see it?"

"Sure."

The two girls followed Maude to the sewing room. Valerie said, "I wouldn't have the patience to do this in a million years." She appeared nervous even thinking about it.

"Once you get started on one, you lose track of time." There was a big, flat, waist-high table for laying out the material. The batting and backing were stacked in bins, and the rolls of colored fabric were in a big box. The sewing machine had its own table. "I've got enough stuff in here to make two dozen more quilts. My output has slowed down since I married Brock."

Joan picked up a Jelly Roll to look at the different colors of fabric. "How long does it take to make a quilt?"

"Superstars can make one in eight hours. It takes me about three times that long." She untied a Jelly Roll and laid out the forty strips of cloth, which were forty-two inches long and two and one-half inches wide. "These strips of cloth are precut and prewashed. A quarter of an inch is lost on each edge to the seam, so the color strips end up two inches wide on the finished quilt. The creative part is designing the pattern. Actually, that's the fun part. The sewing and ironing are a little more monotonous."

Joan said, "The only talent I have is acting. I can be somebody else in two seconds. A quilt never changes once it's been made."

"Well," Valerie remarked, "the only thing I know how to do is hunt for outer space creatures."

"It looks to me like Marcel approves of your profession," Maude threw out. She shut off the light in the sewing room and led the way back to the family room.

The sheriff's phone rang. "Yes." There were thirty seconds of silence. "Did you take him to the hospital? Did he tell you who did it?" More silence. "Okay, call me back after you get a report on him." Connors turned to the group. "The deputy found Montalvo on the floor of his cabin. He'd been kicked in the stomach and face, but whoever did it left him alive. He wouldn't say who beat him up."

"We know who did it. Paul and Silas Newkirk," Brock stated. Truman was standing at one of the front windows, looking out and growling. Brock ran over to see who or what was out there. A car had stopped in the road about a quarter of a mile from the house. Brock looked at the sheriff and said quietly, "We're going to have to move fast. Call two of your men and have them get over here. Tell them to pull in quietly. Follow me."

The sheriff peered out the window. "Who is it?"

"The Newkirk brothers. My guess is Montalvo told them he'd given the money or whatever they were looking for to me in order to save his life."

Connors called the deputies and gave them instructions.

Brock took a sawed-off shotgun and four loaded pistols out of the locked gun case in the office. He handed the shotgun and one pistol to Connors. "I want you to go hide in the master bedroom closet. I'll lure one of them back there. When you hear me say the word okay, pop out and jump the guy."

"What about Marcel and the girls?"

"I'll take care of them." Brock led the way to the master bedroom and put one of the pistols under his pillow on the bed. He motioned toward the closet where he wanted Connors to hide, then ran back in the family room and said urgently, "The Newkirk boys are out front. I'm sure Montalvo told them I had what they were looking for. Let's all go in the kitchen." When there, Brock said, "Marcel and Valerie, get on that side. I'm going to lay a loaded pistol with the safety off for each of you on a shelf by your knees. Maude, you and Joan get in the pantry and close the door. Don't make a move unless one of us calls you out." Panic showed on their faces.

The doorbell rang. Truman ran ahead of his master. When Brock opened the door, the dog barked repeatedly. The brothers were standing there close together. They looked a lot alike, with thinning blond hair and rough complexions. One had a pistol pointed at Brock's chest. "Call the dog off, or I'll shoot him."

"Down, Truman. Why would you do that?"

"Don't mess with me, buddy. Are you Brock Skinner?"

"I am," Brock said with quiet confidence.

"I want the key Montalvo gave to you."

"Your gun is pretty persuasive. I'll go get it."

"No, you won't. I'll go with you."

"Suit yourself."

The one without the gun in his hand asked, "How many people are here?"

"Me, my wife, and her brother."

"There's three cars and a truck out here."

"Yeah, one's mine, one's my wife's, and the red Mercedes belongs to my brother-in-law. The truck is for my wife's business."

"Where are the other two?"

"In the kitchen."

"Let's go see them."

Brock led the way.

When they entered the area where the island and stove were, the man with the gun said, "Silas, yell if they try anything. All right, everybody, stay calm. Once we get what we came for, we're out of here, and nobody gets hurt. Now, show me where it is."

"It's in the master bedroom."

"I'll follow you," Paul said.

He dropped in behind Brock as they walked through the family room. Just as they passed the bedroom closet, Brock said casually, "Okay." The sheriff stepped out and coldcocked Paul with the butt of the shotgun. He fell face first, and his pistol skittered over against the bedroom wall. Connors said, "I'll tie him up."

Brock grabbed his pistol from under the pillow and snuck back into the family room. Silas finally saw him and went for the gun in his belt. Brock aimed at the man and said, "I wouldn't." Silas started to step out of the line of fire, but when he looked over at the two people in the kitchen, they each had a pistol trained on him too. "Throw the gun out slowly." Silas decided to make a run for the front door.

Sheriff Connors came into view and yelled, "Stop! Police! It's no use, there are two deputies out front." Silas, dejected, reached for his piece and set it on the floor. Maude and Joan were told to come out of the pantry after the commotion died down. The sheriff asked, "What is the key to?"

Brock said, "Montalvo just told them about a key to get them out of his house. You want to tell us what this prize is you guys are looking for?"

"I don't know what you're talking about. We just came by to say hello. Where's my brother, by the way?"

"He's in the bedroom lying on the floor." Connors went to the door and waved the deputies in. Paul finally came to, and the deputies cuffed both men, leading them toward the front door. "Take these thugs to jail," Connors said. He was going to get a warrant to search their welding business, but didn't plan on sharing that with them. Skinner gathered up all the guns, including the two the Newkirks had brought in, and locked them in the gun case.

The Cowboys got a touchdown and were ahead of the Lions at the end of the third quarter.

Maude said, "Well, that's the kind of excitement we don't need any more of. We should check on the pastor to see how he's doing."

Valerie commented, "The weather's getting better. He'll be all right."

Brock said, "I'll call over to the hospital and get a report."

Connors came into the kitchen and said, "Don't bother. One of the deputies just told me he was okay. He asked how you were doing, and apologized for causing you any trouble. I told the deputy to tell him, as usual, Skinner's alive and well."

6:30 p.m., THANKSGIVING DAY

The sky had already cleared. Sunlight was growing dimmer, and nightfall wasn't far off. Valerie made a declaration. "The only things that could have been stolen from the Federal Reserve Bank are paper money, coins, or bulk metals. I'm thinking whatever Newkirk took, he must have felt it was too dangerous to sell or get rid of after he took it. I'm also thinking it would be hard for him to get coins or bars through the metal detectors. It's got to be some kind of paper worth ten thousand when he stole it, and more now."

Brock said, "Maybe it's some sort of redeemable gold certificate or something. If so, there's one place it might be; tucked in Montalvo's bible. It could have been in with the twenty-three thousand dollars and he plucked it out and kept it for himself."

Connors returned to his earlier point. "Then why not redeem it before now?"

"Same problem. Not easy to get rid of."

"We're not going over there to look for it tonight," Maude said. "The Newkirk boys will be in jail. The pastor may have had it for fifteen years. We can wait one more day to look for it."

"I'm going to go look something up," Marcel said. He came back in a few minutes and announced, "I think I know what it is that Cedric Newkirk stole from the bank. In the 1920s and '30s, the banks used paper money in large denominations for transactions between themselves. There were ten-thousand-dollar bills, and ten-thousand-dollar gold certificates redeemable for ten thousand in gold coins. A twenty-dollar gold coin today is worth two thousand dollars, or one hundred times face value. That would mean a ten-thousand-dollar gold certificate is worth a million dollars."

"Now we're getting somewhere," Valerie blurted. "I say we go to Montalvo's cabin right now and see if it's in the bible. The drama is killing me."

"There's more," Marcel interjected. "The 1928 version of the gold certificate had Salmon P. Chase's mug on it. There's only one of them and the government has it. It's rumored that other certificates are out there, and several potential buyers are advertising they'll pay five million dollars for one."

The sheriff said, "So it would seem that Cedric wasn't willing to dispose of the bill on the black market, but his stepsons have no problem doing that. They just have to find the stupid thing, which they still haven't been able to do."

"I'm not certain Linus Montalvo knows where the bill is," Brock said.

Joan asked Marcel, "What are its dimensions?"

"You mean the gold certificate?"

"Yes."

"I think it's six and five-eighths by two and five-eighths inches."

"Maude, do you think any of the Jelly Rolls you still have in there are from the Campton church?"

"I don't know. I suppose some could be."

"You did say the rolls were two and one-half inches wide, right?"

"Yes."

"Well, a bill that's two and five-eighths high could have been wrapped up in a roll with only a sixteenth of an inch showing on each side. What if Dianne, or Cedric for that matter, hid it in one of the Jelly Rolls that got donated to the church?" All six of them ran to the sewing room and started carefully inspecting each of the three-dozen fabric rolls in the box.

There were two more left to check out when Maude chirped loudly, "Look! This might be it." She untied the bundle, relaxed the wound material, and pulled the ten-thousand-dollar gold certificate gently from the stack.

Brock said, "Maude, that should make an unhappy Happy Hap Quilter happy."

"Yes, it does! Thank you, Joan, for figuring out where it was." She passed the bill around so everyone could look at it. "Sheriff, who do you think it belongs to now?"

He said, "Possession's nine-tenths of the law."

Brock struck an indignant pose. "I can't believe you said that, being a lawman and all."

"I don't care right now. Let's go back in and watch the rest of the football game. There'll be plenty of time to figure that out later."

The Lions scored a touchdown at the end of the game to win it.

The three sets of lovebirds made the most of the rest of the evening.

RUMBA COMES TO THE CUMBERLANDS

The winery business had come up aces during December in years past, and Maude Skinner braced herself for another busy season of perambulating holiday shoppers tramping in and out from all over Eastern Kentucky and the surrounding Appalachian states. The size of the crowd on any given day depended on the weather. Snow meant bad, and sun good, easily seen by the number of customers parading through the lot, searching for a place to park.

Thursday, the first day of the month, started well. Fifty-seven degrees and a hard blue sky, with an occasional billowy white cloud scudding right over the mountaintop, put a spring in the step, and devil-may-care attitude in the minds of the novice oenophiles shelling out money for Vigneron's brands. Maude had hired a bottle and label consultant who pitched her with shopworn clichés like: "Marketing is the message, and it's about the sizzle, not the steak." Because she had the money to do things up right, her wine bottles made Silver Oak and Opus One "look" second rate.

Joan Brewer came through the door and hurried over to the tasting-room bar. "Maude, there's been an accident in the parking lot. Some old fellow backed into another guy's car. It looks like the one that got hit will have to be towed."

"I better go see about it." After locating the mishap at the end of the third row of cars, Maude stepped around a few gawkers to survey the damage. The rammed car had gotten the worst of it.

The elderly gentleman at fault acted somewhat disoriented and confused. He tottered away from the scene of the accident, talking gibberish. He finally gathered his wits, returned to his vehicle, and found the aggrieved party. "I'm sorry, sir. Shall we call the police?"

"Only if you don't have any insurance." The man whose car had been hit was six feet tall, narrow-waisted, with unusually good posture and combed brown hair like a young Roger Moore. His black pants were fitted and high-waisted. He smiled at Maude and asked, "Ma'am, is this your establishment? It doesn't look as if I'll be able to drive out of here."

"Yes, I can see that. I suggest both of you call your insurance carriers."

Fancy Pants addressed Maude again: "Forgive me for not properly introducing myself." He clasped his hands in front of his chest. "My name's Michael Archer. Would there be any chance I could borrow a vehicle from you? I have a pressing engagement at one o'clock." He was suave, all right. A little too much so, Maude thought. Some of her husband's skepticism about people was beginning to rub off on her.

The older gentleman, who'd completely regained his composure, said, "I think my car still runs. I'd be happy to take you wherever you need to go." He shifted his weight from one foot to the other, waiting for Archer's response.

"That would be helpful. I'll take you up on your offer, sir." Michael Archer retrieved the wine he'd bought from the back seat, and a wrecker pulled up fifteen minutes later to haul Archer's car to a body shop. The two men drove away together in the old man's vehicle, deep in conversation. Maude peered up at the bright sky, shielded her eyes with one hand, and scurried back inside to help thin the crowd of customers standing in line to purchase wine.

~ ~ ~

A cornfield was a rarity in Perry County, not so much because of the paucity of flat ground, but due to the fact that marijuana was a significantly better cash crop. One long section of cornstalks—left standing each fall after the growing season—had been used for bird hunting for years. Barrels of milled feed corn were set out in October to attract the attention of flying creatures, particularly pheasants. Birds, like humans, were lazy and didn't work hard for their food unless they had to, which kept them tethered to the feed barrels. The first week of December had traditionally been the best time for pheasant hunting around the state. Brock Skinner talked Sheriff Connors into bringing his rifle out for a little gunfire on that pleasant afternoon.

Brock's white German shepherd, Truman, was no bird dog, but had become proficient at flushing varmints out of the grapevines at the winery, so it followed that he'd be able to roust pheasants. He had picked up on the retrieving part of the process pretty quickly. Both men were using twenty-gauge pumps with a light-game load to make shooting the birds more challenging. Skinner pulled in behind the sheriff's car at the end of the access road, hopped out of the pickup truck, and asked, "Have you got your twenty-five-dollar bird stamp on you?"

Nathan shot back, "Let me see yours. Nothing would please me more than to write you up for hunting without a proper license."

"There's only one problem with that, Nathan. You ain't the game warden."

"Yeah, but I can still make a citizen's arrest."

"Okay, Gomer Pyle."

Brock had on a brown canvas vest with orange stripes, and pockets for carrying the birds. Connors wore dark green garb under his bright-colored covering. The men split up, each moving to a different edge of the field, in parallel positions. Truman stood at the ready, right in the middle where the stalks began. Brock whispered loudly, "Go, boy." The dog ran headlong into the corn. The men heard commotion in there and out flew the birds.

Shooting a pheasant flying low and away from a hunter with a twenty-gauge shotgun wasn't an easy task, but that was the sport of it. The two friends, with the help of Truman, worked together until each of them got three birds, which was all Brock's vest could hold. He would take the pheasants into town to be cleaned and smoked. Maude used them for hors d'oeuvres and wintertime snacks when people came to visit. The sheriff always donated his to the cook for the annual policeman's ball.

Brock dropped the tailgate of the pickup truck to get a treat from his bag to give Truman for a job well done. The sheriff laid his rifle in the truck bed and said, "Some guy refurbished the vacant place in the four hundred block of Main Street between the bank and Black Crystal Coal. The sign he hung out reads Ma's Dance."

"Dancing? Like a studio where you take lessons?"

"I don't know yet, but if it is, doesn't that seem a little strange to you? There's no way in hell a person could make a living doing that kind of thing around here. Those places have a hard enough time making it in big towns."

"Is Black Crystal the company owned by Tonya Downing, the widow of Rory Downing?"

"Yes. He got drunk, fell down the stairs, and broke his neck. I think Black Crystal leased the space to whoever owns the dance business."

Skinner took the bait. "So, you're on a mission to find out how someone could afford to bring rumba to the Cumberlands? Maybe the person has an angel investor, or doesn't need the money."

"Yeah, right. You always wanted to learn how to dance, didn't you, Brock?"

"Me?"

"Think what a hit you'll be with Maude."

Skinner went to the back of the sheriff's car and laid three pheasants by the trunk. "What, I'm a snitch now, working for the police?"

"Well, it's better than me working for you for once."

"And to think, I invited you out here to do some hunting on this beautiful day, and you have the nerve to ask me to go and take dance lessons. Who's borrowing trouble now?"

The sheriff said, "This is a preemptive strike. If I hadn't told you about the guy, you'd have gotten tangled up with him somehow anyway, and with you, there's always a crime involved."

"You're something, Nathan. You know that?"

~ ~ ~

Brock could tell Maude was completely exhausted when she came in a little after six. He jumped up and said, "Why don't you take a shower and let me fix dinner?"

"Oh, that would be great. There's two pieces of sea bass in the fridge. I was going to pan sear them in butter and bake 'em off at four hundred degrees. If you want to, you can poach the asparagus on the grill with garlic and red pepper flakes."

"I can handle that." He turned on the oven before firing up the grill on the patio. He also found a package of seasoned rice in the cupboard. During the meal, Maude went over what needed to get done for the Christmas season. She planned to keep the winery open until three o'clock on Saturday, Christmas Eve.

Brock cleaned up the dishes after the meal and fixed two cups of decaf coffee. "Nathan and I each got three pheasants today."

"Oh, good."

"You'll never guess what he asked us to do."

"What?"

"Take dancing lessons at some joint called Ma's Dance that just opened downtown."

Maude sat up with interest. "That might be fun. Why's he pushing it?"

"He believes something stinks. Can't understand how some stranger could come into town and open up a dance operation and make a go of it."

"He's probably right," she replied. "Wait a minute. We had an accident in the lot at the winery today, and one of the men involved was named Michael Archer. He was the dance instructor type if ever I saw one. You said Ma's Dance? The name of the place probably comes from his initials, M. A."

"What'd you think of him?"

"Slick."

"Uh-oh. I've never tried dancing. Marcel and I had a friend in college who learned how, and said if he'd have picked it up in high school, he could've had his pick of the ladies."

"Men don't figure things out until later in life," she said.

"Boy, I'll say."

~ ~ ~

The Friday afternoon weather had taken a turn for the worse, temperature-wise. Brock parked the Lamborghini on the street across from the bank. Archer saw the couple get out of the car and angle in the direction of his studio, and then he went back to watching Gabrielle giving instructions to a country boy eager to learn how to dance. She was a nice-looking woman, but didn't much act like one. No matter how you sliced it, the dance business was about the come-on. Maude and Brock were prepared for it when they stepped inside.

"Oh, ma'am, I see you're the lady who owns the beautiful winery in town. This must be your husband." Archer grinned, thrusting out his hand. Brock shook it firmly, but didn't speak. "You said you wanted to hear about the programs we offer when you called. Come in my office and I'll tell you about them."

Ma's Dance had a frosted-glass street-side wall, with the front door on the right that opened into a vestibule. Along the right wall inside were the business office, hall to the restrooms, kitchenette, and music machines. The front left had a heavy, shaggy rug with comfortable sofas around the perimeter. Folding chairs lined the left wall all the way back to the corner of the dance floor. Full-length mirrors had been mounted on the back wall, and the high ceiling was open. Everything overhead had been painted flat black. The dance floor itself was beautiful cherry-wood. The side walls were a soft gray green.

"Okay. Our vision is to teach people how to dance socially. We introduce you to sixteen different dances that cover ninety-five percent of all the music you'll ever hear. We teach the basic and five patterns in each dance so you'll have enough variety to enjoy a three- or four-minute song."

Brock asked, "What are the dances?"

"First, let me explain the way you learn. Our packages are on a thirteen-week cycle every quarter of the year. For twelve weeks, you come in once a week for a private lesson, and as many times as you like for the group lessons. In the thirteenth week, we check how you're doing overall, and on that weekend, we have a formal dance party in a ballroom at a hotel somewhere. At the end of this month, the party falls on Saturday, New Year's Eve, so we'll be doing it up right."

Maude said, "Sounds like fun."

"We're open from one o'clock until nine o'clock in the evening, Tuesday through Saturday. Each lesson is fifty minutes long, on the hour. The group lesson starts at seven o'clock, and on Saturday night, we have a practice party from seven till nine."

"When did you open?" Brock asked, to make conversation.

"The first of October. We add students during the quarter as they come in, but ask them to commit to future lessons for the next four quarters. Now, in the first program, we teach you, in this order, the hustle, waltz, rumba, merengue, foxtrot, swing, cha-cha-cha, and salsa. In the second program, we introduce you to the samba, West Coast swing, bolero, polka, Viennese waltz, bachata, tango, and mambo. The third and fourth programs, we let you decide what you want to learn."

"Sounds like a lot of dances," Brock commented. "What do the programs cost?"

"One thousand three hundred fifty dollars per quarter for each of the first two. Fifty dollars down, a hundred per week, and then there is an additional charge for the formal party. After the first two programs, lessons are one-fifty per hour, at a minimum of one per week for at least two more quarters."

"Well, we'd like to take lessons until the end of the year to see if we'd enjoy learning how to dance."

"You're in luck," Archer said. "We have an introductory special for five lessons at three ninety-five. If you want to get serious after that, we'll review the terms of a longer program."

Brock stood, took four hundred-dollar bills out of his pocket, and laid them on the desk. "Keep the extra five."

"Thank you. Shall we schedule your first lesson? Tomorrow we have a two o'clock available."

"Sold," Maude said.

"Bring some shoes with leather soles. We'll tell you then where to look online for good dance shoes."

When the Skinners got in the Lamborghini, they looked at each other, but neither spoke for several seconds. Finally, Maude said, "I guess the guy could be legit. Did you notice the female instructor?"

"Would have been hard not to."

"I wonder if she's the bait for bilking fat cats in the coal business?"

"She would be if I was in charge. Then again, the business could be money laundering, drugs, or prostitution."

"That's too conspicuous. There's something else going on," she said.

"I'll drop you off at the winery and go check in with Connors."

The sheriff quietly shut his office door after Skinner took a seat in front of his desk. "It didn't take you long to spring into action," he said.

Brock replied, "This one's kind of whimsical. I can't wait to get a load of these dancer types."

"I take it you and Maude stuck your noses in there?"

"And came out with five lessons for three ninety-five. Will the police department reimburse me for that?"

"Hah, hah."

"Well, the first order of business is to run a background check on Michael Archer," Brock suggested.

"Shoot, there's ten thousand people with that name in this country. And besides, there's no way that's his real name. How are we going to figure out who he is?"

"We could waterboard him."

"Nope."

"I could beat him up."

"I really love it when you don't take things seriously. You're a royal pain in the ass."

"Watch it, Nathan, I'll resign from this gig at the drop of a hat."

"Sorry, I lost my cool. Got any ideas?"

"Let's see what tomorrow brings," Skinner said on the way out of the sheriff's office.

~ ~ ~

The lesson began with introductions. "Gabrielle, this is Maude and Brock Skinner."

"Nice to meet you."

Here comes the come-on, Brock thought.

Archer spent a few minutes covering generalities about dancing, and then said, "Gabrielle will work with you, Brock, and I'll work with Maude. The hustle is the easiest dance to learn. Let's try it. March, march, back step. March, march, back step."

After a few more directives, Gabrielle said to Brock, "I can tell you're an athlete."

"Guilty."

"Think about this," she said. "In most sports, all your muscles work together when you move. In dancing, you have to separate the upper and lower body. Most times, the legs are not working in harmony with the arms. Also, strong men can sometimes be too physical. Concentrate on under exerting yourself."

"That, and the ten other things I've heard already. This is harder mentally than I thought it would be," he said.

Michael told Maude, "You're a natural. You're going to run ahead of your husband. You'll have to be patient with him."

When the lesson was over, Archer provided encouragement to them, and handed over website addresses for dance shoes. "Gabrielle, do you have anything to say?"

"Yes. Both of you hear the music and are on the beat. Over half the people who dance learn the patterns, but what they are doing isn't in sync with the music. If you guys keep at it, you'll be great dancers." She smiled alluringly. There it was, the bald-faced come-on.

Archer said, "Why don't you folks come back tonight and observe our practice party. It'll give you an idea how things go. And Maude, we will trot out your wine for a refreshment. Might be good for business."

"We'll try to make it," she said. They scheduled their next lesson for the following Wednesday night at eight o'clock, after the group lesson.

Brock headed to the winery so Maude could make sure things were running smoothly. On the way there, he sought a clarification: "Do you think Gabrielle is Archer's main squeeze?"

"No."

"Why do you say that?"

"I can tell by watching them."

"Woman thing, I suppose."

"Yes. She's a hired gun, and he's paying her well. He's got something bigger going on. He'll only make chump change in the dance business, and he doesn't strike me as a plodder."

Brock turned to her with wide eyes. "Look at you, Sherlocketta Holmes."

"Well, Watson, let's go back there tonight and search for more clues."

"Sounds good. I'm going to go to the gym for an hour or so. I'll pick you up at quitting time. We'll get a bite to eat before we crash the party."

~ ~ ~

At five after seven, the Skinners slinked into Ma's, trying not to attract attention. It didn't work. Archer made a beeline for them. "Welcome! Thanks for coming." They went over and sat on a sofa. A few people came by and introduced themselves intermittently, but didn't put any pressure on them to dance.

Maude and Brock observed the crowd and drew several conclusions simultaneously. There were four couples, two oddball single men, three Miss Lonely Hearts, and three showoffs—one woman and two men. And there was an older woman who danced almost exclusively with Michael Archer. She wore very expensive jewelry and seemed more than casually acquainted with the owner of the studio. Gabrielle worked the crowd, pretty much ignoring Archer.

The Skinners strode over to the kitchenette, expecting to be approached by people skipping a dance. True to form, just about everybody they hadn't met cycled through and introduced themselves. Two of the couples didn't mix with anybody and stuck to themselves. The lady who'd been dancing mostly with Archer came by and said, "Hi, I'm Tonya Downing. And you are?"

"Brock Skinner. This is my wife, Maude."

"Oh, I've heard about you. You own Vigneron Winery. I've been there. Beautiful place, and your wine's good."

"Maude owns and runs it. I'm a ne'er do well," Brock said in jest.

"I can see that. I've heard you drive an expensive car too." She could give as good as she took.

Maude asked, "How did you come to take dance lessons?"

"It's a funny story. After my husband died unexpectedly in May, I figured I should get out and meet people. I saw an advertisement from Michael offering to give dance lessons to anyone anywhere in Eastern Kentucky. He had a portable dance floor and boombox in his trunk and rented space in a hotel for the lessons."

"This place is a far cry from that kind of arrangement. What made him go big-time here in Hazard?"

"I own the coal company next door, and we had this empty space. I paid for the leasehold improvements, and he's paying me rent on the place. It's been a great way to meet people such as yourselves."

"Well, if we can learn to dance as quickly as you have, maybe we won't always be wallflowers."

On the way home, Maude asked, "Do you believe her story?"

"I don't know yet. So far, there's several sketchy characters. Michael Archer doing a gig he can't make much money at. Tonya Downing mixing with the hoi polloi, and the couples who don't care to mix with anybody. I'm not considering Gabrielle to be on the level just yet."

On Pearl Harbor Day, Maude drove the Lamborghini, and Brock took the winery pickup over to Ma's. After the group and private lessons, he waited for Gabrielle to leave and followed her at a distance. She went less than a mile and parked in front of an upscale apartment building on Broadway Street. Brock drove by and headed for home. He told Maude he thought Gabrielle was probably a solid citizen. "Archer must have known she was a hot babe who could dance. Women like that, though, don't usually traipse around without a male escort."

At the Saturday night practice party, the Skinners ventured onto the floor when a hustle or waltz was played. Brock also did a hustle with Gabrielle, and Maude breezed through a waltz with Archer. Brock, in the winery pickup, followed the two antisocial couples when they left the party. They were in one car, drove straight over to I-75, and headed north. Brock turned around and went home when they hit the onramp. He told Maude about it when he came into the house. "The best I can tell, Archer has seeded those couples to have enough people at the practice party. They don't live near here. Whatever's cooking, I'm sure they're in on it."

Tonya Downing invited the Skinners, two sociable couples, and a man she danced with occasionally to her house after the practice party for a nightcap on December seventeenth. She had one hell of a house on Grand Oak Lane, a giant two-story brown-brick affair. "So, Maude, how're you liking dancing?" Tonya asked.

"We really like it. Challenges us physically and mentally, and we get to socialize with fun people."

"I agree."

Brock snooped around the house the best he could without getting caught. There were valuable paintings on the walls, and he suspected expensive jewelry was in a wall safe or drawer in the master bedroom. He took a moment to study the tall flight of stairs Rory Downing must have tumbled down to his death.

Tonya brought out an excellent bottle of Vigneron wine and poured some for each of the guests. The Skinners finished their glasses, chit-chatted for a while longer, and went on their merry way. Maude asked on the way home, "Do you think breaking into her house could be the end game?"

"It's a possibility. I still haven't given up on the idea that she's running some sort of con herself."

"Why do you think that?"

"Because she might have pushed her drunken husband down the stairs."

"I thought he fell down."

"That's what was reported. There's no way to know unless we catch her in some other nefarious activity. I'll brief Nathan on Monday. Maybe he'll see something I'm missing."

~ ~ ~

The sky on Monday morning had the look of winter, and the frigid air was decidedly dampish. Brock told the sheriff, "I'm not sure anything's going on over there, Nathan. The most obvious head scratcher is the fact that two couples, who are not taking lessons, show up for the practice parties on Saturday night, and they don't socialize with anybody. I followed them out to the interstate one night, and they turned north, which means they could live a long way from here."

Connors said, "Have you ever heard of Baker Hobart?"

"No. Who's he?"

"A guy who buys coal properties that have problems. He's going to buy a big piece of land from Black Crystal on the last business day of the year."

"So?"

"The guy doesn't have a bank account. He only deals in cash, which means he'll be walking into Black Crystal with satchels full of bills on Friday the thirtieth."

"How much cash?"

"The asking price was ten million in the spring. He got a contract on the land in June. I don't know why they delayed the closing until the last day of the year. I'm guessing he got the deal for seven or eight million."

"The coal company will just take the money to a bank."

"They may not. When the building they're in was constructed in the late 1800s, the Black Crystal location was built as a bank, identical to the one on the other side of Ma's Dance. It has an impenetrable vault too."

"I don't see how Archer could steal the money."

"I just wanted you to know about it," the sheriff said.

"We can watch the four hundred block of Main Street on Saturday to make sure nobody breaks in."

"Good idea."

"If something's going to go down, it'll be on New Year's Eve, when everybody involved in this affair will be at the same party. We can keep an eye on them. I think Tonya Downing's house is a potential target too."

"We'll watch her place. How are the dance lessons going?"

"Brilliantly!"

Connors couldn't tell if Skinner was being truthful or not.

~ ~ ~

On Wednesday, December twenty-first, at the start of the private lesson, Archer proclaimed, "Tonight, you're going to begin learning the rumba, one of the easiest and most romantic dances of all. It's easy, that is, once you've mastered Cuban motion. Gabrielle, would you care to demonstrate?" Brock wasn't sure if he'd ever want to be seen moving his body like that. It might ruin his manly reputation, but in for a penny, in for a pound. The whole lesson was spent on the basic box step, emphasizing Cuban motion. Their hips and knees were sore afterward.

Gabrielle reminded Maude and Brock that group lessons would be held through Friday, and the studio would be closed on Christmas Eve, so there wouldn't be any practice party that night. The Skinners signed up for the big party on New Year's Eve on the following Saturday, and ordered fancy dance shoes online.

Marcel Sutherland, Maude's brother, had gone to New Mexico to spend Christmas with his girlfriend, which meant Maude and Brock would have an empty house through the holidays. They went to church on Christmas Eve, and upon returning home, Brock stoked the fire and brought out Maude's present. It was a copper lamé outfit for her to wear to the dance party, complete with matching turquoise jewelry and an Italian leather coat. She loved all of it, and thought to herself that she'd never been happier in her life.

Brock liked his present as well. Maude gave him a personalized leather Dopp kit, and inside was a certificate to drive the fastest Lamborghini in the world on a racetrack in Las Vegas next summer. As they were sitting on the couch together, watching the fire, Brock said, "I think I know how Gabrielle figures in this thing."

"How's that?"

"Archer must have told her he had a sponsor, Tonya Downing, who wanted to see a dance studio open up in Hazard. He told her he planned to leave at the end of the year, and wanted her to take the place over. He probably offered to pay the rent next year, or Downing agreed to forgive it, something like that. I'll bet she's got a husband or boyfriend who's as good an instructor as Archer is. He'll step right in, and Ma's won't miss a beat."

"So, what do you think will happen at the party?"

"Gabrielle will bring her love interest. Archer will be Tonya Downing's escort. He'll announce he's leaving and introduce his replacement. When the party's over, he'll drive out of there, never to be seen or heard from again. So will the two mysterious couples who have been hanging around. The question is, what will be in their trunks, and where will they have gotten it from?"

"Surely they wouldn't be dumb enough to have something in the trunk at the party, just in case somebody was on to them. I bet they leave there and go somewhere else to pick up what they've stolen," Maude said.

"Makes sense."

On Christmas afternoon, Brock went to the computer to research Black Crystal Coal Company. Rory Downing had died in May. Hobart got a contract to buy land from the company in June. Another article reported Black Crystal was having to sell properties to raise cash to pay a large loan coming due on January second. Brock kept mulling scenarios in his mind. Most suggested Tonya Downing had, in fact, pushed her husband down the stairs.

The Monday after Christmas, Skinner was back in the sheriff's office. "Nathan, I need you to find out who set the closing date for the Black Crystal property being sold this Friday."

"How am I going to do that?"

"Call up their lawyers and squeeze them for the information."

"On what basis?"

"I don't know, make something up. I've been doing all the heavy lifting here. Help me out."

Connors got a file out of the cabinet to look for a phone number. When he found it, he used his desk phone to make the call. "Is this Hayden Bardoner? This is Sheriff Connors at the police department. Something has come up pertaining to Rory Downing's estate. Can you tell me who decided on the closing date for the sale of the property to Baker Hobart?" Connors listened for a couple of minutes. "Okay, thanks for the information." He looked at Brock and said, "Tonya Downing set it. She negotiated the sale to Hobart, and the closing date was part of the terms."

"That's it, then. Tonya's got something up her sleeve. Michael Archer and the other two couples are for sure part of it."

The sheriff stood and admitted, "I can't believe I'm saying this, but there's a chance you're going to make me look good again. You'll have to put the rest of the pieces together for me, though. And Brock, on this one, I will really owe you."

"Let's not count our chickens just yet. After Hobart brings the money in on Friday, we'll need to watch and see if it stays at Black Crystal, or if they take it to the bank. Here's the license plate number of the vehicle Archer's been driving. Run it and see who the car's registered to."

The sheriff looked it up and reported it was a courtesy vehicle owned by Impact Body Shop.

On Wednesday, the twenty-eighth of December, the Skinners took their last dance lesson of the year. Brock went into the men's restroom and carefully checked the walls. He then stepped into the ladies' restroom briefly to look around. There was only one place where what he was looking for could be, he deduced.

Baker Hobart parked in front of Black Crystal Coal Company on Friday afternoon, the thirtieth. He got out, and it took him two trips to bring the four big briefcases into the building. Hobart came back out empty-handed in a half hour. Connors was camped out down the street, and a few minutes later, he watched two men carry the briefcases to the bank on the other side of Ma's Dance. He dialed up Skinner to tell him the money had been deposited. The bank would be closed on New Year's Eve, so Brock told Connors to go in and get the bank manager's cell phone number, which he did.

Brock parked up the street from Ma's at a little before nine o'clock that evening. Gabrielle came out right at nine and went to her vehicle in the lot across the street. It was nearly eleven o'clock before the two antisocial couples departed. Finally, at eleven thirty, Michael Archer—wearing a bulky trench coat that almost touched the ground—turned off the lights in the studio, came out, and locked the front door. He got in the rental car he'd been driving and turned north on Main Street. Brock followed him to Impact Body Shop, where he parked beside a car in the back. Archer put his heavy coat in the trunk of the parked car and drove away in the rental. Skinner called Connors and told him to get a man over there to stake the place out.

~ ~ ~

The weather had warmed considerably on New Year's Eve. Maude came out of the bedroom with a flourish, wearing her new clothes. Brock had on gray slacks, a black sport coat, and silver tie. He gazed at her and thought she was the most beautiful woman he'd ever seen. "Wow, you look fantastic. I'm the luckiest man in the world. Let's go have a good time and ring in the new year."

The party, starting at nine o'clock, was being held in a small conference hall at a mid-priced hotel five miles out of town. The place had been smartly decorated with spangles and crepe. The four-piece band set up to play behind the dance floor. There were six four-tops with white tablecloths clustered together in the middle of the room. A podium with a microphone stood next to the band. The drinks and snacks were on a black-skirted table, right inside the entrance to the hall.

The Skinners stood around and socialized with the nicely dressed people who took a break from dancing. Brock said, "Maude, I'll be back in a couple of minutes." He stepped outside and got the tracking devices out of the trunk of the Lamborghini. He put one on Archer's rental, and the other on the car the cryptic couples had arrived in. Brock dialed Connors. "The two out here are on. Are you picking them up?"

"Yes, and we've tested the one on the vehicle here at the body shop."

Maude was having a conversation with Tonya Downing when Brock returned to the party. "I was just telling your wife how much I like her outfit."

"Isn't she gorgeous?"

"You're biased, but I tend to agree with you," Tonya said.

At ten forty-five, the band took a well-deserved break. Michael Archer worked his way over to the podium, speech in hand. He said a lot of nice things, congratulating and complimenting nearly everyone in the room before dropping the bombshell that he'd be leaving. The crowd seemed stunned, but when Lonny, Gabrielle's "dance partner," was introduced as his successor, students wanted to know more. When Archer described Lonny's pedigree and told everyone Gabrielle was to be the business manager, the expression on faces in the group turned to delight again.

The Skinners decided to try out their new skills when a song played for a dance they'd learned. The hustle seemed to be manageable, and they emulated some of the simple moves of other dancers. But the waltz made them dizzy. All they could manage were repetitive circles around the room. Archer was correct about one thing; the rumba had it going on. They enjoyed it most of all, and couldn't wait to learn more moves.

Maude saw the two couples and Michael Archer slip out at five minutes till midnight, and said, "There they go." Brock kissed his wife when the ball dropped, and the two of them hung around for another twenty minutes. Gabrielle would be stuck with her first duty as business manager, breaking down the place after the party.

Brock called the sheriff on his car phone soon after they left the party venue. "What's happened?"

"Archer came to the body shop, left the rental, and drove off in his car. I've got an unmarked Mustang behind him, and another one on the tail of the two couples. They're still on separate roads, and it looks like Happy Valley is where they'll meet up."

"Call me when you've got 'em." At twelve fifty, when the Skinners had just crawled in bed, Brock got the call. All five were cuffed and being taken to jail. The coat in Archer's trunk had over one and a half million dollars in it. "Did your man out at Tonya Downing's house report that she'd come home?"

"Yes."

"I guess we better keep an eye on her. We'll be able to pick her up if somebody talks." Brock cut the line and said to Maude, "Nathan's going to owe me big-time. He better think about ramping up his interest in Joan Brewer."

She replied, "Huh. Well, aren't you just the little matchmaker?"

~ ~ ~

Sunday morning, New Year's Day, Brock and the sheriff were standing in front of the bank next to Ma's. "Look, there're people in the dance studio this morning. That's convenient," Brock commented.

The bank manager arrived, keyed open the front door, and turned off the alarm. He asked, "What's this all about?"

"We got a tip someone was going to try to rob the place. This is just precautionary."

He proceeded to the back of the bank where he saw the safe door was slightly ajar. The man panicked. "Why's this unlocked?" He pulled open the two-foot-thick door and rushed inside. "All the paper money is gone!"

Connors said, "Someone must've cracked the safe and stolen the cash."

"There's another explanation." Brock turned to the man in charge and said, "Don't lose heart yet. We might be able to recover the money."

Sweat formed on the forehead of the bank manager, even though it was officially wintertime outside. He said, "I surely hope so. There were over nine million dollars in bills in here."

Connors followed Brock next door where he stuck his head in and said, "Hello."

Gabrielle and Lonny came out from the back, and she said, "Oh, it's you, Mr. Skinner. What is it we can help you with?"

The two men stepped in and closed the door. "This is Sheriff Connors. We wanted to check something in here quickly."

"Be our guest," she said.

"Nathan, help me push these sofas off the rug over here." They carefully shoved them onto the hardwood floor. "Now, let's roll up the rug." When they got a little past halfway, Brock said, "There it is." A hinged door with an eye-hook handle that folded down had been cut in the floor. "Let's go to the police station and have a chat with Mr. Archer." The two of them rolled the rug back down and lifted the sofas back into place. "Thanks, Gabrielle. Maude and I are looking forward to our next lesson. We love that rumba." She waved to the men as they left, not quite understanding what was going on.

Michael Archer maintained a stiff upper lip as he sat across from the sheriff and Skinner in the interrogation room at the police station. Connors said, "If you talk, Archer, we'll try to convince the judge that you deserve a shorter stretch in jail."

"I don't understand why you're holding me here. I haven't done anything," he said.

Brock leaned back in his chair and exhaled. "Okay, if you want to play it that way. The police are going to get you for theft and being an accessory to murder. Let me remind you that when the old man you paid to run into your car at the winery gives you up, things will unravel from there."

"What are you talking about, accessory to murder?"

"You might be the one who pushed Rory Downing down those stairs."

"I had nothing to do with any of that." Archer was beginning to lose his composure.

"Why don't you tell us about it, from the beginning."

He leaned forward, wove his hands together on the table and looked down. "Tonya Downing answered an ad I had online for dance lessons. She called me in April and I came up here from Charlotte. She overpaid for the lessons, and then asked me if I'd like to make a million dollars."

The sheriff said, "I take it Michael Archer isn't your real name?"

"Grant Pomeroy. You don't need to check. I don't have a record," he replied.

"Give us all of it, and we'll try to help you. If we get the bank's money back, there'll be a lot more we can do," Brock urged.

"She called me in May, after her husband had died. She said she'd pay me a million dollars if I'd open a dance studio in downtown Hazard. She told me I could get the money on the last day of the year and leave after that if I had someone on staff who could take my place. I found Gabrielle and offered her the opportunity. She had no knowledge of anything. At the time, all I thought I had to do was get some students in there and crank up the business. In August, she showed me the door to the tunnels leading to the safes in the businesses on either side. She told me the back walls slid open, providing access to what was inside."

Brock asked, "When did she tell you about the plan to move some cash from one safe to the other?"

"Right after we opened, she sprang that on me. I told her I wasn't going down in those tunnels. Then she hired those other two couples you have locked up to do the switch. All I had to do was put the money they brought up in a heavy coat and take it out. There was a million dollars for me, and the rest was for them. I had to hatch a plan to meet somewhere and give them their share of the money. That's when the police nabbed us."

The sheriff said, "We're going to write up a statement, and we want you to sign it."

"Yeah." The remorse he felt was written on his face.

Later that morning, a deputy picked up Tonya Downing and arrested her. During her interrogation, Brock asked, "Why'd you do it?"

"Do what?"

"Kill your husband and steal the money from the bank."

"On Derby weekend, he told me Black Crystal was going broke. He was a drunk, and I was damn tired of him. I wasn't going to stay with a man who had no money. I knew Baker Hobart was ready to buy some property for cash, so I figured out how to steal it from the bank and get them to pay me for my losses. The extra money would make the company solvent again."

"How'd you know about the tunnels?" Connors asked.

"Rory showed them to me years ago when we bought the building." Tonya Downing acted as though there weren't any consequences ahead for her actions.

Brock said, "That was a nice touch, leaving the safe door open at the bank to make it look like a run-of-the-mill robbery. If the bank's money is still in the safe at Black Crystal, and you give it back, you might get out of jail before you get too old to enjoy the rest of your life."

"It's there. You can have it. You'll never be able to prove I pushed Rory down those stairs. I figure a year in jail is about all I'll get." She stood, walked over to the window, and looked out. Sheriff Connors made a fist, thrust it at Skinner, and smiled.

Brock got back to the house by lunchtime on New Year's Day. Truman greeted him first, and then Maude. He suggestively suggested, "What do you say we put on some of that rumba music and practice that Cuban motion?"

She replied, "I can see you have no regrets about the rumba coming to the Cumberlands."